Praise for Ha

When a group of A' Level students go on a field trip to finish their drama script, the experience turns out to be far more emotional, dangerous and haunting than they could have ever imagined. *Happiness Seeker* sweeps you along like the fast and unpredictable tides of Morecambe Bay, where this novel is set. The book is filled with wonderful, three-dimensional characters you really care about, and has a gripping, roller-coaster plot that keeps you right on the edge of your seat throughout.

– Lu Hersey, author of *Deep Water* and *Broken Ground*

Jennifer brings the Bay vividly to life—both its beauty and its danger—cleverly weaving together the drama group's planning and discussions about the piece they've come here to write, with the 'extracurricular' saga that unfolds. Right from the start, I felt I knew Allie and her peers, with their long-standing friendships and rivalries. So it shouldn't have been a surprise when their final heart-wrenching drama performance had me literally in tears.

– Paul Rand, author of *Joe with an E*, coming soon

A thriller. A love story. A political statement. A cleverly woven story of past and present, hopefully not of the future...

What has stayed with me during and after reading this clever YA novel is the danger of Morecambe Bay and its surrounds. The threat is vivid and palpable, and we are highly aware of the perilous sands and incoming tide from beginning to end of this riveting book.

The story cleverly weaves fact and fiction, from the Arthur Miller play our group of A' Level students are studying, to tensions between the teenagers, to the real-life tragedy of people caught in traps not only of nature's making.

A clever, unique, important book that is as enthralling to read for adults as it is for young people. I haven't felt this degree of emotion in a YA book before or seen a place described with such precision.

– Ruth Estevez, author of The Jiddy Vardy Trilogy, *The Monster Belt*, *Erosion* and *Meeting Coty*

It was supposed to be a simple school trip, but this nail-biting story turns into a heart-in-mouth roller coaster as Allie and her friends must navigate increasingly complex dilemmas fraught with danger and betrayal, where the stakes rocket out of control.

Romance blends with risk-taking and literally stepping off the edge into unknown terrain. How can any teenager cope?

Facing the consequences of foolish blunders that spiral into crisis after crisis, Allie is pushed way beyond her limits and faces an ultimate test.

This white-knuckle ride sucked me into perilous depths alongside Allie and her friends – I actually chewed my thumbnail right down during the last twenty pages!

– Jo Somerset, author of *Mission: Find Mum*, out 2024

Dear Lesley · Jonathan

Happiness
Seeker

*see what you think
of this one!*

Jennifer Burkinshaw

*Jennifer
x*

Beaten Track
www.beatentrackpublishing.com

Happiness Seeker

First published 2023 by Beaten Track Publishing
Copyright © 2023 Jennifer Burkinshaw
Cover Design and Photography Copyright © 2023 Jonjo Green

Paperback: 978 1 78645 614 4
eBook: 978 1 78645 615 1

Select quotations from:
Arthur Miller (2010[1955]) *A View from the Bridge*.
London: Methuen Drama.

Excerpt from:
John Donne (2007) 'No Man is an Island'
from *Devotions Upon Emergent Occasions; Together with Death's Duel*.
Project Gutenberg. Retrieved 26 September 2023, from
https://www.gutenberg.org/ebooks/23772.

Beaten Track Publishing,
Burscough, Lancashire.
www.beatentrackpublishing.com

For my dear dad

Preface

This novel deals with topics which some readers may find distressing. However, knowing of these in advance will also spoil some elements of the story. Thus, the choice is yours: you will find the content warnings at the end of the book. See page 323.

This is a work of fiction inspired by real-world events. While it is set in a real geographical location, some elements have been changed for storytelling purposes. These include the topography of Morecambe Bay, elements of Cartmel Priory and, in Grange, the inclusion of a fictional hostel and pub and the placement of the bandstand where it originally came from, on the prom.

Cover Images: Through arched windows, the train station, Grange-over-Sands

All photography by Jonjo Green.

'Map of the Morecambe Bay Area' and 'Plan of Grange-over-Sands' by Douglas McCleery.

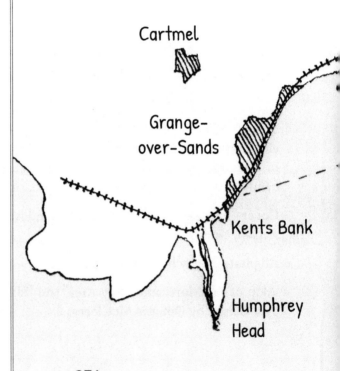

LAND

Cartmel

Grange-
over-Sands

Kents Bank

Humphrey
Head

SEA

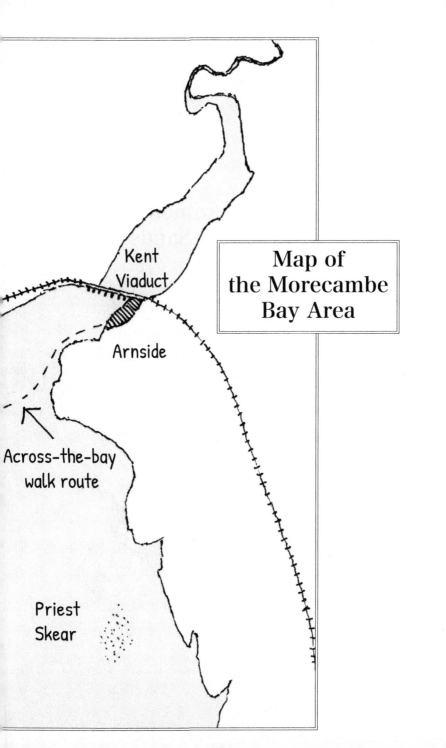

Map of
the Morecambe
Bay Area

Kent
Viaduct

Arnside

Across-the-bay
walk route

Priest
Skear

Plan of the Promenade, Grange-over-Sands

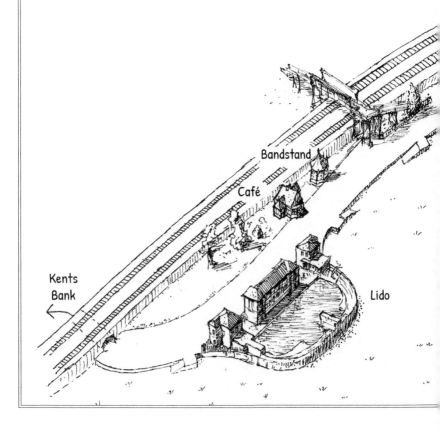

Bandstand

Café

Kents
Bank

Lido

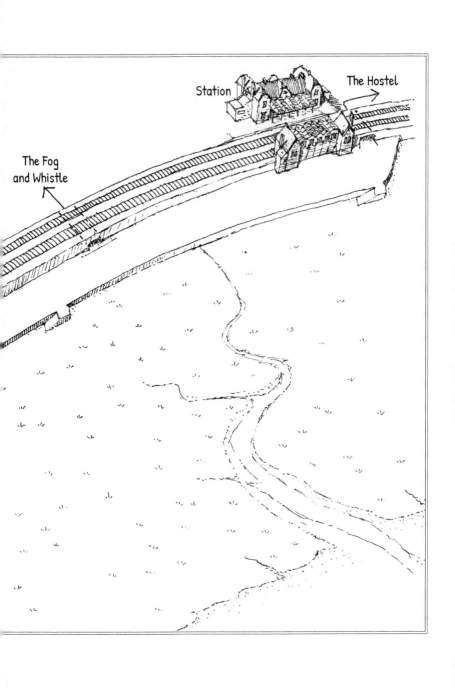

Station

The Hostel

The Fog
and Whistle

any man's death diminishes me,
because I am involved in mankind

From John Donne's 'No Man is an Island'

The foreigner residing among you must be treated as your native-born. Love them as yourself.

Leviticus 19, 34

Remember your humanity, and forget the rest.

The Russell-Einstein Manifesto

Prologue
Day 7
2:08 a.m.

A RARE COMET STREAKS across the sky. Alien-green, it trails a pointed tail. Lovejoy, they call it, but no one sees it. Not this night. Not with all the commotion right in the middle of the Bay.

Close to the inky water, a helicopter circles, adding its beam to the yellow splodges three lifeboats splash onto the waves.

On dry land, a small group is fixated on these distant lights. A girl quakes so violently, the arm around her shoulder tightens over the foil blanket, yet still she trembles.

What chance do they really have of finding her friend in these hundred square miles of pitch-black sea?

As time rolls on, one boat returns to shore. Later, the others must retreat before the grey tide ebbs. The girl too is made to leave, lie down before she collapses.

Jaded now, the moon is a ghost as orange fingers reach over the horizon.

Two more helicopters have joined the first to scour the newly bared Sands. Finally, they too whirr away home.

At last, the Bay is at peace.

The Sands are left to themselves with all their secrets.

In their bottomless depths, so many bones.

And in the bones

the why.

Day 1
Seven Days Earlier

I could have finished the whole story that afternoon.

Alfieri, *A View from the Bridge*

One

THE BEST THING about a best friend is you can't lose them.

But I lose Finn after Carnforth Station.

If only it wasn't to *her*.

"Here, Finn," Courtney says. She pats the seat next to her, so he ends up travelling backwards too, and thrusts her phone in front of both their faces. Knowing she's about to subject us and the whole carriage to one of her weirdly popular TikTok posts, I'm half tempted to duck under the table separating us.

"And now for something different to my usual acting hacks," she tells her camera. "Me and Finn are off for a week of fun at the seaside."

Not quite how I'd describe our sixth-form drama trip, I think.

"So, Finn," she puts her fist to his mouth like a mic, "not long till we arrive. What've you got up your sleeve for our week away?"

"A spot of sea bathing?" He puts on a posh accent.

"Damn," she says. "Forgotten my bikini!"

I clench my teeth at her toying with him.

"Skinny dipping then," he says, his knee jiggling in the aisle.

Courtney laughs. "It's October, Finley. But paddling at the very least! Follow me to find out what—" ironic pause "—activities I've got up *my* sleeve! Hashtag Courtney and Finn's wild week of fun."

And me? The rest of the group?

"It's a wrap, Finn." She lowers her phone, revealing a toothy grin. "*And* on a first take."

"Er, you up for paddling too, Allie?" Finn asks me, sheepish, while Courtney thumbs her phone.

I knit my eyebrows at him. *Me and water?* "I thought this week was all about writing our script?"

"We—" he starts.

"We're talking about *extra*curricular activities," Courtney cuts in. "You know? Oh, no, sorry, Al-e-the-a, you don't. FUN!"

Her pebbly eyes give me one of their best scathing looks as she sounds out the syllables of my name, mocking what she assumes is its poshness when my parents picked it for its meaning, apparently one of the few things they've ever agreed on.

"Scriptwriting *is* fun," I tell her.

For me, creating our own play is the highlight of the whole course. Actors are given their lines and moves; you can't have more control than scripting the drama yourself.

But Courtney's too busy shoving her phone back under Finn's nose, so close her black hair spills across his fair curls. He smirks as he watches their reel back. I've got to accept my best friend's just been cast as understudy for Courtney's sidekick—a role he isn't cool enough for when her usual mates are around.

I root in my rucksack for the play I've brought along.

As I READ Arthur Miller's Brooklyn setting for *A View from the Bridge*, a tragedy, I'm convinced Miss is dead right to bring us somewhere more dramatic than Leeds if we're to write a killer script this week. Only a few pages in and the dramatist's set up a tense triangle of characters in this edgy location right on the brink of the sea.

A few minutes later, the train stops again—Arnside, and the first station on the Cumbrian coast. I tug open the window, and fresh, salty air gushes in.

As we set off once more, the track curving around, I get my first glimpses of Morecambe Bay: no sea but a huge, fudgy beach. It's bathed in orange now the sun's finally elbowed the clouds out of the way. My body buzzes with the rush you get as a kid when you first catch sight of the coast.

"Finn, look!" I exclaim but the two of them, eyes closed, are sharing a pair of earbuds, leaking an unsettling beat.

THE TRAIN MAKES for a narrow viaduct stretching out across the vast Bay in front of us. Our carriage rattles onto the bridge between two lands, and it's like we're off the rails

    soaring across a giant's beach
    the sun sparking off spangled sand
    laced with sapphire water
    all
    the way
    to the
    horizon.
    This is drama!

Dropping my play onto the table, I shuffle across and press my forehead to the window. Everything is golden now.

I LEAVE BEHIND Finn and his wild week,
Mum's parting put-down—
Off you trot, get this drama phase out of your system
And I

fly

ALL TOO SOON, the train reaches the end of the viaduct. The next station is announced: Grange-over-Sands.

I scrabble into the aisle and tug Finn's earbud out. "We're here!"

Grabbing my rucksack, I make for the door. Miss Duffy is already there. My ally. Only last week, she spoke up for me and my UCAS application to study drama while Mum's insisting on 'something sensible with a future'. Which is why I've got to prove myself to her, go home with a gripping play.

"The view from the bridge!" I say to Miss, holding up my copy. "I've never seen anything like it."

She smiles, her eyes gleaming. "Spectacular, isn't it? The Bay's going to add so much to your drama this week."

The Sands now appear in
      jolty
   camera
    shots
       as
    the train
   slows,
  slows,
finally stops.

I press the yellow button to open the doors, and the shore presents itself once again through tall, arched windows on the platform. Once the ramp's in place for Miss's wheelchair, I follow her down, into the week ahead.

Two

"To the promenade!" Sir says, rubbing his hands together before leading the thirteen of back us back through the short railway underpass.

We've just dispatched our luggage to the hostel in their minibus with the centre manager, Mr. Rainer, a gruff man who put me in mind of Charon, the silent guy who ferries the dead across the river to Hades. Now Sir's keen to orientate us and get on with the geography part of the trip.

Blinking in the bright afternoon sun, we stop dead on the tarmacked prom sandwiched between the railway track and horizontal railings to stop you walking off the edge.

"Where's the beach?" Courtney demands, her tone outraged. "This *is* Grange-over-soddin'-Sands!"

What she's complaining about is the thick fringe of grungy grass between the prom and the sand emanating a briny smell.

"We've just crossed several *miles* of what you'd call beach on the train," Sir says, bemused but immune to Courtney's gobbiness. "But this is not a shore to walk on, and here's why."

He gestures left to the colourful panel of signs at the top of a ramp leading down onto the marsh.

In bright-red letters, it shouts: **EXTREME DANGER**
Below that, alongside yellow warning triangles, are the *reasons* for the danger:

Beware quicksand

Beware sudden tides

Beware sudden drops

Next to **quicksand,** in case you don't know what it can do, a stickman raises his arms in terror as he surrenders to the hungry mud. My scalp creeps. These are sands to be admired only from a safe distance.

"Where is the sea?" Shafeeq asks, screwing up his nose.

"This is a tidal estuary," Sir tell us. "The sea will be back soon enough. So, listen up."

We all look his way. He's got his serious face on, and we all respect *Hey Ho*. He's fun, fair, plus he does the lighting for our plays! Though he's warned us he might have to stop when his twins arrive around Christmas.

"You've seen the signs. *None* of you will so much as *dream* of setting foot on these Sands."

It's a statement, but he does a sweep of our faces to check.

Finn nods his agreement, blue eyes wide.

"Hey-ho," Sir says, validating his nickname. "Geographers are coming with me."

Miss decides to go with them to learn more about the Bay, leaving the five of us with instructions to take some photos and even recordings of the shore before meeting her later.

While Hey Ho leads his group down the prom in the opposite direction to the town, trailing phrases like 'coastal systems' and 'five tributaries', Lucy's fixing Shaf over her new, navy secretary specs.

"Bet there's some great vintage clothes in the charity shops in a place like this," she tells him.

Under his trademark Yorkshire flat cap, he gives his lazy shrug, happy to go along with whatever makes Lucy happy.

Next thing, Courtney's making another friggin' TikTok post. The flame tatt licking up her forearm catches red-hot fire on her dark skin as she holds her phone high so only the marsh is in the background.

"So, turns out, we're at this la-la land of a seaside with no sea, and sand apparently…somewhere out there! God only knows why we didn't go to Blackpool instead. So, Finn…" She beckons him.

Enough! I set off down the prom away from all of them.

WELL AWAY FROM Courtney, I stop to take some photos. Leaning against the railing, I allow myself to drift onto the burnished Sands. From here, the viaduct looks like part of a toy train set. A miniature train beetles back across it to Arnside, clear as glass even from this distance. Now I see how the Bay yawns in a giant Y-shape from the viaduct out to open sea.

Footsteps draw me back onto the prom. To my right, a lad pauses at the railings too. Out of the corner of my eye, I notice the calm green of his T-shirt. One hand shielding his eyes against the sun, he gazes out onto the Sands, scrutinising it almost. Maybe it's new to him as well.

As if sensing my thoughts, he turns to smile at me, his face tanned and lean. He makes a sweeping gesture in front of him, palm up, a semicircle between us saying, *All this!*

I smile back and nod. *All this space and beauty.*

We gaze together, the late-October sun surprisingly warm on my shoulders, and a sense of everything being right with this new world washes over me.

A sudden wailing sets up from across the bare Bay like an air-raid alarm. Maybe everything's not all right after all? It's definitely warning about something. My shoulders tensed, I turn to Green-tee, but he's set off down the prom. The alarm stops. I set off in the same direction as him, towards the **Leisure Facilities**, a sign tells me.

AVOIDING KIDS ON bikes, off-lead dogs and meandering mobility scooters, I pass a play park, a bandstand and the café where we're to meet Miss at four p.m.

The lad's disappeared around a corner, so I press on.

THE PROM STRAIGHTENS out, so you can't miss this huge stone semicircle jutting out over the grassy shore. Where its straight edge meets the prom, through a small window, I glimpse a peeling diving tower looming over a pool of murky water.

WHEN I LOOK down the prom, I've lost the lad. I break into a power walk.

Then I see.

The figure out in the Bay.

He's some three hundred metres away—I can make out the green of his top—not so far from the edge of the grass, standing where sinking sand could suck him down at any moment. What if he hasn't seen the loud signs? There aren't any at this end of the prom because there are no ramps. He must have squeezed under the railings, unaware of the risk.

My pulse picks up. *No one* else is around. Now I make out a faint track trodden through the long grass, which maybe attracted him. It'll take me two minutes to jog to the end of the marsh and warn him about the danger.

But Sir's one and only rule for the week echoes in my head:

Don't even dream of setting foot on those Sands.

I wipe my hand across my face as if I can make it all disappear. My pulse is galloping at even the remote chance of the sudden tide coming in anytime soon.

But what if it does and sweeps Green-tee away?

And *I* could have prevented it?

FOLLOWING MY INSTINCTS, I sink down onto the prom.

Once I've twisted onto my stomach, I swivel my legs under the bottom bar of the railings, ease my way backwards down the wall.

The drop's more than I expected—higher than me. Green-tee might have to help me back up.

Under my trainers, the bog's squelchy, unstable. This is sooo not land.

Get a grip, Allie. He's only three minutes away. Tops.

Trouble is, the lad's pacing further out onto the Sands almost as fast as I'm jogging. I speed up, going as quick as I can without stumbling on the squidgy surface.

Breathing hard, I reach the end of the grass. Bang in front of me, the Sands are a big step down. And *I'm* not setting foot on them.

"Hey!" I yell at the back of the figure.

He carries on but then stops and stoops right down.

Now's my chance. I cup my hands around my mouth. "He-eyy!"

He straightens up, turns, looks towards me.

I do this weird criss-cross wave with both hands.

"There's quicksand out there," I call. "*And* a sudden tide."

He strides towards me. Once he gets nearer, he smiles as he recognises me.

"Thanks, but I know this," he says, his accent precise, perhaps Eastern European, though his skin tone's more Greek or Italian looking, jet-black hair on his forearms.

"Oh, okay." I bite my lip. *So why were you out there?* "I thought you might be new to the place and missed the danger signs."

He shakes his head, coming closer again. "I live here."

Where? Who with? I want to ask as he steps up onto the marsh alongside me.

Before I can find a more reasonable question, the siren sets up again.

"What *is* that?" I ask him.

"It warns the tide is coming."

He points behind him, towards open sea. My stomach swoops. A low wall of water stands on the horizon like a battle line.

"We need to get back!" I say.

But something's caught his eye beyond me, back towards the ruined lido.

I turn.

My heart plummets to the ground.

The sea's creeping up behind Finn's back!

Three

"THEY'RE FROM MY school," I tell the lad in dismay. "The tide will be here in three, four minutes."

He starts to run along the edge of the marsh back towards the lido. I race after him. My pulse is racing too, with fear and fury. Telling Courtney *not* to go on the Sands is *the* way to guarantee she absolutely will. But she's dragged Finn after her, and now they're meandering back towards shore, trainers in hand, as if they have all the time in the world.

Can't they hear the sea's low growl?

We're more or less parallel with them. Green-tee stops, pulls out a stubby red whistle from his jeans, blasts out a sharp trill.

Finn's head jolts up, towards us.

"The tide!" I screech.

I jab my arm at the moving wall chasing them. The guy does a much more logical, beckoning gesture with his forearm.

Finn glances over his shoulder. Alarm flashes down his face quick as a mask. He grabs Courtney's arm, and they sprint towards us.

The sea's going to sweep Finn away. Breathing short, I look to the lad. He's still got his eyes fixed on the pair as if assessing the gap between the sea and them. His worry compounds mine.

The freak tide's gaining on them. This isn't a race they can win.

"I'm phoning for help," I tell him, snatching my phone out of my pocket.

"No," he jumps in. "They have a…head start, you say?"

I nod. Enough of one? My gut tells me I can trust this boy, though.

Finn's close enough for me to see the set of his mouth, his wide eyes.

The tide's still hot on their heels.

"We go back to land now," Green-tee tells me.

He leads the way through the spiky reeds while my tummy rolls for Finn.

The prom! The guy gives me a leg up the wall and under the railing. I scramble to my feet to check on Finn.

The sea's followed them up onto the marsh, but its wall has weakened, crumbled, no longer strong enough to bring them down, sweep them under.

The lad's up here next to me now. "They might not have such luck next time. Tell your friends, they need to know what they do."

My breathing's just starting to settle. "They're… Finn's not like that usually."

It's *her.*

The lad looks at me. *The eyes are the window to the soul,* Miss has always told us. His, hazel and lighter than you'd expect given his hair, give me a sense of openness and honesty.

"What are you—" he begins.

"Nearly popped a lung!" Courtney cuts in, landing on the prom bang between us, a beached whale on her belly.

Thanks a bunch, Courtney, I think bitterly. *Now I'll never know what he was going to ask.*

Finn's face appears over the edge of the prom wall.

"Allie!"

I stoop to give him a pull up.

When I turn back to the guy, he's gone. I scan all around, but all I get is a flash of his green top as he vanishes under the railway bridge at the end of the prom.

I gaze after him.

Who are you?

Four

"HARD TO BELIEVE the Sands can become sea in a matter of minutes," Miss remarks, parking her wheelchair at the head of our table up on the café's terrace. Just a few metres in front of us, the long reeds are poking up through the water.

Like a black magic trick, I think, gulping my cold Coke, my first afternoon totally out of control.

"Yeah, proper freakish." Courtney's beady eyes are on me over her Magnum. "The tide raced in almost as fast as you could leg it, eh, Al-e-the-a?"

She's not getting a rise out of me, not this time. Apart from a few wisps of hair escaping her topknot, you wouldn't know she'd just run for her life. Finn, though, is sitting with his back to the shore, his knees doing that bouncing thing, and he won't meet my eye. I stare past him at the calm sea glistening under the mellow late-afternoon sun as if it could do no harm. An all-or-nothing Bay.

"I'm glad you saw it too!" Miss says. "All of you?"

"We were doing a recce of the park," Lucy says, kicking her carrier bags further under her chair.

"Okay," Miss says. "Well, it's called a bore tide. Hey Ho told me…"

She holds up her hand as we all laugh at her finally falling in with our nickname for him.

"It's to do with the full moon and spring tides all this week, which are the fastest, highest and most furious."

Most furious... My eyes slide to Finn. *Look what could have happened, for all you're a strong swimmer.* But he's laughing with the others at Miss waggling her shoulders as she shows off her newfound knowledge.

"Now then." Miss wipes her ice-creamy fingers on a serviette. "We need to narrow down the theme of your devised drama. What thoughts has this unique setting inspired this afternoon?"

My thoughts dart straight to my mystery lad, whose name I don't even know. Not that I can write a drama about him, of course, but why *was* he out on the Sands? How come he happened to have a whistle on him? Where did he go? Most of all, what was he going to ask me?

"Finn?" Miss prompts, pushing back her hair with her tortoiseshell sunglasses.

His eyes flit around. "Erm, transformation? Like you suggested about the Bay, Miss."

"That could fit with the town shifting from a seaside resort to more of a retirement town," Lucy says.

My eyes go to the ruined lido.

"Yeah," Shaf says, "Grange even had a pier once, with yachts. Now it's got a duckpond!"

Over his shoulder, I catch sight of a poster to the side of the café's serving hatch. A single hand claws at the sand's surface, the rest of its body already swallowed down.

"The dangers of the Bay?" I suggest, looking at Courtney.

"Yes. Apparently, the coastguard has to help tens of people each year out there," Miss says. "And sometimes it can't."

I glance at Finn again.

"Where's the conflict?" Courtney says, screwing up her face into her trademark scorn.

I throw up a hand. "People versus the tide."

She scoffs. "The tide's not some monster—not any kind of conscious being. Like Miss said, it's controlled by the moon."

Miss also personified the tide as *furious*. But I should have known Courtney would shoot me down.

"It's people create the conflict," I say, "when they decide to ignore all the warnings about the tide just cos they think they're different."

Courtney groans and scowls at me.

"They're having *fun*, Al-e-the-a. S'a free world. Their choice."

"Your choice," Lucy says, flicking her long, blonde hair out of her way as she hangs up her dresses in the single wardrobe.

I drop my backpack onto the bed under the window.

"You take the middle one," I say. "I've had enough of *her* already."

"The ancient grudge." She sighs melodramatically.

I shrug. Courtney started it, objecting to my southern accent when I joined North Leeds High in Year Nine, objecting to *me* as some 'snotty middle-class nerd'.

"Something kicked off on the prom after we'd gone, didn't it?" Lucy says.

I catch my reflection in the darkened window. The lad. The Sands. Finn and Courtney. It'd be a relief to tell Lucy.

"Allie?"

"Yeah. It was when I saw this—"

The door is flung open and Courtney appears in the doorway, sizing up our bedroom. Her nostrils flare at its fustiness.

"Proper rank! It's as ratty as the rest of this dive in here!" She slings a shiny, red sausage bag onto the bed nearest the door. "Worse, in fact. It's a nunnery."

Lucy laughs. The hostel's male and female accommodation is actually in two separate buildings, each with keypads, the communal areas of the restaurant, lounge and games room separating them.

"There's a single room next door if you want it," I tell Courtney.

"Rude!" she says, for once looking taken aback. "And I'd hate to miss out on all the *fun* in here."

"Kas and Paula are next door but one," Lucy tells her. "Miss D right at the far end."

Courtney nods. Miss needs her rest when she has to measure out her energy in spoonfuls.

She sniffs. "I'm off now anyway, to slaughter Finn at table tennis. Anyone coming?"

"Shaf'll be there too," Lucy says. She'll be with him each waking moment this week; their forbidden romance usually has to be snatched here and there. "Allie?"

I shake my head and pick up *A View from the Bridge* as a decoy from the top of my bag.

"Why you reading that now?" Courtney demands.

"Cos it's our set text and it's more *fun* than watching you play table tennis," I say.

She scoffs and struts off.

But it genuinely is. Two Italians, Rudolpho and Marco, have just made their entrance. 'Submarines', locals call them, as they've been smuggled illegally by boat into New York. This feels like the start of the tragedy.

THE SECURITY LIGHT comes on outside my window as the two of them make their way from our wing to the main building. Once the door bangs to, my mind shifts to *our* drama, and I know I need to see the Bay in the dark.

I scramble off the bed, grab my fleece off the chair and poke my head out into the courtyard. Damn. Right now, Finn's coming out of the boys' wing. Like some tortoise, I pull my head back into the doorway, but he's spotted me.

"Hang on, Mum," he says to his phone. "Allie!" he calls. "You coming?"

I step out, tug the door closed behind me and cross the courtyard. He holds out his phone to me.

"Hi, Poppy!" I say. I love Finn's mum. And, with four sons and even their dog male, she seems to like me hanging out at theirs too.

"How's the drama going, Allie love?" she asks.

This is one question my mum won't be asking me this week, but Poppy knows how much it means to me.

I raise my eyebrows at Finn. "Er...I'd say we've made a good start, thanks, Poppy."

Finn steers his phone safely back to him. "Okay, gotta go, Mum," he says. "I'll check in with you tomorrow night. Hello to the guys."

It makes me smile how Finn has to do a sheepdog-style round-up of all those he cares about. He's giving me a look.

"You weren't trying to avoid me just now, were you, Allie?"

"Maaaybe," I admit.

He sighs. "Okay, you don't need to say it. I know it wasn't best sensible, this afternoon."

"It was *her.*"

He shakes his head. "I do have a mind of my own, you know." He puts his hand on my forearm so I'll look at him, "But I need time out from always being the responsible one. The rest of my life is living up to expectations. All I'm asking is one week when I'm not head boy or anyone's big brother."

My throat catches. I'd never have guessed Finn felt this way when we reckon we know each other inside out, all the time we spend together—the only teens in our village.

"Of course." I try to make light of it. "A week off!"

"Come on then, Alliette." He leans his elbow on my shoulder, ragging me about my height, or lack of, whilst treating me to a Finn beam, all harmony and light. "You may as well join the audience for the Annihilation of Finn Yates."

I give a little shudder. "Far too painful for me. I'm nipping down to the shore to see the Bay in the moonlight."

"Want me to come?"

"You're off duty this week, remember?" I fake a smile because I'd hate to think *I* was ever an obligation to him.

If only he wasn't going off duty with *her.*

Five

THE BRILLIANCE OF a full moon lights my way along the crazy-paved path that tips gradually downhill alongside the lawn at the back of the hostel. The clear night air's refreshing after the warmth of the afternoon.

As I amble, I replay what Finn said. Apart from Courtney, who always speaks her mind, it's rare we know what people are *truly* thinking, even those we think we're closest to.

My brain projects a montage for me; of our water-pistol fights—me and him against his three younger brothers in their garden; running through our drama lines in outrageous accents; the only Monopoly tournament to include a real golden retriever as a player, even though Finn obviously does have to make all Bilbo's moves for him!

If only I could make a TikTok of all that.

#Finn&AlliesFourYearFUNFriendship

It'd get way more likes than #CourtneysWildWeek.

Alongside the fun, Finn's so serious in his humanist thinking, he'll have the next four years mapped out exactly as *he* wants them. So it makes sense, as he says, that he needs a break on this trip, with the responsibility of role model universally thrust upon him at home and school.

SOON, I CAN smell the clean saltiness of the Bay.

And there are voices! Or rather *a* voice.

"Billy!" she says, again and again as if she's calling him. From her tone, Billy's a toddler. But who'd have a young child out at this time of night?

Suddenly, this biggish dog pelts towards me, the whirling white tip of his tail easily visible.

"Billy!" the voice calls. "Where you off? We've only just started!? Oh!"

"S'okay!" I tell who I can now see is a girl around my age. I crouch down to rub Billy's head. His border collie markings feature a perfect white star down his face. "I love dogs."

"Oh, that's okay then," she says. "Come on now, though, Billy!"

She turns abruptly, and Billy abandons me. They head back where they came from. I follow on till the path peters out onto shingle. Beyond, the moonlight catches on patches of water in the Bay. The tide's ebbing again, a giant's bath slowly emptying.

The girl's throwing a ball the full stretch of the little beach, Billy retrieving it time after time. I stand alongside her.

"Allie," I tell her. "I'm staying at the hostel this week."

"Yep, assumed you were part of the school group," she says, distinctly unenthusiastic.

"Yeah, everyone else is playing table tennis, and…" I trail off.

"And what?" she says, surprising me. I'd given up on her.

"And I'm more interested in the drama we're here to write this week. We're going to involve the Bay in some way, which is why I'm down here."

"Aye, there's enough drama out there."

My gut twitches. "This afternoon, two of my...of the group had to run from the tide."

"They're not the first," she says darkly. "When the sun appears, people's brains disappear, and there they are, out on the Sands."

"Our geography students are walking all the way across the Sands on Monday with the guide."

"Ah, they'll be safe enough with Eli."

Safe enough? Rather them than me!

There's a lull while we watch Billy galloping away and back after the ball.

"He's got endless energy," I say.

"Runs like billy-o—that's why I picked his name," she says. "Trouble is, he's a chaser too—sheep, deer, birds, anything moving. Can disappear for hours after them. So I find he's a bit safer off lead in the dark."

Billy drops the ball at my feet this time. I lob it; he brings it back, drops it a stride away so I have to step towards him to pick it up. He keeps on teasing me, each time making me move further to recoup the ball until I decide I've had enough.

"This time, I'm keeping it," I tell him.

He sits and looks up at me, confused by the change in rules.

"You want me to throw it, you bring it all the way back to me."

"You've met your match, Billy!" She laughs.

"He's absolutely gorgeous," I say, bowling the ball as far as I can. "I'd have loved a dog, but my mum refuses cos we're both out all day."

I know that's an excuse. Poppy's always said if I did persuade Mum, she could walk ours with Bilbo.

"I s'pose that's one way we're lucky," she says as if in other ways they're not. "My dad's the centre manager here, so even when I'm at school, he can take Billy out at some point."

"Must be fun, living here?" I bend to throw the ball again.

She scoffs. "Hm, that's the opposite of what Dad and I'd call it. There's usually some trouble kicks off every stay when we have enough to do. Apart from the chef, there's only Dad and me to do all the jobs."

No wonder Mr. Rainer looked so cheesed off when he met us at the station earlier. *And her mum?* I wonder.

"We have different schools in nearly every week of the year so…"

You can't be making friends with visitors, I fill in. But maybe I can be different.

"I'd love to see Billy again if you'd let me."

She sniffs. He nudges his ball right into my hand this time.

"He seems to like you, and he's a good judge of character. I'm Rue. I s'pose you could come and walk with us tomorrow if you really want to."

"I'm sure I can come at lunchtime if that'd work. I could bring a sandwich with me. Could we take Billy to the prom?"

"Yeah. Give me a knock at the lodge when you're ready."

TOMORROW, I'LL FIND a way to ask Rue if she knows a lad with hazel eyes, like Billy's.

Day 2

When a character entered, he proceeded directly to serve the catastrophe.

Arthur Miller on *A View from the Bridge*

Six

THE PROM'S AS busy as yesterday in what Miss described to us this morning as a Hallowe'en summer, which is neat when we're only a few days off the end of October.

Even though Rue's a couple of years younger than us, she seems a lot more mature than some sixth-formers. Turns out music's her thing, which explains why I keep catching her wiggling the fingers of her left hand as if playing some melody she can hear in her head.

"I'd like to actually compose some violin pieces too," she's telling me. "What 'bout you, Allie? What do you…"

I've stopped listening. We're coming up to the café, and it's him! In a slightly darker green top this time, he's sitting exactly where we were with Miss yesterday, with three other guys, small coffee cups in front of them. All in dark colours, they're clearly older than him; one of them, with a shaved head, I'd say is even twenty years older. He and one in a black leather jacket are smoking, which must be banned in the café grounds.

I can smell the smoke as we get nearer, a grown-up, heady smell, dangerous somehow. I hope my mystery lad doesn't smoke.

"Allie?" Rue says, but I'm trying to work out what language they're all speaking. Except *he* isn't. He's leaning back, slightly apart, looking...

Troubled, actually.

"Sorry," I murmur to Rue once we're past the café. "I was...curious. Those guys—what language were they speaking?"

"Polish," she says shortly.

Ah, one of my burning questions answered.

"What do they do then, for work?"

"I don't know." She sounds impatient now, her intense grey eyes shrewd as she turns to me. "I was asking you, Allie, what you want to do with your drama. Cos even though Mum was a great cellist, my dad claims you can't earn a living from music."

"My mum says the same about drama. She's even threatening not to help with my living costs, but I'm not gonna let that stop me having the future *I* want. And I'm lucky my dad supports me. It's not so much acting I want to do, though. I want to *write* scripts."

I'm rabbiting on, I suddenly realise, but I don't get chance to talk about this, other than to Finn, and he's heard too much already.

"Then we're both composers," she says, smiling at me.

We've reached the ruined swimming pool. I peer through the grille properly this time.

"It closed in the early 1990s," Rue says from behind me. "But my mum and dad spent a lot of time in the lido as teenagers, he says. It was *the* place to hang out."

"Are your parents split too?" I ask, piecing together a few things she's said.

She gives a hoarse laugh. "Only by death."

My hand goes to my mouth. "I'm so sorry, Rue. I didn't realise."

"Aye, why would you?" she says and sets off walking again.

I ache for her deep down inside. I can't imagine life without one of my parents. Though Dad's hundreds of miles from us in the north of Scotland, at least I see him in the school holidays. And her poor dad's lost his wife.

"It's a long time ago," Rue tells me. "Eight years. Dad got Billy for me not long after. You were only ten weeks old when you first came to live with us, weren't you, Billy? Mine from the start."

She stops and bends down to stroke Billy's head, and he looks up at her as if smiling. Such a bond between them, and such wisdom and strength in her. Her eyes are on me now.

"He didn't mind being parted from *his* mum. I was his family. Dad loves him too, but not in the way I do. We all need someone who's for us above anyone else. I don't need a person. The someone for me is Billy. And I'm Billy's someone."

"Yeah," I say. "I can see that."

But who's *my* someone right now? Finn's been my constant someone for years. He's the one I always feel at home with, probably because I spend more time at his place than mine. Mum, I'd say is my *intermittent* someone. I know, underneath it all, she's got my back. It took me a while to forgive her after she and Dad split and she dragged me from my old life in Buckinghamshire for her dream job in Leeds. And now she's so opposed to my drama. That's another lofty wall between us.

Which reminds me.

I need to be on time for our workshop.

"Time to turn back, sorry," I tell Rue and Billy.

"So, your drama's gonna be about the Bay," Rue says as we amble back in the direction of the hostel. "But what?"

"Something on its beauty and—"

I glance ahead and see him coming towards us. The lad. *Straight* towards us.

Rue stops. What the…?

He crouches down. "Hi, Billy," he says.

Billy's tail's swirling in actual circles! And the guy, now on his knees—his face is lit up, transformed from the perturbed expression at the café.

"Hugs!" he tells Billy, and next thing both Billy's paws are on his shoulders and some sort of love-in's going on!

"Hi Rue," he says, straightening up eventually with a sheepish smile that she's taking second place to Billy.

A weird stab of jealousy spikes in my chest, but I'm the outsider, only passing through, when these three already know each other and will continue to bump into each other after I've gone.

He's looking from her to me, expectantly.

"Mareno," she says, "this is Allie."

Mareno! I say his name in my head, liking its soft consonants. Doesn't *sound* Polish. Mareno's smiling at me, one of those where you properly look at the person. I smile back, whilst wondering, *is either of us going to say we've met before?*

"Allie's at the hostel on a school trip," Rue adds.

I wait for some detail on him, but there's nothing from either of them.

"Well," he says, after a moment, "I must go."

Why? Where? To do what? As soon as I find some answers, he creates more questions. Such a shame he can't chat any longer, as he seems so much happier talking to us three than he was at the café.

"Oh, by the way," I blurt whilst trying to sound casual, "apparently, there's a band playing at the Fog and Whistle tonight. Our teachers are taking us. Either of you going?"

"I'm playing," Rue says.

"Oh, great!" I mean it too, though I'm surprised. I was imagining electric guitars and drums. "What's the band called?"

She frowns. "It's not called anything. Just three of us…playing. One of the others is my dad."

"Oh, okay." I shrug. So more like a folk group? That wouldn't go down well with our lot!

"Sorry," Mareno says. "I can't."

I wait for some reason, but no. Something subsides in me. I'm hardly going to bump into him a third time.

He raises a hand in goodbye, strides off down the prom.

Rue and I set off again in the opposite direction.

"How do you know him?" I have to ask. Did they used to be a thing, given how well he knows Billy? Yet she's too young for him. Isn't she?

"It's a small town. 'Specially if you're down on the prom a lot, you get to see what's going on."

What is going on? I wonder, especially with those older, dodgy-looking men. I hope Mareno's not involved in something drug related.

"Mareno always makes a beeline for Billy cos he misses his own sheepdog at home."

"But his name—it's not Polish, is it?"

"No!" she says as if I'm being a bit dense. "He's Italian, obviously. It was all the others speaking Polish."

Huh! Well, I did ask her what they were speaking! But no wonder he looked left out. And I was right yesterday in guessing where he might be from. I *love* Italy, at least, the cities I've been to with Mum, and its food, obviously!

As Rue and Billy go in front of me on the narrow track back to the hostel, I take the opportunity to gobble down my tuna sandwich before the afternoon drama workshop. Miss has split us three ways to research a dramatic story set in the Bay, me with Courtney. As if! And anyway, my mind's still working on Mareno. I know his name and nationality, but he's mostly a mystery. If he misses his dog, the rest of his family must still in Italy. So, who does he live with now, and where?

Most of all, how will I ever find out?

Seven

WE'RE OFF TO the Oscars! Or so you'd think, the effort Lucy and Courtney are putting into getting ready for tonight. With no intention of getting dolled up myself, I lean against my headboard and read on in *A View from the Bridge*. I'm up to the part where Catherine, who's seventeen like us, is getting ready for a date with Rudolpho, a scene Courtney unwittingly re-enacts as she lays out different outfits on her bed. Meanwhile, Lucy's in the en suite, doing her face, always an epic ritual.

When they've both finally finished, I get a whole two minutes in the bathroom. While I clean my teeth, I look at my reflection in the little space left above Lucy's massive bag of make-up on the shelf. She uses it like the artist she is—to complement her outfit. With Courtney, it's to build a persona: hard, black lines to her already hard, black eyes.

I don't wear make-up. Other than when I'm on stage, it's What You See is What You Get, and I never do anything different with my long hair either. It's loose and wavy on my shoulders unless I absolutely *have to* tie it back for some practical reason. Poppy often exclaims over it, but I reckon she's just girl-starved! Basically, I'm…indeterminate. I've not got Courtney's startling hair, splaying out from on high, or Lucy's tall, blonde model looks. I'm small-ish, brown-ish. An ish girl.

But that doesn't matter when you're a playwright, does it?

As SOON AS Miss and I pass through the double doors at the rear of the Fog and Whistle, my nostrils flare at the sugary warm-beer smell, and I can feel crisps and the stickiness of spilt drinks under my trainers. I kept Miss company in the minibus while the rest of the group walked with Hey Ho. They're all hanging around the bar with Cokes and OJ, along with locals, mostly with grey hair, I can't help noticing.

Miss treats me to a J2O, and we find a space in the middle of a long, rectangular room where the icky carpet ends and lino leads to the far end. A podgy man is messing with cables and a mic.

"There's Rue," I tell Miss. "Tuning her violin next to Mr. Rainer." A giggle rises up me at him shouldering a heavy-looking black accordion.

Miss bites her lip in amusement. "I'm not sure how this is going to go down with our lot."

"One, two, testing," says Mic-man. He nods at Mr. Rainer.

Phumph! A sweeping accordion chord. Miss and I look at each other, trying not to laugh.

I crane my neck for the rest of our group, still standing around the bar. No one seems to have noticed yet that there are no ingredients here for a rock band.

"Welcome, one and all," says Mic-man, "to what's fast becoming a fixture in the Fog's calendar. So, we're going to kick off with an old favourite, the 'Gay Gordon.'"

"Ooh, I love a barn dance!" Miss says.

"A barn dance?" Courtney will hate that!

Now I enjoy the dramatic hilarity of realising first, as I read Courtney's lips from here.

"*What the actual fxxk!*" she says to Finn, wide-eyed.

He cracks up laughing. After a moment, eyebrows quirked, she joins in.

"Take your partners by the hand," Mic-man says, "and I'll talk you through the moves."

By this point, the rest of our group's caught on. Though none of us would have been seen dead here had we known, it looks like there's an ironic agreement this could be a kind of fun after all.

Hey Ho appears and offers Miss a dance, and she grins.

"I'll power her up," she says, patting the controls on her chair and winking at me. "I reckon she can cope with the moves for the 'Gay Gordon.'"

Mic-man has the couples face each other, anticlockwise, in a circle.

Lucy and Shaf are together, of course, and most of the geographers are paired up too, some in same-sex couples. Finn's all smiles with Courtney. If only they *were* as good together as they look, with their contrasting complexions and him even taller than her.

Once Mic-man has walked them through the sequence, the band strikes up, jolly and rhythmic, dominated by the accordion but with Rue's violin melody soaring above it to make it so much more than a regular beat. It's definitely a good dance to open with. Everyone can manage the forward and backward moves. The polka part's more of a challenge, especially for Miss, but one she looks to be finding hilarious. Finn, all long legs, is in a bit of tizz too.

Not long after the music stops, my phone pings. A new post notification from TikTok:

having a blast at a barn-friggin-dance!
#Courtney&FinnsWildWeekofFun

I shove my phone back in my pocket like it's contagious.

WHEN THE NEXT dance is announced, 'Strip the Willow', most couples stay on the dance floor, including our two teachers.

"I buy you a drink?"

I jump at the deep voice with its heavy accent.

God! The guy in the leather jacket from outside the café. He's slid into the chair next to me, stinking of cheap deodorant and smoke.

I have no choice but to turn towards him, but avoiding his eyes means I have to see his pimply skin and his brown, slicked-back hair.

"I'm…I've already got one, thanks." I hold up my bottle.

He says something to the other guy I've only just noticed on the other side of him, the one with reddish hair who was with him earlier. They laugh, and it's obvious they're talking about me. Leather Jacket stands, looming over me.

"A dance then," he says, brandishing his hand.

I shake my head.

His friend crosses between us and perches on the seat on the other side of me.

"You make my friend, Krys, very sad," he wheedles.

Krys turns out his lip. "I am excellent dancer—for a builder!"

I shrug. "But I only want to listen to the music. Thanks anyway."

His frown lines tell me he's not used to being refused. At once, I wish I'd not made an excuse. Why didn't I tell the truth? *I don't want to dance with you.*

"Cold, eh, Leon? Very cold," he says to his mate, who shakes his head.

"Offensive," Leon says.

I fold my arms and look at the dancers.

So Mareno's a builder too, is he? How are *they* friends of his?

With a last sneer at me, Krys and Leon finally move on, crossing the floor in front of the band, but by now, everyone else is paired up in a circle, facing the same way, men on the outside.

Puh-puh, sings a mouth organ. Mr. Rainer has switched instruments!

"Opposite your partners in two lines," Mic-man says.

I half stand so I can track Krys as he scans the dancers. He clocks someone, scoots around the outside of the circle. I should've have known!

Stand your ground, Finn, I will him, as Krys is between him and Courtney and it looks like he's trying to negotiate. *You wanted to dance with her.*

"When you're ready, folks," Mic-man says, impatient to get going.

What the…? Krys and Finn are in a definite face-off, Krys jabbing his finger towards Finn's chest, taller still than Finn. Finn looks at Courtney, who gives a mock-helpless shrug. Finn shakes his head and takes a step back, stumbling over a chair leg.

By the time he's righted himself, Mic-man's calling the moves and Courtney and Krys are half a circle away.

In dismay, Finn's sits to save face. I go over to sit with him, my fingers curling themselves into my palms at Courtney's expression. She's *lapping* up the drama and attention of being fought over and won by an older guy, no thought for Finn. Exactly why she gets right under my skin. As he studies the floor, I almost wish I'd agreed to dance with Krys rather than this happen to him. *Almost.*

ONCE MIC-MAN'S FINISHED talking through the steps, the music kicks in and it becomes total chaos as couples lose each other when they cast off down the outside. All except Courtney and Krys, who seem to have it completely sussed. Now and again, I glance sideways at Finn, head still down, pretending to check his phone.

I close my eyes against it all and listen to the music instead. Rue's violin transports me out of the room with a wild melody, sometimes with a pure thread of sound, at other times with two or more strings off in some rebellious wandering. I follow her to uninhabited spots—the depths of a forest or even the middle of the Bay—then it's all over.

I open my eyes to a seedy pub and the dancers, looking hot and sweaty, laughing over their clumsiness. The lads perform mock bows, the girls curtsies, all except for Courtney, who bows at Krys at exactly the same time as he bows at her. She laughs in delight.

There's a short pause, and Finn goes over to the band to chat to Rue. She's smiling up at Finn, and I know he'll be complimenting her on her playing. That's Finn, time for everyone.

"Take your partners for the 'Rózsa' couple dance," Mic-man announces.

Finn's back on the sidelines, bobbing his head around in a final desperate effort to catch Courtney's eye, but her eyes are only for Krys.

The walk-through kicks off with couples palm to palm before a half turn involving Krys wrapping his arms tightly around Courtney from behind.

I can't bear to see Finn's face a second longer.

"Not got a partner, Allie?" Miss says, gliding up beside me.

"Not one I'd dance with!" I tell her. "I'm going for some fresh air."

I grab my fleece off the back of the chair, done with sleazy Krys and attention-queen Courtney.

Eight

THE NIGHT'S ICINESS slices into my face and fingers, the purity exactly what I need after the tepid, sweaty atmosphere and condensation clouding the windows. The swing doors settle together behind me, forming a barrier against the seediness inside.

Even though the autumn cold is cutting through my jeans into my thighs, I can't go back in. Not yet. I put several strides up the car park between me and the pub before stopping. I'm still all pent up, especially by the way Krys and Courtney made a fool of Finn. Spreading my fingers by my sides, I close my eyes and try to breathe out the sourness of it.

"Hi, Allie!"

My eyes flash open. "I…I thought you couldn't come."

In a black donkey jacket, Mareno's standing right in front of me. "I finished…quicker than I expected."

"I'm glad," I say, though I'm still wondering what he had to build on a Sunday evening.

"Heard enough of the band already?"

"No, just enough of Krys."

"Krys is here?" He's immediately alert. "What's he done?"

"Firstly, he came on to me pretty strong."

"Came on to you—what does this mean?"

"Er... I suppose, he wanted..." What *did* he want, ultimately? Nothing good.

"He wanted to buy me a drink, then turned...nasty when I wouldn't dance with him."

He tuts. "Are you all right?"

"Yeah." I'm touched he's asked. "But he all but forced Finn out of the way to dance with Courtney—the two from the Sands."

"I'm sorry," he says as if it's somehow *his* fault. "A bad choice," he adds darkly.

"In what way?" Much as I don't get on with Courtney, I don't wish her any harm.

"Krys..." He rubs a palm across his face. "He's not someone *I* would choose to be with."

Yet I saw you with him at the café, I nearly say but remember how uneasy Mareno looked. "How old is he, by the way?" I say instead.

"I don't know exactly. A few years older than me. Twenty-two or three."

That he doesn't know confirms they're not truly friends. And a few years older than him, so, Mareno's what—eighteen, nineteen?

"And Courtney?" he asks.

"Seventeen. We both are."

A pause, but I feel lighter for getting the whole incident off my chest.

"Do you want to go back in?" he asks.

I hesitate. *I'd far rather be out here, talking to you.*

"I was enjoying Rue's music," I say instead.

At that very moment, the band kicks in again, her violin creating a sweet, romantic melody.

"She has talent, doesn't she?" he says.

"You've heard her play before?" I try to ignore another of those envious stabbings.

"During the summer, she would…I don't know the word. She played on the prom, and people put money into the box of her violin, next to Billy."

"Ah, busking."

"Busking," he repeats as if trying to memorise the word. "Okay. And mostly she's…how do you say, when you're not using written music?"

"Improvising? It's called that when actors don't follow a script, anyway. She's improvising tonight, I'm sure. Do *you* want to go in?"

"I'm always happier outdoors."

I smile inside: he came anyway.

"And Allie," he says.

I look up into his eyes through the orangey light escaping the pub.

"I believe, if you don't like something, find somewhere better."

Is this what he's done in leaving Italy to come here? Hard to imagine.

"Where are you thinking?" I ask because I can't go far.

"Come," he says, "and I'll show you."

UNDER THE WHITE light of the full moon, we amble up the slope of the car park, crunching through frosted leaves towards the trees at the top.

"Why has your school come here?" he asks, seeming genuinely interested.

"For the Bay." I suppose that's the short answer. "We're from Leeds, so nowhere near the sea. The geography group's learning about coastal systems." I say it like in speech marks. "The rest of us have to write a short play based on the Bay by the end of the week."

"You don't have long," he remarks.

"I know, 'specially when half my group's distracted by...other things."

"And you're focused. I can see this."

"It's what I've been waiting for, to write something of our own, something new, something to make a difference." I wince. "I must sound horribly idealistic and ambitious."

Will he know those words?

"I like ambition." His breath is misty in the freeze of the night. If Krys and Leon are co-workers, I can well imagine him wanting to be more than them.

"Yeah? What's yours?" I ask at the same time as he says, "What do you want to write about the Bay?"

I leave him space to answer. He doesn't. So I do.

"Something on its power and danger."

We settle on a low wall, facing away from the pub. The moonlight's turning the tall, slim tree trunks silver, like shimmering candles.

"Ah, but please, Allie, don't forget the beauty we saw together."

My heart grows. He remembers the sweet moment between us on the Sands yesterday.

"Every morning, from my bedroom window," he goes on slowly, "the Bay is a completely new sight. Today, it was all shiny…" He does a whirling movement with his forefinger.

"Like rough circles—swirls?" I suggest.

"Yes, swirls, I think."

"It dazzled me when I first saw it from the viaduct," I tell him. "All golden under the sun. Tomorrow, my whole group's going on a guided walk right across the Sands. My drama teacher thinks it will help us with our play, but I'm going to stay at the hostel and do some scripting." And keep Miss company.

"It would be a big shame to miss it." He sounds so adamant.

"Why?"

"Because you need to *feel* it. Especially far from land. The wind on your face, the sand changing under your feet, see the birds, the river…"

I give an involuntary shudder, which he clocks.

"You will be completely safe with Elijah. And after, I would love to know what you think."

I wriggle with pleasure that he wants to meet again.

"I'll consider it some more," I say. "Your English is excellent, by the way."

"My mother would be pleased to hear you say this. She worked hard to teach herself so she could became a guide for tourists. She mostly speaks English with me and my brother."

"Where does she guide?" I'm imagining Rome, Florence, Venice.

He doesn't seem to have heard, tilting back onto the wall until he's flat, his head on his hands. "The moon tonight, Allie!"

I lower myself the opposite way, the tops of our heads so close our hair is all but touching.

"I know. The…extraness of it."

"Extraness," he echoes.

As my eyes adjust, I make out a few stars and patterns. "There's the Plough. You know that in Italian?"

A pause. "*La costellazione dell'aratro*," he says.

"I love the sound of Italian," I tell him. It has rhythm and lilt, nothing like English.

"Later this week," he says, "it could be possible to see a comet. It will be four thousand years since it was visible from Earth and eight thousand before it can be seen again. Imagine!"

"A comet! I *can't* imagine. I'd have to see it."

And we've definitely found somewhere better than the pub, I realise! The enchanting trees, the thrilling purity of the night sky. I leave Earth behind—Finn, Courtney and Krys, my doubts about tomorrow's Bay crossing—and let myself float among the pearly suns, radiant against the sheer black.

EVENTUALLY, I REGISTER the cold of the wall under my shoulders.

I check my phone: I've been out here ages.

"Time I got back," I say, sitting up and swinging my legs towards the pub.

Mareno sighs and gathers himself up too.

"Allie," he says, as we walk back down to the Fog. "What does your name mean?"

"It's short for Alethea. Which means 'truth' in Greek."

"I like the meaning. I'll remember it when I call you Allie."

I like the sound of that. And *I* like knowing the meaning of names too, seeing if they match the person's character.

"And Mareno, what does that mean?"

"Of the sea."

"Cool," I say. He's certainly enthusiastic about the Bay!

"You want to swap numbers?" he asks. "Tell me how goes the walk?"

"How the walk goes," I correct automatically.

"Okay, thanks. I always want corrections, please. And by the way, *I'm* not coming on to you!"

I laugh. This is *exactly* what I was wondering…half hoping. He's the first lad who's ever intrigued me, but becoming involved would be pointless for both of us when I'm only here five more days. Wouldn't it? Anyway, he's not interested in that way, he's said. So what *is* he wanting? Maybe a friendly face since he's saddled with people like Krys.

I stop to find the right screen on my phone, and he gives me his.

"Hey, Mareno." I suddenly realise. "I never said I was doing the crossing tomorrow."

He smiles at me as we swap back phones. "But maybe you will?"

I hug my arms around myself. This half hour I've shared with him, I can't remember anything more magical. If he thinks the Bay is an unmissable experience, if I can meet him afterwards…

"Of course I'll do the walk," I tell him.

WE CONTINUE BACK down the car park, toward the artificial lights.

A rollicking accordion chord blares out through the darkness.

"What kind of dancing is this?" he asks.

"It's called a barn dance."

"Er, why?"

"I guess because it's a type of dance they used to do in barns in the past. More room than inns or pubs."

"You guess? But you don't know, Allie!"

"Busted!" I say, liking this lighter-hearted side to him.

"Busted," he mutters.

We're almost at the swing doors, and the tempo of the music has slowed right down. The last dance. I can guess who Courtney will be sharing it with.

"*This* is not a barn dance," he tells me. "We have this waltz at home." He turns to face me. "You want to try it, Allie?"

"You're a dark horse, aren't you?"

"A horse!" he exclaims. "Why?"

"It means you're a bit of a mystery. First comets, now dancing."

He shakes his head. "I'll never learn all your English expressions."

"Then I'll have to keep using them!"

So," he reaches out his left hand for mine, "the dance?"

Like practically everyone, he's taller than me, but he doesn't loom the way Krys did.

It's only a hand, I tell myself. *He must be lonely, so far from home, and it seems to mean something to him, this waltz.*

I stretch out my hand towards his.

The swing doors suddenly burst open, releasing a stream of bright orange light.

In a spume of riotous laughter, Courtney stumbles forward, Krys following, his hands on her hips.

"Mental!" she's shrieking.

I snatch my hand back; Mareno steps away from me.

Day 3

As long as you owe them money, they'll get you plenty of work.

Eddie to Marco and Rudolpho

Nine

"THE BIGGEST GRAVEYARD in the north," Elijah tells us, brandishing his staff towards the Sands. Reassuring from our guide! "Aye, quicksand's swallowed down planes, carriages, horses. And people. Lots of people."

The hairs lift on my arms. Robert Harrison, the young guy I'm researching for our play, his body was covered by the Sands for seven weeks, but at least it was then recovered and buried at Cartmel Priory, not far away.

I gaze over Elijah's white hair, trying to distract myself with the houses rising from the shore of Grange opposite, distinct in the fresh morning light. Mareno's somewhere in the town, perhaps waking up to the view I've just had of the untouched silver Sands wiped clean by the tide overnight like one of those magic slates. The whole train journey from Grange, across the viaduct to Arnside, took only five minutes; it'll take four hours to walk the eight miles back. I want to have *done* the trek across this wild, beautiful landscape, leapfrog the next few hours.

Elijah sets off along the pebbly beach towards the sand; I scurry to follow him in his battered, yellow sou'wester tied with string at the waist, his lower legs and feet brown and bare, despite the stones. He stops abruptly at the edge and has us all line up. Most of us take off our trainers and socks here, but somehow, I want a barrier between me and the sand.

"One rule," Eli says. "You *never* go ahead of me. And remember." He holds up an ancient finger. "The Sands will *always* win if you don't respect them."

The low stomach pain I woke up with this morning intensifies: if this is the verdict of the guide, the Sands really *are* our enemy. I glance along the line at Courtney, leaning against Finn, likely hungover after Krys buying her vodka and oranges last night. *See?* I want to tell her. *We **are** battling against the Sands. There **will** be winners and losers.* Now my pulse patters.

I'd rather not, I think. *Genuinely. I could tell Hey Ho I'm not well, catch the train back to Grange.*

Yet Miss says experiencing the Bay close up is crucial for our method acting.

And most of all, how can I see Mareno again if I haven't done the walk?

Steeling my whole body, I step through the Sands' force field down onto the seabed.

Beneath my soles, it's uncertain and unpredictable, one step yielding and squidgy, the next hard and ungiving. I try to keep my mind totally on the here and now. Not with Finn and the others behind me. Not even on Mareno and the glittering times we might still share.

Under a pale morning sun in a clear sky, a strong wind is blowing straight in our faces, forcing me to inhale lungfuls of the freshest, saltiest air. The gusts are growing ever stronger as we trudge parallel to the shore towards open sea.

Open sea!

The tide's not going to return for hours, though, I remind myself. Hey Ho explained earlier how the walk begins at six hours' ebb, so even if the crossing takes us four hours—which it will at Shaf's rate—it'll be three hours until the sea starts to flow back in.

As far as the horizon, only sand and pools of seawater and overhead the biggest of skies marbled with clouds. I'm almost enjoying the space and freedom, the wildness of it all. Not far to my right, a flock of tall, white birds are busy dipping their long beaks into the sand for their breakfast.

Whoa! I'm suddenly dizzy and have to look down. It's like I've walked across a sheet of cardboard that tipped me side to side. I glance over my shoulder at a glistening patch. Sinking sand, I reckon.

See?! I want to shout as I scurry to catch up with the Elijah. *It's so breathtaking out here but absolutely lethal— the last place we should be walking.*

In a few minutes, Eli stops in front of a stretch of water a few metres across.

"Is this the Kent?" I ask him.

Hey Ho told us earlier the Kent's the principal river emptying into the Bay.

Eli scoffs. "You'll know about it when we meet a river."

Now I dare look properly, this isn't *living*, moving water. The sea's left this behind as a reminder it's been… and will return. But this I can handle.

"The Kent is much nearer't far side," Eli adds. "The final hurdle."

My stomach contracts.

"You might want to get 'em trainers off first, though," he advises.

I wriggle out of them, trying to shove the prospect of the river to the edges of my mind. I peel off my socks and roll my jeans up above my knees.

My bare feet sink into the sharp cold of the waterlogged sand, the mud oozing between my toes and over the top till they're buried. It's oddly intimate, like part of me is part of the Sands.

As I stuff my socks into my pocket, the back of my hand brushes the smooth metal of my phone, which Mareno held not twelve hours ago, making a typo in the dark. Will he get in touch after the walk? Will I if he doesn't?

Finally, the others are lined up on either side of us, Finn holding hands with Courtney, Shaf with Lucy, the geographers forming their usual little clan.

Pheerr! Elijah whistles.

And we're off!

"Yeoow!" Shaf yells when, after a few seconds, the pain registers.

It doesn't bother me: the still water only comes to my ankles, and my toes are gripping firmly into the smooth, sandy bottom.

ON THE OTHER side of the channel, Elijah leads us in almost a ninety-degree turn so we're no longer walking out to sea but towards Grange. Straggly clouds have drifted in front of the sun, marring the blue. The buildings opposite are no longer defined, and without the sun to pick out their gold, the Sands are a matt sludge brown.

We're deep into the Bay's territory, as far to go back as to go on. The still hush—no birds even—is more menacing than calming, as if lulling us into a false sense of security. The whole expanse is barren, not even shells to brighten the bleakness in front of me.

Finn draws alongside me, still hand in hand with Courtney.

"All right, Allie?"

I grunt. *No thanks to you and the threat of the river hanging over me.*

Courtney passes me, dragging Finn after her.

Elijah said not to go in front of him, I almost say, but she's hardly going to take any notice of me, is she?

Pheer! Pheeeeeeeeeeeeer!

Elijah again.

We all stop. Ahead of us all, Finn freezes, turns, his face blotchy with mortification. Courtney won't look back, though, oh no.

Eli marches after them, and we all fall in behind him. I'm sorry Finn's embarrassed, but she—she deserves whatever's coming.

"So, Madam," he says, "you know what to do if you walk into quicksand?"

Even the word ushers in a stillness among us.

The face on her! How many times have I seen it, her 'I know better' look? Not this time, Courtney!

"I thought not," Elijah says. "You don't know the first thing about it, do you? For a start, what does 'quick' mean?"

"You sink in quick," she says cockily.

Lips pursed, Elijah fixes her. "Quick's an old word for *live*. And if I hadn't stopped you, *you'd* be in living sand. Look."

We all gaze after his staff. Not more than a metre ahead, the sand's surface is wobbly and puckered, a vast crème caramel. It's shiny, same as the patch I walked over earlier, and slightly indented from the sand around it.

I shake my head in frustration: she could have led Finn right into this hungry mud.

Elijah strides forward and plunges his staff into it like a stake. It disappears right up to its curved handle.

"So, lass," he says, catching Courtney's eye again. "What if you'd stepped into *that*?"

She brazens it out but, for once, has no answer.

"I'll tell you what. You'd sit on thi'arse."

She grins, and the whole group laughs, the tension dispelled.

"Next, you throw your coat to one side of you and roll out onto it, away from the sinking sand. And you do it fast—afore you become cement."

"What then?" Finn asks, wide-eyed.

"Then it's hours of a job while you wait for the coastguard—if the tide don't get you first," he says. "So, Madam, don't assume because I'm here, you're safe. Not if you break the rules. If you're up to your ankles in sinking sand, it's a job an' a half to get you out. Up to your waist?" He pauses; every face is on his. He purses his lips and shakes his head. "Well, the odds are against you."

Most people have a 'the worst way to die': shark attack; avalanche; plane crash. Drowning—and this way in particular—is mine. Unable to run for it, totally trapped, the long, slow wait for the water to cover you, enter you.

Far worse even than the tide taking you suddenly.

"And understand this," Elijah adds. "A patch of quicksand can be *any*where. Far out, near the shore. And even if there were a map to tell you where, it'd have to change every day. It takes a sand-born person to be able to read these Sands, the most dangerous in the world," he says before setting off on a wide trajectory around the danger zone.

'The most dangerous in the world' echoes in my head. *But we won this particular battle with the Bay.* If only because we had Elijah to guide us through the minefield.

A SHIVER SHRUGS across my shoulders. The temperature's dropping, as it does before rain. Heavy charcoal has coloured in the clouds, and Grange has become a grey ghost town.

"Gather round," Elijah says. "We're at Priest Skear, skear an old Norse word meaning a bank of rocks in the sea. The night the Chinese cockle pickers drowned, they were out on this sandbank."

Thin drizzle weeps from the grey clouds onto the straggle of equally grey rocks.

Each one of us is glued to Elijah's face, but it's like he's speaking a different language.

"A group of young men and women from China were out here gathering the shellfish at night," Hey Ho explains. "They went out too close to the tide." He pauses. "Drowned."

My skin crawls. Ambushed by the tide in the dark, right where we are now, in the middle of the seabed, and all for the sake of some shellfish?

"Back then," Elijah says, "we found their craams scattered round where they'd dropped 'em—the rakes for bringing cockles to the surface."

"I thought they grew on trees," Shaf stage-whispers behind us so I don't know whether he's joking or not. Lucy shushes him.

Elijah stoops for a moment; rises with something in each hand.

"This is a wheeat," he says, holding a small shell between his finger and thumb. "A teeny young cockle, too young to harvest. They have to be at least two years old afore you pick 'em. Which is why, the day before yesterday, Fishery Patrol declared the cockle beds closed for a few months, so the wheeats can breed and mature. No more cockling allowed for some time now."

He passes the shell in his other hand to me, as the nearest person. "*This* nice big un's what they were cockling for."

I hold it out on the flat of my hand, next to the mini shell on his.

Ridged with various shades of brown, the cockle is cool and damp; it fills my palm, heart-shaped yet so light for what's caused so much heavy grief.

Eli lays the wheeat back onto the Sands. I do the same with my shell.

As he leads us on, towards Grange, I'm relieved to be leaving Priest Skear behind with its vibes of a priest giving the last rites.

As I TRAMP on, I try to judge the relative distances behind and in front of us: the cockle beds are as far out as you can go from land in either direction. But at least the clouds are less dark and dense now. Grange is clearer; in it, Miss, Rue and Billy, and Mareno.

But first, I have to cross the river.

Ten

ALL TOO SOON, we're at the Kent's edge. Only a step away, water flooding down from the Lakeland hills is gushing out to sea. Soon, it will collide with the tide coming in the opposite direction.

What I have to wade through right now is at least as wide as a swimming pool across when this *live* water's my horror. Churning and unpredictable, it dizzies me even as I stand on dry land. In either direction, with a mind of its own, river or sea water is rushing somewhere. It has an agenda, and if you're in its way, it'll take you with it.

Elijah has us all line up along its bank so we don't wear the sand to quicksand in any one place. I hitch my jeans up higher still.

"Once you start into the river, don't stop, not for anything," Eli says. "If someone else gets stuck, leave 'em and carry on or you'll get stuck too."

Quicksand in the river! I look at Hey Ho in horror. *What were you thinking, bringing us out here?*

"I'll come and get them out," Elijah adds.

I'm not convinced. How, exactly, in deep water?

"Best way to keep your balance is to look ahead, not down," Finn says, coming alongside me.

I stare at him, speechless. I'd do anything to avoid this, but there is no alternative.

So, pulse thumping in my ears, I fix my eyes on the other side and think of Mareno.

Eli whistles.

We all wade forward.

I don't register the cold, only the force from both sides, buffeting, bombarding me, stronger with each step deeper. And underfoot, instead of sand to anchor you, *things* are growing—river life.

I grind to a halt, exactly what Elijah told us *not* to do. He's way out of reach to my right, Courtney and Finn ahead of me, her shrieking as they splash each other. I stare down into the churning water, remembering even after all these years how it feels to be tumbled over and over under it, till you don't know up from down, only that time, my dad was with me, and lifeguards came and fished me out of the wave pool.

When I look up again, *everyone's* ahead of me.

Stop! Wait for me! I want to yell.

The more I make of it, though, the worse it'll be.

I gulp down my panic, focus on my breathing, steady, in and out, fix my eyes ahead; plan what I will say to Mareno, later.

And yes! This step takes me shallower. I'm past halfway.

But the rest of them are already on the sand, all of them facing away from me so they wouldn't have a clue if I fell!

Keep it together, Allie.

The water's only halfway up my calves; I'm nearly out.

My pulse slows; sun warms my face; I smile at the sight of the buildings, clear and close.

Each heavy push takes me closer and closer till I'm out the other side.

I jog to catch up with the others, on the home run now. *I've done it!* I think, exhilaration streaking through me. *I'm the winner today.* Now I've got all the experience of the Sands and the river I needed to write about convincingly, I'll never have to set foot in the Bay again.

"How many miles to the hostel?" Shaf is grumbling as I walk up the path through the reeds with him and Lucy to the little station ahead of us. "A ten-mile hike isn't what I expected from a drama trip."

"You expected a doss of a week, didn't you?" Lucy says.

Shaf grins and throws up his hands.

"You've got to admit, it was unforgettable," I say, still buoyed up. "So much we must pass on to Miss and can put in our script."

And I can talk to Mareno about.

"Yeah, more hard work. It's…agggh!" Shaf shrieks.

This black-and-white blur is hurtling towards us.

"Keep that wolf away from me!" he yells, shoving me in front of him!

"It's only Billy," I say, squatting down. "Hey, Billy lad." I scratch his ears as he licks my nose.

Lucy leans down to stroke his back while Shaf hangs back.

"I'm just home from school," Rue says, mainly to me, "and Billy and I thought you'd appreciate a welcoming committee."

I beam at her. I do, I really do. It's been more of an ordeal for me than anyone could know. And strange to imagine it's taken a big chunk of Rue's school day to do the crossing.

"We've even brought biscuits, haven't we, Billy?"

"Thank God," Shaf says, reaching for the packet she's offering. "I'm dying here."

"This is Shafeeq, and he's melodramatic!" I tell Rue.

"Really!" she says as Finn arrives to say hi to Billy.

Courtney grabs a wodge of biscuits, but she's so not interested in dogs—or Rue, though I catch her curling her lip at Rue's bird-nest hair.

Hey Ho sweeps the geographers on, leaving us six to make our way back to the hostel in our own time. As we walk up the ramp at the end of the salt marsh, Finn's making Rue laugh with his spot-on impressions of Elijah.

"I still can't believe there are no cockle bushes out there," Shaf tells her.

I smile to myself. It's good to see Rue having some human friends.

Soon, we're at a level crossing and the suitably named station, Kents Bank.

THANKS TO BILLY, Rue, Finn and I soon leave the others behind on the track that runs alongside the railway all the way back to the prom.

Finn pauses outside the lido and peers in through the window.

"Pity this is closed. I love swimming outdoors."

"Yeah," Rue says. "My mum did too. I was telling Allie, she spent a lot of time here when she was our age. One of my favourite pics is of her lolling on the steps around the pool. Most of my memories of Mum are from photos."

Finn looks stricken. "Oh, Rue, I hadn't realised." He puts a hand on her shoulder; he'll be projecting how *he'd* be without *his* mum, they're so close.

"Anyway," she says, her face brightening, "soon, they're going to renovate the place, so if you come back in a few years, you should be able to have your swim."

He smiles at her, thoughtful, hand on his chin. "But wouldn't you like to see it first, as it was in your mum's day?"

"Well, yeah," Rue says, "I've always wondered about it. But how?"

She glances up. Its high wall is topped with barbed wire, and the metal rails are covered with anti-climb paint, a sign tells us.

Finn walks around to the curved side of the lido and looks down at the marsh.

I can see where this is heading. "Finn, have you not read the warnings?"

Yellow signs are placed all around the front of the lido, shouting:

DANGER KEEP OUT

DANGER DEEP WATER

DANGER OF DEATH

I know Finn's partly trying to do something for Rue, but it calls to that wild streak in him too.

He suddenly stumbles forward. Courtney! She's snuck up and leapt onto his back, her legs around his waist.

"Yeeha! So, we're going in, are we?"

My shoulders slump. We are now.

"In where?" Lucy asks, finally catching us up with Shaf.

Courtney jerks her head at the little window. He and Lucy go to look.

"Why would we want to go in there?" Lucy asks, wrinkling her nose.

"S'a bando, innit?" Shaf says, uncharacteristically enthusiastic.

"Not abandoned if we visit it," Finn says. "We only need a ladder. If we scale the walls from the bog, there's no barbed wire on that side. Plus no one can see us."

Still on Finn's back, Courtney looks down at Rue pointedly. First time she's spoken to her now she's useful, and she definitely doesn't know her name. "You gotta be able to find us a ladder."

Not even a question! I cringe inside.

Now Courtney's hijacking it, this is no longer a meaningful experience between Finn, me and Rue to connect with her mum.

Rue looks at me. I give a little shrug. It's up to her.

"I *would* like to sit where Mum sat," she tells me almost apologetically. "See if it sparks any…feelings in me or inspires some music."

"I've just been Googling it," Lucy says. "There could still be some art deco tiles in the old changing rooms."

Rue looks at Finn. "My dad's got one of those telescopic ladders."

"Shuuut up!" Courtney crows as if the whole thing had been her idea. She slides down Finn's back. "Tomorrow night then, prison break?"

Eleven

AFTER THE HOSTEL'S unusual take on fish and chips, I let the others drift off to the games room and linger behind with Billy. Ever since we got back, I've been seesawing: do I keep waiting for Mareno to message or do I make the first move? He's the only person I can relate to at the moment. Billy looks up at me with his bewitching eyes as I stroke his head, and I know what I'm going to do.

My tummy's all nervy as I thumb my first ever message to Mareno.

I keep deleting words—it's harder than drafting a whole *scene* in a play! I don't want to come across as keen, and I'm trying not to use words he won't know.

Soon, Billy's had enough, scratching at the door to go out.

"Hang on," I tell him and press send.

> ALLIE: So, I survived the walk! I can escape
> the hostel if you happen to be free some time.

It's lame but will have to do.

AFTER I'VE TAKEN Billy back to the lodge, my stomach's still tumbling, both in case I do or don't hear back from Mareno. I resort to the games room to distract me.

The cheers hit me as soon as I open the outer door. A row of backs screens the ping-pong table from me; heads swing from side to side. Courtney's got her determined face on. But who's good enough to make such a riveting match for her?

My stomach twists.

Krys doesn't belong here. He's not right for our group, even apart from being far too old. Do I go tell our teachers? They'd kick him out pronto, no question, but then I'd be the snitch, which never ends well.

Finn's sitting on the floor in the far corner, glum. Studying the carpet, he doesn't notice me, but he must be gutted, hearing Courtney exchanging low balls with Krys and everyone cheering her on. It's the dance all over again, poor Finn, all gangly arms and legs he hasn't quite grown into yet, trainers that are never trendy, replaced by a 'better' option after she's been cosying up to him all day.

I should go over and sit with him, but it'll only make things worse, like saying *I told you so*. Nor can I stay here, seeing him miserable like this.

I head back to the bedroom to try to reach the end of the first act of *A View from the Bridge*. Finn's like the protagonist, Eddie, both losing the girl they care about to the new guy, the superficially more interesting foreigner.

All at once, there's a knocking at the window, right next to me. My shoulders jerk. Krys's face, in close up, waggling his wide tongue. Averting my eyes, I kneel up quick as a flash and draw the curtains against him. My pulse is still skittering as I sink back on my bed.

"I win!" Courtney brags two minutes later, slamming into our bedroom.

"Does Hey Ho know *he's* been here?" I ask, even more riled now she's brought Krys right onto our patch. The pub was one thing, the hostel another entirely.

She marches to the mirror and undoes her topknot.

"Hey Ho doesn't own this place. And, anyway, there are *lots* of things he and Miss don't know," she says, her reflection giving me a strange look. "Aren't there?"

"Why was he leering though our window?"

She shrugs. "He'd left his motorbike outside."

Motorbike, of course! Krys is such a cliché! He must have wheeled it there; I've not heard it arrive or leave.

"You're taking a risk getting mixed up with him," I say.

"Proper kind of you to worry about me!" she says, fixing me through the mirror with those hard eyes. "But *I* know what I'm doing on the lad front."

I shake my head. She's got it all wrong just because she saw me with Mareno last night.

"Where does this leave Finn?" I say, diverting her attention from me.

"Finn's a big boy now," she tells me, shimmying at the mirror. "*He* can make his own choices too."

What *is* his choice with her? Take it or leave it, however she treats him?

"Besides," she goes on, "Council-flat-Courtney's from the wrong side of the tracks for Finn."

I scoff down my nose. "Finn doesn't even see any tracks."

She almost smiles. I suspect she agrees about Finn, but there *is* a divide at school between those from the urban council estates and those of us who, like Finn and me, live in posh rural villages. And it *isn't* fair someone with Courtney's talent can't afford to do a drama degree like I can, thanks to Dad. Knowing her, though, and all the work as an extra she's clocked up on TV dramas, she'll make it one way or another.

She comes to the foot of my bed.

"Allie..."

That's a first! As is how she's looking at me, not mocking but...normally.

"What do you really know about Mareno?"

I blink in confusion. So she knows his name now? She and Krys must have been discussing him.

Brrrrrrrr! My phone vibrates against my thigh, saving me.

I dive out of the room and back into the courtyard.

"Hello?" I'm all breathless.

Twelve

"THIS IS A cool place to meet," I tell Mareno.

We're in the bandstand on the prom. Sitting on wooden seats angled towards each other, we're near the entrance so we can see another full moon mirrored in the still black of the sea.

I passed no one on the prom, so we have the whole place to ourselves.

MARENO PICKS UP a backpack from the other side of him.

"I've brought coffee. You want?"

"Do you want some?" I say automatically.

"Yes, I would, thanks!" he laughs.

"Me too!" I blurt for some reason. I don't even like it.

He pours some from a flask into its cup.

Liking the bitter, slightly spicy aroma, I take my first ever sip of coffee.

"Do you like it?"

I pass it him back. "Honestly, only the smell."

He laughs.

"So," he says, "how was today?"

"Crossing the Bay?" I pause. So hard to sum up. "The view from the bridge, it was breathtaking again, all fresh and new. But I felt so nervous on the Sands. I'd never go out there without Eli."

"No, of course. You need an expert."

Someone 'sand-born', Elijah said.

"Nearer to the middle, it was so grey and miserable, and it actually rained over Priest Skear. Have you seen those rocks?"

"Yes," he says.

I wait, but that's it.

"Next was the Kent, the river. And I *really* don't like fast water."

"I think I know this of you already," he says, teasing a little, about Saturday, I suppose.

At 'already', I go warm inside. "Yeah, I do like things… under control."

"Maybe this is why you like to write drama."

Oh. I blink into the darkness. It sounds so obvious now he says it, but so far, it's not been among the many reasons I'd thought of for wanting to be a playwright!

"Ha!" I say, trying to make light of it. "How did you know?"

When I have to try to *tell* Finn how I feel and why.

"I…I think…" He sounds suddenly embarrassed. "Because usually, I hear *my* head too. But sometimes, you have to hear your heart, no?"

My heart gives a little hiccup. Listen to your heart about what?

"I think…my heart took such a battering when my parents split, my head took over."

"Hm," he says. "I'm sorry—your parents."

We fall silent.

"You think today, walking across the Sands, it will help you to write your drama?"

"Hugely. Our drama teacher was right. You do have to go out there to know something of how it feels. But now we need to agree the theme and a structure."

"You can do this, Allie," he says. "I know how determined you are."

"Thanks." I'm chuffed by his belief in me. "I have to be to show Mum I can write."

"You have courage to do what you want without her support."

"Me, courageous?" I've never thought that before. "You're the courageous one, coming here alone."

"Yes, but my parents support me."

"Yeah, but still…"

It was hard enough for me moving *within* England with Mum. It must be so tough starting in a whole new country, all alone.

We're quiet again.

"What did *you* do today?" I say after a while.

"I studied."

"What are you studying?"

"Geology."

Geology? I was expecting him to say something like a BTEC in construction.

"What interests you about geology?"

His hot coffee breath clouds in the clear night air. "Our ancient, changing planet. The fact, for example, that once there was only one huge continent, Pangaea. One Earth."

"I love that!" I tell him. "It means we're all from the same place, doesn't it?"

"Yes," he murmurs so very quietly.

"It's exactly what this poem said we studied only last week. 'No man is an island…every man is a piece of the continent.'"

"I do not know this poem," he says.

Across from me, he suddenly looks achingly alone. We might be all from one place, but Mareno's adrift from his family, 'a part of the main…washed away by the sea'.

"You must…" I stop, rephrase. "Do you miss Italy, home?"

He swallows. "I miss my family."

He fiddles on his phone and holds out a photo to me: on a white-gold beach with a turquoise sea, his mum, I assume, with an arm around each of her sons; his dad, sitting next to Mareno, the same height, both with the same short black hair; in front of them, a border collie.

I study it for a long minute, an ache in my chest. As an only child of split parents, there are no happy-family photos on *my* phone, and he's left his far behind.

"Lovely!" Both the setting and his family. "What's your dog called?"

He hesitates for a split second. "Jonida."

"Jonida," I repeat, trying out the new name in my mouth. "I like it. A girl, I suppose?"

"Yes, or my mother would not be happy!"

I laugh. Still not as outnumbered as Poppy, which is why she likes having me around, I reckon, even down to suggesting ways of doing my long, wavy hair.

"She's a beautiful dog," I tell him, handing back his phone.

He does some scrolling. "And here are my father's parents."

They look to be on the same beach, but instead of sea, mountains rise up close behind them.

"Your family must all miss you too. But you'll see them in your holidays?"

"No, Allie. Now I'm here, I must stay here."

He puts his phone back in his pocket.

"What! You'll never go home again?"

"Difficult," he says shortly.

Why? I can't imagine never seeing my homeland again. Maybe they'll visit him here instead. But who does he live with now?

"Were you on a special holiday in the photos?" I ask instead.

"No, this is near where we live. My family, I mean. The bay where I used to fish with my grandfather. We don't have money for holidays."

I don't know what to say. Mum's taken me all over Europe and even to New York once with work.

"Well, you don't need holidays when you live somewhere as stunning as this," I say after a moment, still worried I'm being tactless.

"The nature *is* stunning—the mountains, lakes, sea."

"Whereabouts in Italy? I've been a few times."

Another beat. "You wouldn't know it. Northwest."

"Do you always have hot summers?"

"And cold winters. With snow."

Of course. The Italian mountains are famous for skiing.

"I love snow, but England hardly gets any. And you still want to live here, where most of the time it's…bleurgh?"

"I come where the opportunities are. And anyway, Pangaea. The sea here smells the same as at home."

"Yeah," I smile at him through the darkness. We've found a way through geology and poetry to make him feel at home.

"My family could even see the same comet as us later this week," he says.

Us?

He stands and looks out into the Bay as if trying to spot the comet already.

I stand up beside him.

"It's a once-in-a-lifetime happening, I think you call it?" he says, turning to me. "We need to go away from all light."

"But where? Up on the fells?"

He smiles at me. "We will find the perfect place."

I'M DANCING MY way along the prom, hugging to myself my secret hour with Mareno, our comet watch yet to come. We haven't arranged anything; I just know it will happen.

It's only as I creep into the courtyard at the hostel that I remember the comet that appears in *Julius Caesar*; how it's thought to be a sign of his death.

MAREN: Is this the right poem?

No Man is An Island

No man is an island,
entire of itself;
every man is a piece of the continent,
a part of the main.
If a clod be washed away by the sea,
Europe is the less,
as well as if a promontory were:
as well as if a manor of thine friend's
or of thine own were:
any man's death diminishes me,
because I am involved in mankind,
and therefore never send to know
for whom the bell tolls;
It tolls for thee.

John Donne

ALLIE: You found it! Yes, that's the one.

Day 4

Now there was a future...there was a trouble,
which would not go away.

Alfieri

Thirteen

"WE'RE WRITING A f…flipping tragedy here," Courtney complains.

"Tragedy makes for great drama," Lucy says.

"A docudrama would also complement your work on *A View from the Bridge*," Miss says. "That too is based on a true story Miller heard."

Right now, she's got her back to the view—a literal Bay window in the lounge—of another high tide.

"Tragedy's no fun." On a twin floral sofa opposite me, Courtney drops her head into her hands.

"Nope," Finn laughs. "Drowning's not a whole lot of fun, I suspect."

"We've found a tearjerker of a true story, haven't we, Shaf?" Lucy says.

"What?" he asks, still half asleep. He reluctantly shifts his flat cap back from over his eyes. Basically, he's doing drama A' Level to be with Lucy more, though he's genuinely a natural actor when it comes to it because he doesn't sweat it.

"Does it involve love by any chance?" Courtney says.

"How did you know?" Lucy asks.

"Go on," Miss says.

Lucy stands between the two sofas.

"Henry Turner was nineteen. He lived in Arnside in the 1760s and had a special present for his fiancée, Isabel Crosfield, who lived in Grange. But this was nearly a century before the railway, when it took at least a day to walk round the Bay by road."

"But he's lived by the Bay all his life, innit?" Shaf says, forcing himself to stand. "He knows to check the tides. What he doesn't know, what no one can, is where the sinking sand is."

Melodramatically, he flashes big, round eyes at us all. Courtney sniggers.

Finn leans forward.

"Only his corpse arrived," Shaf says. "Washed up on the shore three days later, all marbled and swollen."

"Isabel got the locket," Lucy says, tears streaming down her face, "but not her Henry." She can cry at will, imagining Shafeeq drowned this time, I bet.

After a quiet moment, Finn holds up a photo on his phone of an ancient-looking volume with a leathery cover. "There's this whole *book* of drownings at Cartmel Priory— at least four hundred and fifty since the registry began in the sixteenth century."

"If this is what you want to focus on," Miss says, "I can ask Mr. Rainer to take us there in the minibus. It's only a few miles away."

"The gravestone of the guy I'm researching is there," I say.

Courtney groans again and lolls back on her settee, eyes closed. She's all about performance and naturally good at it, I'll freely admit, but she hates research, whereas I love gathering ideas and content.

"There's these graves at the priory too," Finn says, "of six boys and three girls aged between fifteen and twenty-eight who drowned together in the Bay in 1846."

"Why were *they* out there?" Miss asks, encouraging us to delve deeper. "As ever, it's the why that matters."

"They were coming back from the Whitsun Fair," Finn says.

A highlight of their year, perhaps.

"Ellen Inman had been to buy her wedding dress there. The following day, she was supposed to marry one of the others in the group, Thomas Moore."

Lucy gives a little cough, and her eyes well up again.

Finn looks at each of us, demanding our attention. "They'd borrowed a horse and cart from one of their parents. The day was sunny and still, and some of them were from fishing families, so they knew what they were doing as regards the tide and sinking sand. So, they got to the fair safely, enjoyed a carefree early summer day…"

My mind conjures up stalls selling hand-embroidered stuff, herbs, beer and cider; coconut shies and a tin alley, all fun when you're in a group.

Courtney huffs. "Cut to the chase, Finn. We know it don't have a happy ending. So, was it the tide or quicksand got 'em first?"

He looks at her. "Neither." A dramatic pause. "Their horse and cart, in the dark, it went careering into Black Scarr, a deep sinkhole, so called because you can only sink— no clambering out."

I swallow a gasp. A sinkhole? Yet another weapon in the Bay's arsenal.

"William Anson," Finn continues, "Henry Croasdale, Helen Holt…"

Naming them makes them even more real.

"At least their bodies were recovered," Lucy adds.

"Thank you, Finn," Miss says quietly. "Even though it was so long ago, doesn't make it any less tragic, does it? Young lives lost, just for wanting a little fun."

Miss always pushes us to find what we have in common with people, real and fictional. Our shared humanity is where empathy starts, she says.

"Let's hot seat one of them," she says, "because though these nine were like you in many ways, what they went through before they died is something you can hardly begin to imagine."

Last time we did this form of questioning, it was Miss in the hot seat—of her wheelchair, which she'd just started using as we went up to sixth form. She invited us to ask her questions, and we began to understand something of how she was having to adjust to seeing the world from two feet lower; how people talked over her head like her brain had stopped working; how she'd had to shift her whole mindset: to save what energy she did have for doing the things she enjoyed. Like teaching us and taking us on field trips.

"Allie, would you be one of the group in the hot seat?" Miss says.

"How about Jane Inman, Ellen's sister?" Finn suggests. "She was fifteen, like Rue."

Holding Rue in my head, I try to sink into Jane's mind: she'd have been looking forward to being home; Jane showing their mum her wedding gown; the family sharing a special meal before the wedding the next day.

"What did you talk about together, when you knew you were going to drown on the Sands?" Courtney demands.

Fourteen

A RE YOU FEELING any connection with your mum yet?" I ask Rue.

We've already walked around the pool and lingered on the terrace where the deckchairs would have been. Now we're standing at the highest point of the lido, the diving tower, with its bird's-eye view over the dark, dark Sands in one direction, in the other, the pool's precinct, curiously silent at this moment as the rest of the group explores the buildings inside the crumbling brick wall directly opposite us.

Rue sniffs and shakes her head as we gaze past the diving board to the water far below, fragments of ancient deckchair lurking in its murky waters.

"What happened to her, your mum?" I find myself asking.

"It was sudden. Instant, Dad said. A freak brain aneurism."

What can I say? No time for goodbyes and last words.

"I'm so sorry. It sounds so…brutal."

A pause.

"It was…unbearable," she says. "But now I can hardly remember her. It's all a blank when I try to picture her face or hear her voice. I can't recall how it was to *be* with her anymore."

That I *can* imagine. Though I do at least spend school holidays with Dad, I no longer remember how it was to spend everyday life with him.

I turn to the other direction, scanning from the streetlights of Arnside opposite us to across the Bay, matt under our first cloudy night.

I catch my breath and clutch Rue's arm. "Look! A light winking. Someone's *right* out there in the pitch-black."

"Aye, p'haps," she says. "Not a lot we can do about it, is there? None of our business."

I frown into the dark. Here I am again, back in Donne's 'No Man is an Island' poem. What was that line near the end after 'any man's death diminishes me'?

"Hey!" a loud voice cuts in from below. "Come on join the conga! Come on join the conga!"

There they all are! A chain of people waving phone torches careers out of the left-hand changing block. Heading up the stupid dance is—no surprise here—Krys.

Poor Finn. Krys just 'happened' to be passing at the exact time Courtney was insisting on being the first to clamber in from the marsh by the Rainers' ladder. Krys was second, of course.

Finn's not part of the conga, I notice. It coils me up inside each time that sleaze bag appears and Finn has to witness Courtney turn, Hyde-like, into some flirtatious moron. At the same time, she knows how to throw Finn enough crumbs of attention when Krys isn't around so he doesn't entirely lose hope.

I *tried* to mask my dismay at Krys turning up, but he looks at me like Courtney does, as if somehow, he knows a lot more about me than I do about him, though I reckon I know his character more than well enough.

"Na naanaa na, na naanaa na! Hey!…"

Trailing his line of silly dancers after him on our right, Krys bounds up and down the steps. Arms out like plane wings, he veers close to the pool edge, pretends to fall in, then leads the laughing conga to the left-hand steps before careering right to the top of them, till they're not far below us.

BACK AT POOL level, they've finally burnt themselves out and the chain breaks up, everyone finding random places to collapse. Krys, though, he's still hyper like he's on something. He darts to his backpack and hands out cans; him turning up like this was well and truly planned!

I spot Lucy and Shaf, not interested in alcohol, peeling off back towards the changing rooms. A group of lads drift off to the steps with their cans.

Courtney struts to the edge of the pool, opposite the diving tower, and dangles her legs over the side. Finn goes to sit with her, taking advantage of Krys having disappeared off somewhere. He pops a can and knocks it back.

"Allie! Rue! Come see!"

It's Lucy, who's finally caught sight of us as she emerges from the changing block. Rue follows me back down the steep steps.

AFTER WE'VE PAID dutiful homage to Lucy's tiles— the original ones from the 1930s, all peaches and muted greens—we agree it's time to set off back to the hostel, not least because Shaf is already stretched out on a step, cap over his eyes, asleep. As we go to tell the others, the clouds have cleared a little, allowing the moon to shine through onto the pool.

Krys has taken Finn's place next to Courtney, the faintly dangerous smell of his cigarettes hanging in the air above them.

Now I see what he was off doing: straight across from them, blood red against the grubby white of the diving tower, he's spray-painted in massive letters:

Krys
Kortni

I look at the two of them. What *is* going on? Is she sleeping with him? No wonder Finn was necking cider! Nine cans are lined up on the side of the pool, though I can't be sure he emptied them all.

"Where's Finn?" I ask Courtney, coming up behind her.

She shrugs.

"Courtney!" his voice rings out, right on cue.

Courtney! Courtney! Courtney! boomerangs back to us from the high walls so we don't know which direction to look in.

"Up there." Lucy points to the diving board.

Finn's waiting for everyone's attention, Courtney's most of all.

People gather, all gazing up at him. The cloud's fully drawn back from the moon now, providing a natural spotlight for Finn.

Courtney's thumb appears high up in the air. He places one foot on the diving board; it flexes; he wavers, hamming it up.

Now both feet are on it, and he's stepping forward like a tightrope walker. For a second, he looks like he'll trip but whirls his arms around as if to regain his balance.

Next to me, Rue catches her breath.

"Go, Finn!" Courtney yells, punching the air.

Someone whistles with their fingers.

Fin-ley! Fin-ley! A chant starts up. *Fin-ley! Fin-ley!*

My shoulders tense.

Enough, Finn, I breathe. *You've shown you've got nerve.*

Unable to watch, I turn to Rue. She grimaces.

There's guffawing all around us, and I look up, discovering why. Finn's turned sideways on in a strong-man pose. Courtney hoots.

I recognise this side of Finn from the 'wild' swimming that winds me up no end, the part of him that loves a thrill, but nothing on this scale. He's doing what it takes to win Courtney's attention back from Krys, and the cider is masking his sense of danger.

Facing us again, he bounces on the board so it emits a loud *boing!*

Laughter ripples through his audience, and he makes a sweeping bow.

Now he stands still and looks straight at Courtney.

Quiet.

My hand goes to my mouth. The realisation punches me in my solar plexus. I unstop my mouth: it's not too late to save him.

"NOOOOOOOOOOOOOOOO!"

Fifteen

THE WORD ELONGATES through my lips.
  My heartbeat roars like the tide in my ears.
Am I the only who knows what could happen? The only one who cares?
Too late.
Finn's toppling.
Headfirst.
Tombstoning.

THE START WAS so abrupt, but now time slows, exactly as they say.
My eyes are glued to his figure.
He needs to be *feet* first.
If it's not deep enough…
If he hits the water at this angle…
He'll be broken.
Or skewered by a shard of wood.
At the very least, the cold will shock him, his clothes drag him down.
If he wasn't drunk, he'd have had a chance.
I can't move, only watch his tumbling body.
He hits the water.
Goes under.
Droplets shoot up in the air. Water ripples out.
Don't lose the spot.

But he's come up already. If he was hammered, the cold's snapped him out of it.

Cheering, then the chanting strikes up again.

Fin-ley, Fin-ley!

Courtney squats down as he swims casually towards her. "Mental, Finn! Way to go!"

He props his elbows on the edge and grins up at her. And I see exactly what's been going on. She's filming, will have recorded the whole goddamn diving dare.

I dread to think what the caption will be on TikTok. **#FinnsMentalMoment**?

"That's living!" Finn gasps as he heaves himself out onto the side.

It could have been dying! I want to shriek at him. But if I open my mouth, all sorts of other things will spill out too. Not the time.

I linger at the back of the crowd while he strips off his hoodie and Courtney puts her jacket around his shoulders. Spectacle over, the audience breaks up.

A HAND ON my arm draws me gently around.

"Okay, Allie?" Mareno says to me quietly, an eye on the others.

"What you doing here?"

"I heard the shouts…saw the ladder."

Courtney leaps right between us, Finn forgotten. Mareno removes his hand from my arm.

"Yo, Mareno," she says as if she knows him, a bit sarcastic and her voice slurred as she swishes her hair. "Come to join the party?"

She offers him one of Krys's cans. He gives a quick shake of his head.

I'm aware of Rue next to me now.

"What brings you out at this time of night?" Courtney asks, undeterred, still right in his personal space.

"Walking," he says, clearly reluctant to be drawn in.

"Walking, eh?" she echoes.

Don't even talk to her, I think. *Let's get away from all this.*

"I've just set Finn a bit of a challenge." She laughs, jerking her head between the diving board and Finn, who's wringing water out of his hoodie a couple of strides away.

"I saw," Mareno says, disapproving.

It's not how it looks, Finn's nothing like this, I'll tell him later.

Krys's voice suddenly booms out in Polish from behind Courtney.

I jump. I'm not sure whether Polish always sounds threatening or if he's being intentionally hostile.

Mareno's nostrils flare, but he looks down at the tiled floor. Krys stares at him.

"I ask you, *Mareno,*" Krys says in English, his voice too loud. "I ask, are we too childish for you?"

Mareno seems to have to force his eyes up to him.

"Too foolish."

Go Mareno!

Finn's come over, his expression bewildered. Lucy appears.

Krys is bristling; the tension notches up. Next someone'll chant *Fight! Fight! Fight!*

"Foolish, is it?" Krys asks. "Well, you *are* the one always stud-y-ing."

He cuts the word into mocking syllables like Courtney does my name.

Courtney pouts at Krys. "Mareno didn't like me daring Finn," she says with an exaggerated whine.

"Well, I don't like him giving his girlfriend a false name," Krys says, flicking his snake look between me and Mareno.

"No... I'm not..."

A false name? What the HELL? If Krys means the typo in my phone contacts, so what? But how could *he* know about that?

"Coming, Allie?" Mareno asks. From the corner of my eye, I see he's edging out his hand low down, reaching for mine.

"Aw, do you *have* to go, Maren?" Krys calls after him, oozing sarcasm as he enunciates his name but without the o.

Maren? Is his name Maren? My hand goes automatically to my phone. *Did* he make a typo in my contacts? I glance at Mareno—Maren?—but his eyes are down, his head too, almost like he's submitting to something, though I can tell from his breathing he hates it.

"Oh, so sorry, little Allie," Krys says, stepping closer to me. "Did you not know your *friend's* real name?"

My nerves are tingling. I've never felt so confused and at a loss, and Mareno's giving me no clues, simply standing as if waiting for me to decide what to do.

I don't know what's going on with him. What I do know from seeing him alongside Krys for the first time is what polar opposites they are. I know in my gut Mareno's good. And so very alone.

I grip my phone in my pocket and take in a deep breath.

"Of course I know his real name," I tell Krys.

As proof, I flash 'Maren' at him from my contacts.

Krys's mouth shrugs a surprised acknowledgement at me before he turns his focus back to Mareno.

"So, he tells you *everything*?" Krys's gaze bores into him.

"Enough." Mareno…Maren cuts in. "Allie?"

At last, he looks me in the eye and reaches out his hand to me again, a longing in the movement.

What am I saying if I take his hand? What will it mean?

I'm in a freeze-frame. Everyone's still, silent and waiting—*for me.*

On the other side of me from Maren, Rue's and Lucy's astounded faces give me no clue.

Finn, somewhere behind Krys, I can't quite see.

I tip my head back for the moon, so clear right now I can make out its landscape, as if *it* can tell me what to do.

It can't.

My eyes lower, to the diving tower. Up there, Rue claimed that what other people do is none of our business. It's the poet, Donne, in direct opposition to Rue, who gives me my answer:

Because I am involved in mankind.

I stretch out my hand to meet Maren's. It's dry and, as you'd expect from a builder, rough. Palm to palm, our connection's *live* as his hand supports mine.

Together, we march to the lido wall. I sense all eyes on our backs every step of the way. We drop hands so we can climb.

I'M IN THE dark as I pause on the outside lip before slithering down onto the bog.

For these few seconds as I wait for Maren, I'm the one completely alone. I've just walked out on my oldest friends. And Rue, a new friend who matters to me. For this…new, unfathomable Maren, the missing o no typo. I'm all tight inside at his deceit; at the position he's put me in.

His walking boots appear at the top of the ladder. What else do I not know about him? Things Krys, and apparently Courtney, seem already to know. What if he's like the Sands—lures you in on appealing first impressions only to betray you with hidden horrors?

Here he is! After fiddling around in his pocket, he puts on a head torch to light our way across the marsh.

As soon as we're on the solid prom, I stop and turn to him.

"Who *are* you?"

Sixteen

H E NODS TOWARDS the bandstand. "In here?"

I follow him and we sit deep inside, near the back, on benches much further apart than last night. He places his head torch between us.

Ruffling his hair, he gives me a hollow smile. Now I can see his eyes, my indignation—and hurt actually—give way a little.

He shrugs. "I'm the same person."

"Called?"

"Maren."

"Oh-kay. So why are you ever called Mareno?"

He leans forward onto his thighs, his face in shadow; rubs a hand across his eyes.

"Good grief, how bad is it?" I ask, only half joking.

"Depends how bad *you* will think it is. This is part of the problem."

Him being so concerned with what I think softens the new hard edge I've grown towards him. But only for a moment.

"It's bad you've been deceiving me. You're not Italian, are you?"

He catches his breath.

I realise now, his English accent doesn't *sound* Italian. It doesn't have that emphasis and upswing at the end of words.

"I didn't lie to you, Allie. I never told you I was Italian. I even put my real name into your phone."

I sigh. "You're splitting hairs."

We almost smile at yet another confusing idiom.

"What I mean is, you let me *think* you were Italian— when you talked about home, showed me photos of somewhere not Italy at all."

My brain's rewinding all kinds of snippets, including so many of his awkward pauses.

"Jonida—I bet that's not an Italian name either, is it? And what was all that about remembering *my* name means truth when you call it me? I look pretty stupid now, don't I?"

"Oh, no, Allie, please no." He leans towards me, his whole face tight with concern. "I'm sorry, I truly am. I *hated* not telling you my truth. The fact is, I'm…"

Ukrainian? Russian even? Draft dodging?

"Albanian."

Uh-oh, my head throws in, shortly followed by an image of cannabis plants.

My brain's still buffering. I get it, why he wouldn't broadcast this. The news is full of Albanians at the moment—how single young men make up the majority of migrants arriving in the UK, some with criminal records back home, who go on to become involved in drug dealing in cannabis or even cocaine.

"I've got questions," I tell him.

"Er, okay." Though it doesn't *sound* like it is.

I'm having to work out exactly what my questions are, so many are cramming my mind.

"So, you're pretending to be Italian as a sort of camouflage?"

He shrugs. "You know how people here like Italy and Italians. They like them, as they do Poles. *Trust* in them. Can you say the same of Albanians, especially at the moment?"

I can't pretend my imagination hasn't connected lovely images with Mareno—a musical language, passionate nature, sunny Roman buildings, pizza, pasta, gelato! And what did my mind conjure up for Albania? Criminals and cannabis!

Maren sits straighter and raises his eyes to mine. "This doesn't mean I'm ashamed I am Albanian. But we can receive so much hatred, sometimes it is better to *be* Italian, and easy to do because we look similar and most of us speak the language well."

More of my exasperation seeps away. It's horribly sad to be better off pretending to be a different nationality from your own.

"Your poem," he says. "It says 'each is part of the main'. In Albania, we don't feel that we are…"

A motorbike roars on the prom. We look at each other. Krys. A Pole, one of the supposed 'good guys'.

"It's…prejudice, that's what it is," I pick up, "to make you feel this way. To assume one nationality is all good whilst tarring all Albanians with the same brush."

I hit my forehead with the heel of my hand at using yet another idiom.

"I can guess what it means."

"It's assuming all Albanians are…dodgy, simply because some are."

I check his face to see if he's understood 'dodgy', whether it offends him.

He smiles now. "I knew you were different, Allie. But I have to ask you to keep to yourself, please, where I am from."

"Of course," I tell him, affronted. "I hardly go round talking about you, you know."

Voices reach us, ever louder. Maren twists to see. I can make out Shaf protesting loudly he's carried the ladder for long enough; Lucy tells him tough, she's not up for it. Jay offers to take over. The familiarity brings a sad smile to my face. I'm concerned for Maren, but I need to process what I've just learnt about him, and what happened in the lido with Krys, it affects me too. I need… *want* to see my friends; put things right. I never again want to be as isolated as I was a few minutes ago.

"You go," Maren says, standing as if he understands all of this. Is that because he feels isolated all the time?

"But we haven't finished," I tell him. "Have we, Maren?"

He smiles as I use his name for the first time. It sounds and feels surprisingly natural. More *real*.

"No, I'll see you again soon, Allie." He falters. "If you still want to."

I smile. Of course I want to.

"You'll be all right? When will you have to see Krys again? At work tomorrow?"

One of his hesitations. I open my eyes wide and give him a look. *Now let's have the truth.*

"Soon. I share a house with him and others."

You live with him?! New questions queue up, but my friends' voices are fading fast.

"Go, Allie," he repeats.

I PUT ON a spurt to catch up with the group, but they're in a clump and I can't face them all together. Somehow, I need to talk to Rue and Lucy each in separate conversations. Finn—*waaay* too much for tonight.

As I trail them, my brain continues to rerun Maren footage. Rue believes he's Italian. But then, that was the whole point, wasn't it? I'm genuinely not fussed what nationality he is. Yet one of *my* first questions was where he came from—a lazy shorthand. How would I ever have got to know Maren properly, though, if Krys hadn't outed him? If he'd continued with half-truths and hesitations? And isn't Maren living up to stereotypes of Albanians in his sham?

What's in a name? Juliet asked about Romeo Montague. Nothing, she wanted to think when she'd just found out who *he* was, and look how that turned out! Both dead at the end, taking at least three others with them. And he didn't even deliberately mislead her.

Yet I do understand Maren's reasons, and maybe he was protecting me to some extent. Because now I too have to deceive people.

Seventeen

J UST ALONG THE prom, Finn's spotted me and is hanging back. And I'm pretty sure it's not out of concern. My body sags. I don't want his questions, especially when I won't be able to answer them.

"What are you playing at, Allie?" he jumps in. "Going round with that guy from the Sands who can't decide what his name is?"

My hackles rise. "Diving right in's becoming a terrible habit," I tell him. "You're asking what I'm playing at when if Courtney says jump, you jump. Literally!"

"I *wanted* to."

"Finn! I *saw* her thumbs up! She'd dared you—she said so openly."

"She dared me to go onto the diving board. *I* decided to dive in."

"More fool you. It's called tombstoning because throwing yourself into a rubbish-filled pool of unknown depths can put you *in* a tomb."

"I know what I'm doing where water's concerned, Allie. You know that. I'm a life-friggin'-guard!"

"Lifeguards can't guard their own lives! You were jealous—pissed off by Krys turning up, then the graffiti. You'd been necking cider and wanted to impress Courtney."

"I was having *fun*."

"Really? How much fun is it now Courtney's disappeared with Krys?"

A low blow. Even in the heat of this moment, I know it.

"Whatever. I was having more fun than you're having with this Mareno, Maren or whatever he's called."

"You sort yourself out," I tell him. "Don't let her make a fool of you, Finn, when she's so obviously besotted with Krys."

He shakes his head sadly. "Oh, Allie, who's really being made a fool of here? You seem to be forgetting, in four more days, neither of you will ever see these two lads again."

"So? I'm not bothered. I had no idea he was going to turn up tonight."

Adamant, he shakes his head. "Then he's using you in some way."

"Using me?" My voice is shrill. "Using me for *what*? Don't even answer that when Courtney so blatantly takes up with you only when Krys isn't around."

Now I've shut him up. I've gone too far, but I can't allow myself to soften.

"It hurts how you want to be with her at all after she's persecuted me for years."

"Persecuted!" He scoffs as if the verb's too strong for how she mimicked my southern accent every time I opened my mouth, convinced practically the whole year group I was a posh geek who didn't need friends and definitely couldn't act.

His ridiculing tone smarts. He *knew* how I felt at the time.

"You can't hold it against her forever," he goes on. "It's more than two years ago."

"But she hasn't changed. And—"

"Give her a chance, and she will," he says, quietly now.

"She'll never deserve you," I mutter, but the heat's subsided in me too.

Realising my motivation here, Finn pulls me into a decidedly damp sideways hug, "Oh, Allie, I don't want you to be hurt either," he murmurs.

"Gerroff, Finn," I tell him. "You're making me all soggy!"

I link arms with him instead, and we tag on to the end of the group. This is the first time *ever* we've spoken to each other like this. We've never even argued mildly before this week. Finn in particular is all about peace and harmony. As he pulls my arm tighter through his, I know whatever romantic mistakes he may make, our friendship will *always* survive.

FINALLY, WE ALL sneak back into the courtyard. Leaving Paula and Rue to return the ladder to her dad's garage, we disperse. It's looking like we've got away with the whole escapade. Without it, I may have never known the truth about Maren, I realise.

I steal into the girls' wing with Lucy. Slumping wearily back on her pillow, she wipes off her make-up.

"Thank God Finn was okay earlier," I say, sinking onto my bed too.

She gives me one of her searching looks.

"What's going on with you, Allie? Who is this Mareno, Maren guy?"

It suddenly hits me; she's never even seen him before.

"Maren," I say. "We met him on the shore the first afternoon. He knows Rue and Billy. Then I just happened to bump into him a couple of times."

"*Just happened*? Krys thinks you're his girlfriend."

"Well, he's wrong."

Lucy raises a delicate eyebrow at me. "You have each other's phone numbers. You were holding hands."

I shake my head. "It was only a hand, Luce."

She narrows her eyes at me. She's right not to believe me. Accepting Maren's hand must be one of the most significant things I've ever done, but not for the reasons she's thinking.

"He...needs a friend. Doesn't fit in with Krys and the others from the barn dance."

"Why doesn't he? What is all this aggro between him and Krys? It's more than, well, like you and Courtney not seeing eye to eye."

I shrug. "Dunno, but I think it's says a lot for Maren that he doesn't get on with a...a piece of work like Krys."

Why he ever ended up with Krys and his mates, I have no idea, I think as I button up my PJs, but Krys knowing the secret of his nationality is giving him a hold over him that's dangerous.

"Yeah, maybe so." Lucy gropes under her pillow for her eye mask. "You've got to admit, though, it's a headline. You suddenly becoming the rebel and going off with a mystery stranger! Very un-Allie!

"I don't feel *un-Allie!*" I don't even feel like I'm breaking rules, though I know I am. I can't argue Maren hasn't been mysterious, yet despite it all, I trust him. He's gently beckoned me into this new, more significant world of his, a new kind of drama I have to be part of. "I can't explain," I finish weakly.

"Don't get hurt," she says, "that's all."

"No chance," I tell her, snuggling under my duvet. "He's simply someone I've crossed paths with."

"Hm. I've seen the way he looks at you, Allie."

No, you haven't, Lucy. You just look for romance everywhere.

What Maren needs is someone on his side, if only for a week.

"And he *is* quite a looker," she adds sleepily.

Weirdly chuffed, I turn out the light.

Day 5

There are times you want to spread the alarm but nothing has happened.

Alfieri

Eighteen

"THE LIVING DEAD!" Hey Ho, says casting his gaze over us at breakfast.

He's not wrong. Every single face is wan, some clearly more hungover than others. Typically, Courtney looks the best of a bad bunch. I've no idea what time she came in last night, and I was awake way after Lucy, Googling where Albania is, discovering something of its traumatic past.

Our teachers may suspect something was afoot last night, but not what. We are all sixth-formers, after all, and what they don't know can't hurt them.

My toast pops up. I grab a plate.

The door slams back. Hard.

Rue stands in the doorway, white and wild somehow, her hair madder than ever and her clothes the same as she had on for the lido last night.

"Billy!" she calls, scanning the room. Next, she sinks to her hands and knees and crawls around, checking under all the tables. "Billy, Billy!"

I crouch down beside her. "He's not here, Rue. He's not been in this morning."

Hey Ho comes over. We all know Billy by now. He's become our mascot.

"What's happened?" he asks.

She scrabbles to her feet, collecting herself.

"Billy's gone missing. Dad and me've been searching all night. Anyone seen him?"

She looks at every single person, challenging them to think. Every single one shakes their head or says no.

I go over to Miss. "Can I go help look for him?"

She has her considering face on. I know what's going through her mind. We have loads of work still to do on our script. But what's the priority here? I know of Billy's tendency to run off.

"You can have an hour, Allie. No more."

I nod, sandwich my slices of dry toast together and grab my fleece off the chair.

"WHERE ELSE SHALL we look?" I ask Rue out in the courtyard.

Ashen, she closes her eyes, leaning against the wall. "There's nowhere left to look. This is all my fault."

"How can it be?"

"S'karma. It happened while we were in the lido. I'd told Dad I needed an early night so he didn't check on me. But when he let Billy out last thing, of *course* Billy knew I wasn't in the house and came looking for me."

I clench my teeth, wishing we could rewind and skip the whole ridiculous night.

"He must be somewhere, Rue."

Now she looks at me.

"Aye, somewhere. He'll have sniffed me out at the lido, not been able to get in, then likely got distracted by a sheep."

I shake my head. "Where've you *not* looked?"

Her shoulders slump. "We've been all along the shore from here to the prom and around the lido—I had to tell Dad about it—then on to Kents Bank. But now the tide's in so..."

So, if he's caught or stuck somewhere, it's too late.

I scour my mind for ideas.

"If he got the scent of something, he could have followed it anywhere, couldn't he? Including inland. The geographers are going up...Hampsfell? I think that's what they called it. Let me ask Mr Hazleton to search for him up there. And Maren too? He'll want to know, and he could have some thoughts."

She nods, weakly, not even bothering to bring up last night's revelation about Maren. She seems to have given up hope. But I won't let her! We swap phone numbers.

"Right. You go and sleep for a few hours while I sort it. And I'll walk through the golf course."

It's between here and the station and another possibility for Billy to have run off into.

"I won't be able to sleep," she says flatly.

"You won't be able to keep looking if you don't," I tell her.

Sick to the core, I go back in to talk to Hey Ho. I'm not as convinced as Rue there's no hope for Billy. Some dogs run a long way away, don't they? Sometimes they get injured or trapped and it takes them days to find their way home. But even the possibility something...fatal has happened to him is unbearable. I hate to think how Rue will take it if she doesn't get her Billy back.

So, I've got to all I can to make sure she does.

As I scoot down the road to find a way into the golf course, I ring Maren.

He sounds so shocked and sad. He's going to search around Kents Bank, where he lives, he tells me, and Humphrey Head, a headland a few miles south where there are deer. It's possible he tracked one all the way up there and…and what? We don't know.

BY THE TIME I'm back at the hostel, I've been more than the hour Miss allotted me, unsurprisingly. Nearer two. Maren's going to search all day. Why he's not working today is another question to add to my never-ending list.

A hopeless aura hangs over my drama group, a grim mix of exhaustion, hangovers and fretting about Billy. As I try to catch up on where they're at with our script, I sense a distrust between us too—well, Courtney and me—a huge worry in an ensemble. For all we will never agree, we've always trusted each other on the drama front, and anyway, she always tells the truth, painfully so. I'm the one hiding things, I have to admit. All of them about Maren.

"We've decided this morning," Miss tells me, "to piece together a montage of the different story strands you've researched so far. And we've been trying to pin down how we depict the Bay—the Sands and the tide."

I nod, but it's agonisingly close to home when Billy's disappearance seems more likely to be related to the Bay than anywhere else.

"We're gonna waft bits of grey material from the sides of the stage," Courtney says.

I nod again, not listening.

Courtney erupts into sniggering. "Could you be any more naïve, Al-e-the-a!"

"What?" I ask Miss, bewildered.

She smiles at me, her eyes kind. "Billy being lost, it's really upsetting you, isn't it?"

"It's a bleeding dog!" Courtney chunters.

Lucy tuts. "What we *are* going to do, Allie, is project some real footage of the Bay as the backdrop and have silhouettes of figures in tableau of the various stories in front of it. We can have voiceovers in the form of reporting."

"And a chorus linking the different stories," Finn adds, "like in Greek tragedies and Alfieri in *A View from the Bridge*."

I shut my eyes. What if Billy's story, happening right now, ends as a tragedy?

I try to bring my mind back into the room. "We could use sounds effects too, like wind and rushing water, and some music overlaid to add depth?"

"Good thinking," Miss says.

I glance over her head out the window and can't miss the sea covering the Sands. For the millionth time, I wonder where Billy can be. Where he took off to last night.

My hand touches my phone in my jeans pocket, but I know it would have vibrated if Rue or Maren had got in touch. I can't imagine what Rue's going through. Billy's not 'only' a dog. He's her someone, bought for her as a young child as some consolation for the loss of her mum. Two unbearable losses. And if something has happened to Billy, she'll blame herself. Needlessly. Forever.

AFTER A LONG lunch break, in which I have to nap, Miss puts me with Finn to research the Chinese cockle pickers Elijah told us about yesterday.

"Shall we go over there?" he suggests, nodding towards the radiator under the window. I puff out a breath of relief at the kindness in his voice.

Cold and miserable, I sink down to the floor with my back to the radiator. And the Bay.

Finn slides down next to me, bumps shoulders with me.

I manage a smile and lean against him.

"I can't believe it about Billy," he says.

I knew he'd be upset too. He'd feel the same if Bilbo was missing.

"There's still hope. You know how dogs can go missing for...weeks."

He tries to smile, but we both know there's no point kidding ourselves. Billy could also already be lying somewhere. Dead.

A gulp escapes me.

"People are searching, Allie. Rue and her dad, the geography lot..."

"Maren too."

His shoulder alongside mine stiffens.

Time to change the subject.

"I've found out the Chinese cockle pickers had these bosses who *forced* them to go out working in the dark far too near to the tide," I say.

He shudders. "The worst reason of all to go out there. Because you have to. I wonder *how* these bosses made..."

The door bangs open; all heads snap towards it.

Hey Ho.

He holds up a hand to quash our expectations. "No news, I'm afraid. We didn't find Billy on the hills, despite dividing up and covering as much range as we could. It's practically dark now, so that's it for today."

I CAN'T SIT around doing nothing. As soon as Miss lets us go at the end of the afternoon, I dash through the rain to the bedroom and message Maren.

Grabbing my kagoule, I start off along the road, keeping my eyes peeled for flashes of black and white. While Billy never leaves my mind, an undercurrent persists too—the conversation Maren and I have to finish.

He meets me in the railway underpass. Above a wet blue kagoule, his face looks drawn and strained in the artificial light.

We both shake our heads.

"What you thinking…?" I ask, my voice wavering.

His mouth turns down in a wince. "It's… It's not hopeful after nearly twenty-four hours. But it's not impossible. Dogs sometimes find their home even after a long time."

I nod. "It'll kill Rue, the not knowing."

He sighs. "Somehow, she will find a way to bear it. She has no choice, I am sorry to say."

A pause. This is how it is. We both know it.

We agree we'll comb the shore path back to the hostel. Maren puts on his head torch, its wide beam lighting our way as we scramble over the rocks, all the while calling for Billy, hoping for a flash of white fur or a bark.

Nothing, all the way to the little beach at the bottom of the hostel grounds where I first met Billy. The rain's stopped, so we perch on a rock.

"Maren, I've been wondering, when did you come here? To England, I mean."

"I am here since June."

"Ah, okay, so not so long then. And you've been working with Krys and the others, I suppose."

One of his bloomin' hesitations.

"Mostly."

I'm not being nosy. Miss always says questions are the route to understanding others, and how can we be friends properly if I understand so little about him? So, I go for it.

"*Why* are you here?"

When you've got a loving family in a beautiful location.

He throws up his hands, suddenly animated by a question he *does* want to answer.

"So many reasons. Most people our age in Albania don't have work, and those who do are mostly in farming on very small wages. So much corruption too. Rama, our prime minister, is pretty much a successor of Hoxha, the dictator."

"God, that does sound desperate."

"It is. People are…depressed and anxious." Maren's speaking slowly, searching for the words to describe it to me. "And for us younger ones, no hope for better."

"Yeah, I knew it must be bad if you would leave your home and family."

He looks relieved that I get it. "Exactly, Allie."

"Maren," I say, suddenly shy. He looks at me. "You're much more you as Maren than Mareno."

He breaks into a wide, relieved smile. "This is the best thing you could say to me."

I beam back, happy he's happy.

The huge moon's appeared through the clouds now, gleaming on patches of left-behind sea in front of us. We sit, breathing in the salty night air. But for Billy being missing, this would be another of our sweet moments.

Eventually, Maren stands. "I need to…get back now."

"More study?"

He raises his hand in a goodbye, which he's done before, but only now do I recognise it as an evasion tactic.

THE MOOD AT dinner is worse even than this morning. At least then there was the hope we'd have found Billy by dark. A dead, hopeless evening lies ahead. We're all too knackered from last night to contemplate table tennis or anything remotely energetic and loll around listlessly in the common room. I've brought *A View from the Bridge* with me. Even Eddie and Marco hurtling towards what can only be the tragic climax is less painful than what's happening in reality here.

Someone must die, but I still can't decide who it will be.

Nineteen

I JOLT AWAKE. LIGHT. In the courtyard. The security light.

I poke my head between the curtains. A tall figure in black glides across the courtyard, stops at the minibus. Mr. Rainer?

My pulse trips—something to do with Billy?

BY THE TIME I've pulled my fleece on over my PJs and got out into the courtyard, the figure's in the bus, which lurches forward, stops.

I dash to it and press my face up to the passenger window. My mouth gapes.

Rue.

But on her own.

In the driver's seat!

I yank open the door and jump onto the passenger seat. "What's going on?"

"Out!" Rue hisses, her features scrunched up in anger.

I blink and blink again. "But…what are you *doing*?"

She dives across to pull the door closed.

"*You* can't drive this," I tell her. "If you need to go searching, let's get your dad."

Perching on the edge of the driver's seat, totally ignoring me, she grinds around for a gear.

"You *can't* drive," I repeat.

"I can. I often move the bus for Dad. And now he's given up on Billy," she says so quietly I can barely hear. "I never will."

At that instant, the bus hops forward again. She dips the clutch, tugs the wheel to the right, and we grind our way up the drive.

My pulse is skittering. This is lethal—for her and for me. Got to act. Once we've left the hostel, I'm on my own with her.

Damn. The courtesy light's gone out!

Narrowing my eyes, I try to make out where the horn is. There? In the middle of the steering wheel? I pounce.

She grabs my wrist. I gasp. She's astonishingly strong.

Now she veers left, onto the Grange Road.

"Lights!" I urge her, or we *will* end up crashing on these dark roads.

As she gropes around, we swerve into the kerb.

"Let me," I say, my pulse hectic as I grope to my side of the steering wheel and manage to twist the lights on. Thank God I've had my first few driving lessons. I finally click my seat belt in place.

By now, we've passed the station and the bus is whining along, still in first, the only gear she's ever used, it seems. We pass the duck pond and labour up the shop-lined hill.

"Why right at this minute?" I ask her.

She's hunched forward over the wheel like something demented.

"Tide's out. I have to. Have to find him. Have to know."

My chest's leaden. She's going to drive out onto the Sands. In the *dark*. She'll never make it. The whole bus will go down, taking her with it.

But not me!

At the roundabout at the top of the hill, she swings left, still only in first gear, along the Esplanade. The Bay stretches beside us, moonlight gleaming on patches of water the tide has left behind.

Suddenly she swipes the wheel! We veer to the left once again, downhill, towards the shore.

"Brake, for God's sake!" I scream as we gather speed.

I stop breathing.

The white gates of the level crossing are hurtling towards us...

"Ruuuuuuuuuuuue! Middle and left pedals!"

At the very last second, we jolt to a halt in an emergency stop. Her first? The gates of the level crossing are bang in front of us, the crossing she, Billy and I walked together on Monday. Here we are, full circle, only without Billy. And now she's set on mounting some doomed mission to find him. Which I won't be part of. She's not taking me out there to sink without trace in the dark.

My heart races ahead of me.

She sighs out a ragged breath. Her head tips onto her arms in exhaustion.

"Let's go back," I say gently.

"And abandon Billy?" she cries.

She tears out of the bus to open the gates of the level crossing.

I jump out too but stand at a safe distance. So she knows I won't be going with her.

"Don't you betray me," she half orders, half threatens me. "This is my last chance."

I throw up my arms. "I haven't got my phone."

If I had, I would.

I can only stand and watch as the bus limps over the railway track. I follow her across and watch its taillights shrink down the slipway, doomed.

I'M IN A *nightmare*, I think.

But I'm not, unbelievable though it is.

Rue's out of her head with fear and grief.

What can I do?

By the time I've run back to the hostel, it could be too late.

Something tells me I need to stick nearby. She's surely not going to manage to drive even down the bog. I need to be here to pick up the pieces, get her home.

Now IT HITS me. Maren! He lives at Kents Bank, he said. He'll know what to do.

My heart swoops. Without my phone, I've no way of contacting him and I don't know his address. I can hardly go knocking at random doors, can I?

I cross the tracks and pelt down the ramp at the other side. Powered by love of Billy, Rue's going at some speed along the marsh, the minibus lurching from side to side.

I suck in air. If she stops soon, she'll be safe. We can fetch her dad. He'll recover the bus and—

Oh God! It's lumbering from the ledge onto the Sands now, and she's driving even faster.

I run through the bog as fast as I can without a torch, all the while the rear lights dwindling further and further into the distance.

Her life's in huge danger. At any point the bus could run into quicksand, tumble into a sinkhole.

I stop at the boundary between grass and sand. It benefits no one for me to risk my life as well.

The strangest thing! Almost as strange as Rue making off with the bus in the first place. It makes a wide sweep around so it's facing back into shore. Now it's purring its way back towards the path. And me.

ITS HEADLIGHTS DAZZLE me. Yet I'm still pretty sure, and it's the only explanation. I put my arm up to shield my eyes.

Someone else *is* driving.

So, someone *else* has seen her, somewhere between the hostel and Kents Bank. A resident with a view of the Bay who's gone out there to investigate, maybe?

The bus is nearly back, slowing as it approaches the marsh. Buzzing with relief now, I dash to the passenger door and throw it open—again.

I peer across Rue, slumped forward onto the dashboard, and freeze.

Twenty

"MAREN! YOU WERE out looking for Billy too?"

He looks straight ahead, not at me. Rue's body's wracked with sobs. But thank God she's safe.

I squeeze my eyes closed. I don't want to see Billy's body in the back of the bus. They've found him. They must have.

"Get in," Maren says curtly.

His face is set and grim as he focuses on driving us back up onto the marsh.

I can't take in what's going on. *So, you saw the minibus setting out onto the Sands? Or were you already out there, searching for Billy?* This is a time for grief, not questions.

But Billy. Billy. I can't look around into the back.

We wend our way up through the marsh and soon are at the level crossing again.

A sort of shudder ripples through Rue. I can feel it where the sides of our bodies are pressed together. However distressing it is to her to have her search attempt thwarted, it's better than *her* lost to the Sands too. Eventually, she'll understand.

Once we're on the road, I look over Rue to Maren.

"Who...who found Billy? You or Rue?"

He shakes his head, irritated. Not the Maren I know. "We haven't found him."

My shoulders slump in relief. It's not as if it means Billy's safe, of course. We still don't know. We can hope, though.

So why is Maren so angry? Does he think I'm part of Rue's grief-crazed escapade?

I sink back into my seat. A large part of me wishes I'd never got involved—with either of them. Yet somehow, I didn't have a choice.

As Maren reverses our journey from Kents Bank up the hill to the Esplanade, I can't wait to drop Rue back at the hostel and talk to Maren alone. He's got to know I did my best to stop her. And I want to hear his part in the story.

I become aware of a sort-of unwashed fug emanating from Rue. Glancing sideways at her, it looks like she's still in last night's clothes. My heart contracts in pity. I can totally understand why losing your someone would make everything else pointless.

WE SWING DOWN into the courtyard.

"No, this way round," Rue tells him, speaking for the first time, her tone sullen and flat, as he makes to reverse the bus. She means so it's how her dad left it.

He ignores her, pulls on the handbrake and waits for her to climb out, staring straight ahead. She gives him a strange look, still angry, I suppose, for scuppering her would-be search.

I clamber out to let Rue past. "You'll be okay?" I ask her.

She ignores me as she squeezes past me in the bus doorway.

All at once, she spins back and sticks her head inside the bus.

"Think about what you're doing," she urges Maren, her voice quaking. "Just think..."

I stand, gobsmacked, as she slumps her way towards her house. What *is* he doing?

Stunned, I climb back into the front seat.

He's studying his phone.

"What *are* you doing?" I ask him. "What did she mean?"

"No time. I'm already late."

I blink. Late for what? I don't know this cold, harsh Maren with clandestine appointments.

"Allie," he says, pointedly, wiping his palms down his thighs.

He's waiting for me to get out.

"You're...you're taking the minibus?"

First Rue, now him! What next? My ears pound.

"I must. But I'll bring it back soon."

"Then you're taking me too."

I'm never going to be able to sleep, wondering what the hell is going on. I glance sideways at him; he's glaring at me. I fold my arms. No way am I budging till I've got to the bottom of this. Him.

HE SIGHS MASSIVELY, slams the bus into gear, and we're off, out of the courtyard.

Groundhog day—towards Grange again, the same route. Duck pond, shops, Esplanade, down the hill to the coast. To Kents Bank. To his place?

"Where are we going?"

He says nothing.

At the station, we turn right, past a farm with outbuildings. He turns on the full beam to light our way along a lane with grass up the middle. No more buildings; the hedges close in and the road peters out. We come to a standstill, the nose of the bus up against a wooden gate.

He turns off the lights. My chest drums in the dark silence. No one knows where I am.

Don't be so melodramatic, I tell myself. Maren's hardly a murderer or a rapist. Is he? This is no different from being at the edge of the woods or shore with him. It *isn't.*

He breathes out, wipes his palms on his jeans again and turns to me for the first time tonight, though I can't see his features.

"I'm late," he tells me. "Because of Rue. Now I don't know if they came already or not. We wait."

We? Now *we.*

"Who for?" I ask, trying to breathe normally. "Who's they?"

His attention's already diverted from me. He's staring into the driver's mirror.

"Down!" he commands as he makes to get out. "Right down."

Twenty-One

I SHRUG INTO MY seat. Is he deliberately putting the fear of God into me? If he is, it's because *he* feels it too; the air's thick with apprehension.

In the wing mirror, harsh lights creep up, a giant insect with fiery eyes reversing up to us.

My stomach knots. This is the stuff of thrillers.

The Jeep stops right behind us, its boot to ours, blocking us in. I catch my breath. I can't see Maren, but the bus sags slightly. Wriggling to my right, towards the driver's mirror, I locate the black outline of his head and shoulders as he leans against the rear door.

The full beam of the other vehicle narrows, dips. A short, stocky figure climbs out of the passenger seat, then the much taller driver from his side. They leave the doors open and converge slowly on Maren.

My pulse hammers for him. To cut them down to size, I name them Stumpy and Stringy, which almost gives me nervous giggles.

The three of them form a dark triangle in the mirror. Deep, muffled words seep through to the front.

All at once, the volume ramps up. Stumpy thrusts his arm towards me.

My heart slams painfully.

Maren lowers a hand, palm down, as if to quell their concerns. The bus shrugs as he leans up off it. His face flashes in the driver's mirror as he turns to raise the luggage door.

I hold my breath.

As it opens, cigarette smoke wafts to me, seedy and threatening, sending my pulse sky high. I'm out of my depth, a child in a dangerous adult world Maren is somehow part of.

Stringy opens their boot too. A deep, savage barking breaks out and a clawing on metal. My shoulders leap.

I clutch at my chest. My God, are they going to release some killer dog on Maren?

Stumpy growls a short order I can't make out. Instantly, the dog shuts up.

"Dog fighting next," Stringy comments to Maren.

Stumpy snarls something at him.

Stringy's face instead of Maren's appears in the mirror. The skinhead from the café on Sunday!

There's a rustling from the rear of the bus.

I daren't look around.

But in the mirror, Maren's straight back reappears instead, his arms a wide hug around something bulky. He waddles it over to the boot of their four-by-four and slams the door.

The two slip into their Jeep, which shoots rapidly back along the lane.

It's over.

I kneel up, twist around to watch through the open back door, with Maren, as the lights recede…and are gone.

We're back in darkness.

THE COURTESY LIGHT comes on as he climbs in beside me. When he raises his right hand to wipe his forehead, it's shaking. My whole *body's* trembling.

"What *was* that?" I ask.

Something Rue clearly knew he was doing.

He folds forward onto the steering wheel, head on his arms.

The light goes off. I grope around on the ceiling to switch it back on.

He stirs.

After what seems minutes, he looks up at me, his eyes narrow. "You don't know?"

He shut me out again and slumps back onto the head rest as if exhausted.

My brain gropes around towards something it's *almost* known, like a child who, deep inside, knows there's no Santa and now must face the truth.

The heavy, bulky object in the back, the secrecy, him being on the Sands when we first met, 'busy' on the night of the barn dance, passing the lido last night.

Nothing to do with Billy or even walking. And no wonder he's so interested in the tides!

"It was…you were…selling…cockles," I whisper.

"Turn out the light," he says, screwing his eyes tighter shut.

Such pleading in his voice, I do.

"So tonight," I say, slowly, "you were already out on the Sands with your…haul when you saw the bus, Rue, rescued her."

Saved her life, most probably. My mind replays images of his impatience: constantly checking his watch; speeding us back to the hostel.

"But Rue made you late for your meeting," I realise.

"If I'm not here at the right time," he says quietly, "my bosses go with the rest of their stock. They can't wait for me. The cockles must be fresh when they arrive at France or Belgium."

"But the cockle beds are closed. Elijah told us they closed Saturday, the day we arrived."

As soon as I say it, I regret it. For the first time, I'm… wary of him.

"This is why they can't know you're here."

"They didn't see me?" I interrupt, nerves on edge again.

"No. They're angry I have this bus. No one must know I am cockling. They have a licence but only for when the beds are open, of course. So now I must go out at night."

"Why?" I blurt out.

Why on earth would you take your life into your hands on that black minefield? And *illegally*. For shellfish. I remember the cool hardness of one on my palm on Monday.

"Because I think, how can you *close* nature? And I only take the large cockles. They are fruits of the sea, free to those who will take the risk."

Another evasion! "I'm not worried about the cockles! We all know what happened to the Chinese cocklers, and they were in a group. Why do it in the dark?"

Maren looks me in the eye for the first time tonight.

"It's the only way I can make money."

I swallow. Our foreignness rears up between us—my privilege, all the opportunities I have without having to leave my family and homeland.

"Why can't you find some other way of earning a living? Building like Krys and Leon. Even…car washes."

I know of Albanian-run ones in Leeds.

"I can't."

I sigh. *Can't or won't?* I don't know if he's being stubborn or even greedy. Cockling must pay well, but there has to be a better option than dicing with death.

"I'm worried for you," I whisper almost without meaning to.

"Your worry doesn't help," he says flatly.

End of.

He slams the gear lever into reverse. As the bus moans back along the lane, I unwind what I thought I knew about him.

So, was he cockling before the barn dance? Last night, it must have been *his* light I saw from the diving tower. If so, no wonder he's been sleeping in the day.

And those 'bosses': they clearly make him highly nervous, fearful even, something I'd never have associated with him. I suppose he wants to keep hold of his livelihood.

As he drives back along the Esplanade—my third time tonight—I look out at the moon, now clear of clouds, tinting pewter any water left behind in the Bay. As the Sands have been laid bare by the ebbing tide tonight, so has Maren—so tempting until you find out their truth.

He's withdrawn into himself, his face closed off against me. I know so much more about him than I did, yet there's still much more I don't.

I glance at his profile again, his mouth set under his straight nose, and I *know* he's in some kind of fix. A snare, making him hard.

HE DOESN'T SAY another word all the way back to the hostel.

I tell him how the bus needs to be positioned. He turns off the engine.

"Listen, Allie," he says, looking straight ahead. "Forget you ever knew me."

My blood fizzes. "How am I ever going to forget what I've seen tonight? Or not wonder whether you're dead or alive?"

"I should never have let us get…involved."

He may as well have slapped me full in the face.

"Involved?" I grope for the door handle, buzzing now. "We've never been involved! Though I wish to God I'd never come onto the Sands that afternoon."

I leap out, remembering in the nick of time not to slam the door.

I jump. He's there, at the back of the bus, holding out the keys to me. I'm to get them back to Rue, I understand. So here he is, involving me again.

You get them back to her, is on the tip of my tongue. It's because of *his* cockling he still has the keys.

But he did rescue Rue.

I snatch the keys off him and stride away.

"Allie," he whispers.

I stop but don't turn.

"Tell no one of tonight."

I'm so very glad we'll never see each other again.

Carrying on past the girls' blocks, I go down to the shore where I first met Billy and Rue and hurl pebble after pebble at the Sands, putting all my strength into each lob.

"This is all your fault!" I yell—full-on yell—out into the Bay.

Your tides, your quicksand, and your bleeding sinkholes that have taken so many. Perhaps Billy. Maybe Maren next.

But then I think, *it's those bosses too*, and I search for an actual rock, find one I can pick up and fling it.

My blood cools as my mind clears.

What exactly am I so mad with Maren for?

The deception? He had reasons. What's he's doing is illegal and his bosses are scary.

Chilled and weary, I turn to go back to the hostel and finally to bed.

Day 6

There ain't nothing illegal about a girl falling
in love with an immigrant.

Alfieri

Twenty-Two

"COME ON, SLUGABED," Lucy's voice says, a looong way off.

"Not now," I mutter, pulling the duvet over my head.

"Now," she says, ripping it off me.

"Bad night?" Courtney asks, giving me a stare as she struts out of the bathroom.

The pain of it slams back into my brain.

Rue; still no Billy; Maren.

FINN SITS WITH me at breakfast, though I can hardly eat. As soon as we'd re-found our usual comfy way of being together, last night happened, and it's changed me. Seeing what grief can make someone do, witnessing the desperate fix Maren is in. None of which I can tell Finn. Can I? Still, I'm comforted, him being next to me, and he senses I need him.

As we trudge back to our rooms to prepare for today's drama sessions, I pause in the courtyard, turning my face up to the rain to shock me out of my numbness. Finn does the same.

"Might wake me up," he mutters.

We stand there for a few minutes, trying to…come to.

"Allie…" His voice is suddenly *too* awake, urgent.

I follow his gaze towards the drive.

A figure. Maren. Trudging towards us. In his arms, his black-and-white coat slicked against him and his head lolling against Maren's chest, a beautiful border collie.

For two seconds, I'm numb. Then I yelp in horror.

I run towards them. Maren stops. I stretch my hand out to Billy's neck. It's sodden. Ice-cold.

Maren shakes his head, his mouth turned down and his eyes without light.

My hand still on Billy's shoulder, I meet Maren's gaze over the pitiful body, his eyes so similar to Billy's in colour. It's Billy our eyes speak of. Billy, Rue but Maren too.

"Where?" I ask.

"On the bank of the Kent. He'd been swept into the side."

A spike of pain shoots across my chest, for Maren on top of Rue, that he should be the one to find Billy.

"I'll come with you," Finn says, his voice choked as he rests his hand on Billy's head for a moment.

I'd forgotten him. The three of us look at each other, at a loss. There *is* no answer to how to break this to Rue.

We trudge, Maren between us, towards the Rainers' lodge.

As the rain wets the four of us still further, tears roll down my cheeks.

For Billy, for all who have and will have drowned in the Bay.

And for the anguish of those they leave behind.

IT'S MR. RAINER comes to the door. His face crumples. Rue appears right behind him.

She makes this cry, one long mewl, like an animal, a mother finding her cub dead, and slides to the floor.

Her dad receives Billy from Maren. Rue reaches out for Billy. Mr. Rainer lays him gently across her legs. She wraps her arms around his neck as if he was still alive, not flinching, even as she kisses the cold of his face.

None of us can say a word.

THE DAY CONTINUES to weep for Billy. Miss has told me to take a little time. I wish she hadn't. I'm back in bed, aiming for the oblivion of sleep. But my mind insists on leading me along these ugly paths scarred into it. I struggle up, lean against the headboard, try to think up a distraction, but I'm too tired to have the discipline to work on our script alone. I can't face the others either. They'll be sad for Rue, but they won't feel how Finn and I do about the loss of Billy and the suffering of Rue.

Maren. What he was doing last night, all I now know of him, stands as a barrier between me and my friends. If only I could purge it from my brain. Go back to how I was when I arrived.

But would you want that innocence back, Allie? I ask myself. It was a fool's paradise. These dangers exist—in nature, in people like Maren's bosses and the hold they have over him, making him vulnerable.

I shake my head. Vulnerable. Maren would *hate* me even putting such an adjective in the same sentence as him, but I can't help him. Like Billy, he's going his own way.

I scrabble out of bed again. Got to break free from these pointless cul-de-sacs my brain is dragging me down. Out in the courtyard, I don't know where to go. At least the rain has finally eased.

Is…is it…faint, on the wind?

Yes, a violin.

At first, I can't tell where it's coming from. Rue's house, an open window?

No. Of course.

I follow the path back to the shore where I first met Billy.

SWEET AND PLAINTIVE, the pure sound of the strings is becoming louder and clearer. It tugs at my chest as it's so evidently about Billy. I slow so as not to disturb Rue. Now the melody is high and light, mimicking his playfulness and spirit; the Billy I remember, teasing me with a stick, full of the joy of being alive. But minor notes are pushing their way in. Delicate to start with, they're ever stronger, louder, angrier. As I come out onto the beach, Rue's a dark, lonely figure, her chin tucked so tightly over her violin as if it's all she has left.

Elbow out, she saws at two, then more strings together creating painful discord, again and again in a grating glitch of agony, every sound declaring the aching wrongness of Billy's loss.

Until it's over.

I had no notion music could paint emotions so vividly.

Her arm droops: she's spent.

I don't speak. Daren't.

Finally, she notices me.

"Requiem for Billy," she says without looking at me.

"It was so…him. And so you." *Your sorrow.* "I'm so, so sorry, Rue."

"I already knew," she says, walking towards me. "I could tell he was no longer in the world from Monday night."

I shake my head sorrowfully. Would Billy still have been with us but for the inane lido escapade? But what-ifs—that way madness lies. Billy could have run off after Rue multiple other times.

She's looking at me now, stronger than I ever expected. And I realise it's because she can let her emotions out in her music. Catharsis. Whereas mine, for Billy, for Maren, are all stoppered up.

"Allie." Her voice is urgent. "We can't lose another. We have to make sure the same doesn't happen to Maren."

My shoulders drop, and I cover my eyes with my hand. Rue's mission makes absolute sense, ensuring Billy's death hasn't been in vain.

And what an aim—to save Maren!

"Think about what you're doing," she urged him last night. She found out only minutes before me, of course, when he had to put his sack of cockles into the back of the bus.

Rue, who only the other night at the lido, before Billy, said it was no business of ours what people got up to. She can't afford to lose anyone else.

But this has to be *her* mission.

"I'm going home in less than forty-eight hours, Rue," I remind her. "And…and I'm…done with Maren. I can't help him. But you can. He's in terrible danger, cockling at night."

She gives me a knowing sort of smile. "It's you he'll listen to, Allie."

I shake my head vehemently. "He absolutely won't. We…fell out last night. And we were both clear we won't see each other again."

Not that there was anything between us.

"There's no telling him anyway," I say to her.

"We can't give up on him."

"I've had to, Rue. But please, do what you can."

She nods, pondering as she cradles her violin.

Twenty-Three

TOUGH TIMING COMING here today, Allie," Miss says, lingering to have a word with me outside the towering priory at Cartmel.

In more ways than you'll ever realise.

"Billy, the registry of drownings," she continues. "Sometimes, though, sticking to the plan can help life feel a bit more normal, even when all around you seems to be shifting for the worse."

I smile at her, my first for a long time. This isn't some platitude. Day in day out, Miss does her job, follows her usual lifestyle as closely as her body will allow her, and always without self-pity.

"Shall I say it or will you?" I ask, teasing her about one of our well-worn drama catchphrases.

We end up saying it together. "The show must go on!"

I'M ON PHOTOGRAPHY duty, so as she heads inside to join the others, I meander towards a small area of fenced-off gravestones in front of the priory, where some sheep are acting as happy lawn mowers. Surrounded by their quiet grazing, cheery birdsong and the already-dead, I'm strangely soothed as I wander around trying to read some of the gravestones. The lettering on many of the mossy slabs has been worn away by the centuries; the one I run my fingers over is cool and smooth.

I wander towards the edge where a row of higgledy gravestones all but leans against a mossy wall. Oh God! This is partly what I came for, but now I've found it, my newfound peace dissolves. Lying side by side are the nine from the sinkhole at Whitsuntide, their graves the only way left for them to be with their friends. Reading the 4*th* *June* date over and over again hammers home the cruelty of them being denied even one last summer.

All of them are around Maren's age.

But I'm not thinking about him anymore.

I take some photos as fast as I can for Finn; move on.

A TALLER GRAVESTONE with a long verse in swirly, Gothic writing catches my eye. It takes a while to read, as some of the letters are faded, but this is the other one I needed: Robert Harrison, whose body was lost for weeks on the Sands.

It reveals a shocking new truth.

"What does it say?"

My shoulders leap at the voice from behind me.

I turn slowly.

Both of us look anywhere but at each other.

What are you doing here? Questions are on my tongue, as ever with him. But what's the point?

Instead, I turn back to the gravestone. He comes to stand beside me, suitably funereal in his black jacket.

"Here lies the body of Robert Harrison…"

I read, painstakingly, to him.

**"…who Drowned on the Sands
the 19th day of January 1782 in
the 24th year of his age…**

**"Also here lies Margaret Harrison
who was drowned January the
17th 1783 near the same
place where her son was
drowned."**

"She dies a year after her son?" he checks.

"It can't have been a coincidence," I say. "Two days before the anniversary of his death, in the same place, dying in the same way…it's not unusual. A mother of one of the Chinese cocklers took her own life on the first anniversary of *her* son's death."

I'm thinking now of Maren's mum; of course I am. I *know* from his photos he's a much-loved son.

I sweep my arm behind us, back along the row of nine graves.

"This group, their horse and cart went careering into a sinkhole in the dark. You know about those? Thomas Stephenson, aged sixteen, Ellen Inman, aged twenty—"

"All right," he interrupts. "I have the idea. But Allie, *I* will not be in this graveyard. Or like Billy."

I shake my head. He found and carried Billy's corpse. He saw Rue's devastation. Why doesn't he get it?

"You can't be so sure. You aren't invincible."

Let him work that word out!

"But I *am* careful."

"This graveyard's packed with bodies of people who'd have said much the same things to those who...cared about them. And yet here they are because none of these dead learnt from what happened to those who drowned before them."

At 'dead' and 'drowned', he flinches, retreats into himself again.

"I make sure it's almost no risk."

"Why take *any* risk with your one life?"

He rubs his eyes. "Rue told me you wanted to see me here. But..." He shrugs. "We go in circles."

"Why would I want to see you? You're the most infuriating person I've ever met!"

The ghost of a smile plays on his face. Why? It's nothing to smile at.

"There is no choice," he says, serious again.

"There are *always* options. It's you won't take them."

He throws up his hands. "What options?"

"You find other work. Yes, even a car wash. Extract yourself from these bosses. Anything other than...what you're doing now."

"It's not possible."

My blood fires up. His obstinacy makes me hot and tight inside. I will *not* ask him any more questions.

He toes at the grass with his walking boots, then looks at me properly for the first time.

"Do you trust in me, Allie?"

I sigh, look back at the gravestone in front of us, then into his eyes, as readable as ever to me.

"I do trust you. But I know there are still things you're not telling me."

His face is tense with torment, but he doesn't say *anything*. We're quiet for a long moment. Impasse.

"When do you next go out?" I ask finally.

"Tonight."

"Then I'm coming with you."

His lips pressed together, he shakes his head. No way.

"Why? Too risky. If it's not safe for me, it's not safe for you."

He strides away from me.

"Rue has wasted both our time!" I yell after him.

Twenty-Four

E VENTUALLY, I REALISE I can't stand here any longer, gazing unseeing at a gravestone whilst I rerun, over and over, every word Maren and I said to each other, unable to change any of them. I *told* Rue I couldn't influence him. So, I trail up over to the porch, with scarcely the will or strength to heave open the massive wooden door.

THERE'S NO ESCAPING death here either. The funereal scent of incense combines with a sickly, sweet odour of chrysanthemums. My instinct is to bolt back into the fresh air, where the dead at least are sleeping peacefully in nature.

But now I register signs of life. To my left is a busy little gift shop selling cards and souvenirs; a long way to my right, a team of pensioners is polishing brass work around the altar. And there's Lucy, taking a close-up of what looks to be an image of Isabel Crosfield's locket, fastened to a thick stone pillar.

Isabel, yet another life blighted by grief. Because it *is* those left behind who suffer, not the unfeeling dead who don't know their lives have been terminated; who don't know anything. As I walk forward, memorial slabs beneath my feet are testaments of more deaths, though centuries of footsteps have erased most of the details.

Together with the high, high vaulted roof above me, this priory and its graveyard puts you in your place, insisting on your mortality.

Directly opposite me is another huge wooden door I'm assuming leads outside to the back of the priory. Tentatively, I make towards it, stepping on the memorial stones, across the first aisle and along the middle section between wooden pews. As I reach the pillar before the second aisle, a movement to my diagonal right catches my eye.

Through the dark wood fretwork of a side chapel, I glimpse snatches of a figure. A figure in a black jacket.

I was so sure Maren had gone.

He's inverting a short, white candle to light it from one of several others already burning. This he sets carefully in a black, metal holder and bows his head for a long moment. He repeats the process for another. He kneels, clasps his hands together, bows his head again. So earnest, so...exposed. His brow furrows.

My skin creeps. In his face, as clear as glass to me— fear.

It must be two minutes before he stands, crosses himself. The nape of my neck chills as he makes the sign down and across his chest as if to ward off danger.

He's moving, taking the few steps up out of the chapel to aisle level. I slide behind the pillar, hold my breath again. But he doesn't pass. Instead, I hear the creak of the door, the back door I'd already decided to take.

So I'm not following him, am I?

THROUGH YET MORE gravestones, a mossy path leads around the back of the priory. Glancing all around for Maren, I kick my way through orange-bronze leaves till I come around the corner and almost jump. His back to me, he's sitting on a grey drystone wall, gazing up at a distant fell topped by a narrow crop of trees.

When I haul myself up next to him, he doesn't seem surprised.

"Two candles," I say. I have nothing to lose now. "One for Billy, one for you?"

For God's protection.

He glances sideways at me, doesn't deny it.

His hand edges along the stone between us, till it finds mine and covers it. Now I know his palms are callused not by building but by cockling.

"I like the work in the daytime. I am at home on the Sands, and free. The four nights since Fishery Patrol closed the beds has been okay so far."

I turn my hand over to thread my fingers through his as he continues to stare up at the summit.

"I'm as careful as I can be. This morning, I was putting out branches to mark my way tonight. But then I found Billy. And I know, over the months before the cockle beds open again, something can...go wrong." He glances at me. "I can't let fear stop me, Allie."

Why can't you? Why?

I look at our joined hands. For him to admit his fear to me is a massive moment. My heart's giant with need to help him with what he believes is unavoidable.

"Why can't I come out with you? Or even only to the shore. Then I'd know if you weren't back when you should be. Could get help."

He opens his mouth, bites his bottom lip. Tries again.

"My bosses."

"What is it with them? How can they make you do something so dangerous and illegal in the first place?"

"You honestly don't know?"

I shake my head. Even as he asks, though, I *do* know. It's something I've hidden my head deep in the sand about. He raises his eyes to mine.

"It is because *I* am illegal."

I hold his eyes.

"I...I...I tried not to think too closely about it, Maren." Tears prick as I realise something. "Because I needed to hear it from *you*."

His teeth tear at his bottom lip again, and he looks to the side of my head for a moment. Now back into my eyes. "I'm sorry..." He shakes our hands as if there's too much to say. "So much to lose."

I nod. "But it's not the most important thing about you. Not to me. And *you're* not illegal—just here illegally." He smiles now and grips my hand tighter. "Cos who decides who can live where? Who owns any part of our planet?"

He shrugs. "Your government decides. And I understand why. But I don't cost your country anything, and I'm not a criminal."

I wince. The cockling almost seems small fry. "But if you're caught living here undocumented…?"

"Deported," he says. "Which is why I couldn't tell you."

His cover story makes even more sense now. As part of the EU, some Italians, like Poles, were given settled status after Brexit. Albanians, never. Finally, I understand why he can't go home.

"Couldn't you apply for asylum?"

"Albania is not at war. I am not persecuted there…but hopeless."

'Here' is turning out hopeless too. And far, far more dangerous. I sigh and look to the trees on the horizon for inspiration. How can I help him out of this fix he's in, at the mercy of brutal bosses?

I shift my eyes back to his. "Tonight. Let me come and wait for you at the shore. I'll go before you have to deliver the cockles to…them."

"Allie," he says gently. "I will be hours and you will be cold."

"I don't care about the cold."

"And when you go on Saturday, who will look out for me then?"

"This is one night I can help with. One night less."

He gives me a sad half smile. "You are very…"

"Determined."

He says an Albanian word instead. "What is it in English?" He claps his other palm to his forehead. "Stubborn."

I laugh.

"The pot calling the kettle black."

He gazes at me bewildered. "The what...?"

"It means you're calling me exactly what you are yourself."

He smiles at me. Properly. "I think watching for me, it's your heart speaking, Allie."

"Definitely not," I tell him. "It's pure logic that someone should check you come back safely."

He gives me a sceptical smile, then drops his head on my shoulder. It's heavy, as if he's tired by more than lack of sleep. And so alone.

I'll be your someone, I think, releasing his hand to wrap my arm around him. *If only for this week.*

We stay this way for some time.

AFTER TEA, FINN and I meet up on one of the sofas in the lounge, trying to recoup time I've lost this week, with Billy. But now, thoughts of Maren roil my stomach as I wait for him to tell me when and where I should meet him ahead of him going out on the Sands.

Finn's busy on his laptop, trimming the images of the Registry of Drownings he took at the priory and of the graves I forwarded. Meanwhile, I force myself to Google the Chinese cockle pickers, agonisingly close to this night and Maren's reality. But is there something to help me understand Maren's situation with his bosses?

All who went out that terrible February night were here undocumented too, all from one of the poorest areas of China, the Fujian province, risking their lives for a better future for themselves and their families back home. As Elijah told us, twenty-three of them drowned.

Their Chinese bosses were convicted and imprisoned. Bosses, I discover, is a euphemism for gangmasters— 'ruthless, exploitative, *greedy* gangmasters who oversee the work of casual manual labour', Google tells me. In reality, the debt the workers owe to their bosses leaves them no choice but to follow orders. Any order.

As I open various links, these words appear on my screen:

> *My dear wife, I am in great danger. I am up to my chest in water. Maybe I am going to die. It's a tiny mistake by my boss.*

A bubble forms in the pit of my belly.

He mistook the time. He should have called us back much earlier.

But the water's up to my neck, under my chin. Their prayers will be in vain.

It's too close. I am dying...

The bubble rises up and escapes me in a gulpy sob. I drop my phone like a hot brick, face down on the sofa, as if not seeing the screen will mean the words didn't ever have to be spoken.

"What, Allie?" Finn twists towards me.

"This, this..." I gesture towards my phone, unwilling even to touch it.

He picks it up and reads.

"Guo Bing Long's final call home," he murmurs, his tone stricken. "His last words."

I wipe my cheeks with my hoodie sleeve but can't stem my tears for the twenty-eight-year-old farmer with two little children at home, thousands of miles away.

For Maren.

Finn reaches across to put a hand on my shoulder.

"It's all too much this, isn't it?" he says. "First Billy. Now this. And..."

I stiffen as he pauses.

"Maren too."

I pull away and bury my face in my hands.

"Allie, I'm guessing from this, and where Maren found Billy, that he's risking *himself* cockling too?"

"I...I can't discuss it," I burble through my tears.

"Okay, but it's a lot for you to shoulder on your own."

I straighten up and glance sideways at Finn. I'd only be confirming what he's already worked, wouldn't I?

"He *has* to," I tell him, praying he won't ask why.

He shakes his head. "Other fishermen won't like it when they've lost their work for months. They could even report him to Fishery Patrol."

"Nobody will know he's doing it. He only goes out at night since the beds were closed last Saturday."

Finn gives a low whistle. "At *night*? And alone?"

"I know. I'd do anything to stop him."

"Anything? You're scaring me, Allie." He blows a huge, reeling kind of sigh. "Promise me you're not going to take any risks."

My phone buzzes. I thrust out my to take it back from him.

"Is this Maren?" he asks.

I read the screen. "I've got to go to him."

"Allie!" He blinks at me. "Be careful, *please*. In fact, let me come with you."

For a moment, I'm tempted. He could wait on the shore with me. But I want, I *need* to be alone with Maren before and after.

"Thanks, Finn," I say as I unfold myself, "but I'll be fine. I'm not going out on the Sands. You know how scared I am of the Bay."

Twenty-Five

A S I APPROACH the little terraced house Maren's given me the address for, a little way uphill from the level crossing, singing reaches me from an upstairs window. It's opera, a soprano with a yearning tone reminiscent of Rue's playing earlier, even though I can't understand the words.

The front door opens as I walk up the short path intersecting a scruffy garden with grass as long as on the marsh. On either side of the door, the two window frames are all splintered, rotting away.

You're going in there? my head asks me.

I hesitate on the doorstep.

"The house is empty," Maren says, smiling at me, a proper, open smile now he's not hiding anything anymore. I catch the outdoor-otherness of him as I pass him and step into a fusty hallway with a stained beige carpet that makes even the hostel look plush and fresh. Yet the singing, drifting from upstairs to us, elevates it out of the tacky.

"Krys's room," he tells me as we pass an open door on the right. "He has the biggest."

"I s'pose he's with Courtney again."

I glance into the room: a huge, curved-screen TV and a massive bed.

"Kitchen." He nods to the left.

I glimpse a wonky stack of pans and plates next to a sink already full before following Maren upstairs.

Maren's room is right at the end of the landing, past two more doors.

The boxroom.

I push the door closed behind me.

Seashore replaces fustiness in here; salt and ozone flood through the open window.

As he stands in front of me, I realise we've never been *inside* together before.

"What a great sweater!" I tell him. It's fern green with a cable pattern, I think it's called, and a wooden button at the V-neck.

He looks chuffed. "My grandmother made if for me to come in. It's extremely warm."

He's wearing thick green socks too, which make him look vulnerable, somehow—there's that dreaded adjective again—without his usual walking boots.

Collecting his phone from a rickety-looking desk, he turns down the volume as the singer picks up her tragic-sounding lament again.

"An Albanian song?"

He shakes his head. "Czech."

"You understand Czech?"

"Only this one song—the favourite of my mother. 'Song to the Moon'. It's a sense of *mall*...our word for missing someone."

"Yeah, I can hear it."

I know that tight suffocation from when my dad went to live so far away.

Maren moves to the open window.

"The singer asks the silvery moon to tell his loved one she is hugging her. She begs the moon not to disappear."

I go to stand by him. "The moon's been on your side this week."

He's still melancholic; we gaze out at the round moon as the singer continues, articulating Maren's longing for his home, family and perhaps especially his mother.

I won't let your mum lose you, I vow. *To face a lifetime of grief, like all those others whose loved ones have had their lives cut short in the Bay.*

THE SONG'S FINISHED, but Maren stays at the window. I turn into the room, greedy for clues to fill out what I know of him. It won't take long. A chair with his blue kagoule draped over it at the tiny desk, holding a single book—geology by the look of it; a small, folded towel with a plastic bag on top, holding a toothbrush and razor. He's a man, I realise. Not like baby-faced Finn, who I'm almost certain doesn't need to shave yet. Or not so often.

And this. "I was wondering at the priory, Maren." I point at a small wooden cross. "You're Catholic then?"

"Some of us are, especially in the north where I'm from, though most Albanians are Muslim."

On a shelf above the desk is one thing only: a wooden chess set with all the pieces laid out, one set a darker shade than the other.

"This is exquisite!"

He lights up. "It's oak. My grandfather made each piece. For me, when I started playing."

"Can I?"

He nods, and I pick up the lighter king, running my fingers over its intricate shape.

"It must have taken ages to make this one piece alone."

"Yes, and he kept it secret from me for months and months. Until my seventh birthday, when he said I was ready to learn to play."

"I play," I tell him, putting the king back in his place, "with my dad. But we don't have much chance, now he doesn't live with us. Mum doesn't play, and I'm an only child."

"You could start playing again, with Finn?"

I smile. "Monopoly's our game."

"Another friend?"

Our eyes meet—one of those moments when you can read the other. *He* can't be that friend because what should be such a small thing, to play chess together, is impossible for us. I go home the day after tomorrow, and this evening we have…work.

To my left is his bed—a single mattress on the floor, taking up the whole length of it—covered with a neatly straightened duvet in a grey-checked cover, his pillow at the window end.

At the foot of the mattress wait his backpack, stuffed with what I suppose is his cockling gear, his walking boots and a pair of trainers. On the back of the door is his wardrobe: his donkey jacket and a pair of jeans carefully placed on hangers.

Now I find his eyes, and his are waiting for me as if he's allowed me to see how meagrely he lives and is defying me to…what? Pity him?

He shrugs his needless defence of it. "I have my own room, with a view."

I smile. It's not luxury, of course, not homely, but the Chinese cocklers lived literally dozens to a house.

A shrill sound screeches. I jump. Maren freezes. It shrieks on and on. He finally moves to his phone; stops the racket; looks at me.

"It's time."

My heart stabs. Maren's life's ruled by the tide. The tide and his bosses.

He leaves his phone on his pillow. "No point taking it with me when there's no signal." He pushes up his shirt cuff and holds out his wrist. "Papa gave me his watch."

So much thought and care went into Maren coming to the UK, but does his family know how his life here is turning out?

Passing Krys's room adds to my sense of unease. I can't forget how much he relished revealing Maren's name— out of some kind of spite, it seemed. What does Courtney know, then? How can we trust either of them?

ON THE PATH outside the little house, Maren tilts his head to where whisps of cloud are now scudding across the moon.

"We want the moonlight while I'm on the Sands. But later, we welcome clouds so we might see the comet from the shore."

"It could be tonight?"

His eyes flash their excitement at me as he nods and starts walking, almost skipping backwards, so he can see both me and the sky. I grin, loving how intensely he lives, despite…everything. Maybe *because of* everything. After Billy, we're both extra aware of how precarious life is.

As we walk together down the hill towards the level crossing, he points out a ramshackle, farm-type building on the corner of the lane we drove up with the cockles on Monday.

"This is the house of Elijah," he tells me. "If I'm not back by one, you come for him."

Oh God. That wipes the smile off my face. Maren's really had to think about this.

"Not the coastguard?"

"Allie, no. Elijah would know what to do."

Does he know Maren's here illegally? That he's cockling by night?

Knowing I can't call the coastguard even if he does end up in trouble, I realise my role's even more important tonight.

We reach the level crossing and have to focus on stepping over the gaps between the rails in the near-dark. The glow from the streetlights at the station won't help us much further than the ramp, and the moon isn't enough. Maren puts on his head torch to light our winding way through the grass.

All too soon, we're at the border between marsh and the Sands. They're as menacing as I sensed them on Monday when I first followed Elijah onto the seabed.

Sinkholes and the graves outside the priory suddenly flash into my mind.

I rub my eyes. I don't want Maren out there.

He catches me in the spotlight of his head torch.

"Tired already?" he asks, swinging it away from me. "I will be less than two hours. I'm not even going as far as the river. I've found a bed far nearer than Priest Skear."

"Great!" I'm buoyed with relief.

He tugs the collar of his black jacket closer into my neck—he insisted I put it on over my fleece, while he wears his waterproofs. His jacket smells gritty somehow, like it's known work.

"I'll be fast because you're here," he says.

"Don't be fast," I tell him. "Be careful."

AS HE STRIDES out onto the Sands, his head tipped to read them, he's a soldier, armed only with his backpack and head torch going into battle with this Bay, a battle I know, especially after Billy's death, strikes fear into him too.

I check my phone. 11:03. If he's not back by one a.m. then...

I try to imagine knocking Elijah up in the middle of the night.

It won't come to that, I tell myself as I hug my arms, safe up on the marsh.

MAREN DOESN'T WALK directly out into the Bay but follows some safe route he worked out earlier. I track along the marsh with him. For a while, I can make out his shape, the beam of his head torch in front of him. When he reaches a certain point, his torch appears only when he faces sideways, the brightness dwindling all the time.

As I keep vigil, pacing back towards Grange at the moment, my mind's turning over this whole conundrum Maren's in, questions still bouncing around my brain. Will I ever *fully* understand the enigma of this boy?

How did he come to the UK? Can't be on one of the small boats or he'd be detained somewhere, wouldn't he?

How did he meet his bosses?

How did he end up living with a bunch of Poles who barely tolerate an Albanian in their midst?

And are Maren's bosses Krys's bosses too? Do they find the others their building work? Do they *all* gang up together against Maren?

MAREN'S LIGHT, THOUGH intermittent as he moves around, remains in the same area. He must be at the beds. Finally, I sit, listen to the silence, enjoy the cool, calm air on my face. It's good for Maren. Beneath my thighs, the long grass is squishy, itchy. I breathe in its unique smell, some grass still living, some dying off. That time of year.

My eyes strain into the darkness, trying to imagine what Maren's doing right now. Will he be bending, straining his back, or kneeling? Using a jumbo, the short plank of wood I read the Chinese cocklers used to bring the shells to the surface? Then that short rake to gather them. Finally, into the sack. Over and over again until it's full and his fingers are rubbed raw by the salt and harsh sand.

My chest burns. Maren won't be a victim. Though he's on his own, he's savvy and experienced. He'll have double-checked the cockle beds for sinking sand. When he sets off back, the tide won't even start to flow for another three hours. That's his rule, and on the walk back, he can see precisely what's in front of him with his head torch.

Breathing more easily, I lie back, my hands, deep in Maren's pockets, warm. It's so still, so tranquil.

Twenty-Six

WHERE AM I? When my brain catches up, my stomach tumbles over. I've been sleeping on my most important job ever. I jerk up, sucking in a breath as I scan the darkness for Maren's light.

Nothing.

I scramble to my feet.

I've failed. Failed Maren completely. If he's stuck, lost, how will I ever find him?

How long have I been asleep? I grope in his jacket pocket for my phone. No! Not in my jeans either.

On my knees, I scrabble blindly in the long grass, wasting crucial time.

I keep glancing out into the matt black, willing a twinkle to show, still rifling among the reeds, trying to be systematic.

My fingers touch something, something cold and metallic.

I snatch up my phone, never more precious.

12:31

You've gone and slept nearly half an hour, Allie.

I scrabble to my feet, stamping my legs to get the blood flowing, scouring the deep darkness. Maren should be well on his way back. Alarm bubbles in my veins: no speck of light anywhere.

There! A mere dot of yellow. But moving. Moving this way, a little further towards Kents Bank.

I dash in the same direction, eyes fixed on Maren's head torch.

The prick of light is becoming bigger, fast, till it's a white star on his forehead, making for shore, to me.

But the star's fading. Even as I watch, his battery's failing.

The star vanishes, its fire dead.

My hand goes to my mouth, my heart quickening.

I try to clock the spot. *Have* to remember where he is.

If his torch has stopped, *he* will have. Won't he? He'd never risk walking into quicksand. But he's not to know I've seen the exact moment it gave out.

In the time I've run to Elijah's place, God knows what Maren will feel compelled to do. We'd never locate him. I can be with him in a fraction of the time.

Using my phone as a torch again, I peer from the ledge of the marsh onto the Sands. No surprise his footprints are no longer there. I can only guess at the angle he took. My pulse banging in my ears, I've never felt more alone. I can't do it.

So don't, my head tells me.

I wish to God I'd let Finn come with me. I could have gone for Eli while Finn…

Finn what?

You know what you have to do, Allie. Maren's stranded.

The first step must be the hardest.

It's all right, I whisper to the shore. *I respect you.*

176

As I take my first step out, I pass again through the Sands' force field like a ghost through a wall.

I SHINE MY phone torch ahead of me. Gritting my teeth doesn't make its beam any broader, but the sand is firm for each next step, which has to be enough. The further I go, the calmer I am. As long as I can know my next footfall is secure, this isn't so terribly dangerous. Maren's right. Armed with knowledge and the right process, you're safe—if you've taken a spare set of batteries! It's him I'm terrified for. What if, unaware I'm coming, he sets off in the dark?

I stop, casting my beam at head height so he'll see it.

"Maren!" I yell into the darkness. "Maren, I'm coming. Where are you?"

I stand stock still, straining for even a whisper.

Nothing.

The hopelessness of our situation seeps into me: I could be going in completely the wrong direction. Only the streetlights of the town behind me and the minuscule ones opposite give me any confidence I'm even advancing *into* the Bay rather than along it.

I swallow hard. Elijah might not find him any better than I can, but a helicopter's floodlights could.

A helicopter that would catch him, cockling illegally, *living* here illegally.

I look at my phone.

12:57

Shall I? Ring 999?

Come on, Allie—you're risking his life with your indecision.

I glance up at the moon for guidance, close my eyes for a blink; set off again.

Five minutes more.

If I still don't see him, I'll make the call.

1:03

The time he'd expected to be back with me.

"Maren!" I scream into the darkness. "Maren! Where are you?!

As I hold my breath, it seems the whole *world* is silent. Waiting with me.

Was that…

Was it something? Or just wishful thinking?

"Maren? I'm here! Shout again."

"Allie!"

This time, I know it's real.

"Here!" the ghostly voice calls.

And then his whistle, clear and pure, cuts through the dark.

"Don't move!" I yell. "Keep whistling, and I'll come."

Twenty-Seven

THE WHISTLE, EVER louder, and his voice, ever stronger, spool in the distance between us.

I stop; breathe. No panic. Nearly there. Next time I stop and look up, my beam will catch him. His voice is at one or two o'clock.

I duck my head again to check out my next few steps.

My foot halts in mid-air.

Bang in front of me, the surface is creased, like slack cling film, exactly like the patch Elijah showed us, deep as the length of his staff.

I toe at it with my trainer.

It wobbles.

My heart knocks so hard I'm nauseous.

"Quicksand!" I scream to Maren.

Morecambe Bay has the most dangerous quicksand in the world, Elijah's voice warns in my head.

"You can find a way around," Maren yells to me. "But, Allie, so, so slowly, only one foot at a time."

I'm shaking and weeping, and now it comes to making a move, I can't do it. Even if Maren were with me, I'd be petrified. If quicksand seizes me by the leg, I'm dead. Even if Maren managed to bring help, it'd be too late. My last hours will be alone, in terror. The tide will come for me long before the dawn. I'll hear it from far off; its roar growing louder as it marches to claim me and...

I sink down onto the safe sand behind me, trembling violently. Why in God's name did I not phone for help when I could?

"Allie?" he calls. "All right?"

"No," I croak into the darkness.

"Allie?"

He hasn't heard me. There's alarm in his voice now.

If I don't so *something*, we're both dead. I push myself carefully to my feet.

"I'm okay. But...I don't think I can...I think I should...it'd be safer if...I went back. Got help."

He's gone quiet.

"Allie, listen. Only a few metres are between us. I'm on safe sand. You are too. This patch can't be big."

My throat's bone dry.

"Allie? Allie..." followed by a word in Albanian.

There's such tender concern in his tone it's as if he knows the depths of my terror.

"I know you can do this," he tells me.

Is he saying so to save his own skin? my head asks me.

Yet that sweet-sounding word in Albanian was spoken with such caring.

"I'm coming," I tell him.

"One foot," he says. "We have so much time, Allie."

Crouching, I spotlight the grotesque sinking sand again, alive and quivering at me, and track it around to the right. It continues at least to the length of my beam.

Maren's wrong about the size of this patch.

I swivel around to my left to inspect the surface. No creasing or movement as far as I can see. I thump it with my fist. It gives, of course. It's sand. I straighten up now, lean all my weight on my left foot and place my right lightly down, ready to fall backwards if it sinks more than it should.

It *feels* like what's behind me. I take another step, and another.

"Okay?" he calls.

I flash the torch in the direction of his voice. The sand there is puckered still. I am going to have to go towards nine o'clock before, somehow, I can make for two.

"Not yet," I shout.

One, two, three, four, five paces along on this firm line. Feeling faintly sick and my forehead clammy, even in the cold, I daren't pause between steps. I might not be able to start again.

"I'm here, Allie," he calls, as he must see me travelling away from him.

"Keep shouting."

It's like walking the plank between the lethal patch on my right and going too far out of my way to the left. All the time, I'm trying to veer back towards his voice.

It becomes only those two things—the next step in front of me and his words reeling me in.

Until, until, one time, his voice is so close that when I stop and look up, he's there, a few metres away.

"Careful!" he warns.

My legs tense. To stumble into quicksand at my final steps…

Blocking my inner voice, I light the small stretch between us. It *looks* harmless.

I run across it like hot coals...

All the way to Maren.

He reaches for me, pulls me to him tight and safe. My body's limp, shaky, like low blood sugar. But *his* body's firm, his arms strong.

I'VE NO IDEA how long it took me to reach him. And if you could trace the route I'd had to take, it'd form some weird, zigzagging line.

Still holding me, he's rubbing the top of my arm, the warmth and weight restoring strength to me bit by bit, like a transfusion.

"Thank you, Allie," he murmurs against my ear. "What if you didn't see my torch stop working?" Now he's stroking my hair.

My heart warms in waves in his arms. When he needed me, I didn't fail him. The candle he lit yesterday flickers in my memory. I've never before believed in prayer, but was *I* the answer to his tonight?

"Thank God you had a whistle," I murmur.

"It's what I was searching for the afternoon we met. I lost it on the Sands earlier in the day."

Now I'm recovering, I'm aware of how *good* it feels to be held by him. This is not like Finn's quick hugs *at all*.

"What happened to the girl who didn't even want to cross the Sands with Eli?" Maren asks.

"She met you!"

He pulls me tighter still. And I think of how, in a matter of just a few Maren days, I've gone from being an observer or reader of life to doing the most dangerous, dreaded deed.

When we finally have to pull part, I'm cold again, weak, but we've got to manoeuvre around the sinking sand together. I take his rucksack for him while he hauls the cockle sack onto his back, grunting under its weight.

WE CAN'T WALK side by side, not in this quicksand-infested area. I lead, shining my phone torch ahead of us, he following right behind.

At the soggier borders of the weak sand, my footprints have already vanished. Crouching to scrutinise the surface, I take short steps before turning to light the way for him.

At last, it's consistently firm and he can come alongside me. We walk on a little way together.

"Rest!" he says out of the blue.

He sets the sack on the sand, lets his shoulders sink.

"I can take them from here."

"Can we stop, talk?" he asks.

"You pick your places!" I try to joke.

But his tone is serious.

Twenty-Eight

AFTER WE'VE CHECKED the sand, he spreads out his waterproofs, and we sit side by side in our circle of sanctuary. He turns off my phone torch. Clouds are completely veiling the moon now, so we're in darkness, facing out to sea, unable to glimpse any lights, any land, anyone.

Open sea. I swallow a surge of panic. It must still be at least an hour and a half before the tide will start to flow.

"Allie."

I brace myself.

"You had to rescue me tonight. Probably saved my life."

"Maybe, maybe not. But I'm so glad I was there."

"Thank you," he says quietly. "I know now I have to stop...fishing at night."

You do! Yes! Thank God! I want to yell into the space.

"But it's complicated," he says.

I keep still and wait as I sense him struggling to sift through his situation.

"My family saved for six, seven years, ready for an opportunity for me to come to Britain when I was eighteen because I will never have work in Albania, as I told you. Babi—my grandfather—his friend, Armend, fishes further up this coast. His boss, Bosko, was looking for more people who know fishing, know the tides and sands. Armend suggested me. And it also helped I can speak English and Italian, so I could pass as Italian."

Gazing out into the night, he pauses as if he can only recount his story in short chapters. Some of this I knew, some is news. There's a certain logic to how he came to be here, but the innocence and hope of how it started rips something inside me, when I know how it's developing, the key turning point when the cockle beds were closed last weekend.

"As we only had saved a few hundred pounds, Bosko paid the rest of my transport here, in a lorry on a freight ship to Liverpool."

Maren stops again, scraping at the sand in front of us with his forefinger. My skin's all goosebumped. Lorries, freight ships are for transporting goods, not people. I wait. Does he wants to tell me where from, how long it took, how it was?

He doesn't speak, and I realise, to go into any detail at all would be to relive it. Does his need for the outdoors and space come from being confined in a lorry, unimaginably claustrophobic and airless? On the other hand, I know he's always relished fresh air and nature, so being enclosed would be especially traumatic for him.

He sniffs and clears his throat. "So I have to repay the debt. It's much more than he said it would be. Thousands to organise an…entry into the UK. I can't work in building with Krys and the others because I don't exist here. Cockling is all I can do, using a licence Bosko has for the Poles."

'Don't exist' here? Somewhere in his account, he's disappeared as a person and become some…commodity.

"I'm no use to them if I'm caught for illegal cockling," he says slowly as if trying to reason through something. "The fishing authorities would find I am illegal too, and I'm deported. The only way I can repay my debt is to cockle for Bosko."

I shake my head into the darkness. I can't accept there is no alternative. Maren clearly had no idea what he was signing up to.

There's so much I want to say about what's not right here, but it won't change anything. I reach for his hand. He squeezes mine.

"So, this is the only idea I have, Allie."

I hold my breath. He's going back to Albania?

"I will tell the bosses," he says, "I will tell them, I'll continue to cockle for them but only in the day. After all, I'm no use to them dead! It isn't a crime to walk on the Sands, and I can make sure no one sees me fishing."

It sounds so simple, and after what almost happened tonight, why wouldn't his bosses accept his plan? Maren's right. They need him alive!

My whole body is lighter and lighter, like it's been carrying weights I wasn't fully aware of. We survived the quicksand. Maren's never risking his life in the dark again. Right now, we're sharing this wild, remote spot.

I've never felt more alive.

This elation's building up in me; it won't be contained. I release his hand and scramble to my feet and, head back, arms outstretched, spin around and around.

Laughing, Maren joins me, catching me around the waist and spinning with me.

"We have our waltz now?" he says as we slow.

He offers me his left hand; my other hand goes to his shoulder and his to the small of my back, under his jacket.

"*One*, two, three," he murmurs. His hard thigh nudges the leg I should move backwards until I've got it and we're slow dancing, as one.

He nestles his head closer to mine. "Allie," he murmurs, "it's all right to listen to our hearts."

As I tilt my face towards his, it's like stage fright, my churning mix of thrill and nerves. "You *know* how I feel, Maren."

I shift my hand from his shoulder up to touch his cheek for the first time.

And we kiss.

It's aching and sweet, his lips so soft and gentle when the rest of his body is hard and strong. I love his faintly spicy taste; he's both new *and* familiar. At once deep and fizzing, we've uncorked something rare.

As we pause, I find I'm clutching his sweater; I open my eyes to smile up at him.

But wow!

Over his shoulder.

For a second, I gape, unable to find the words.

"Look!"

A hazy green orb is streaking across the sky

arrow-fast

trailing a wriggling, pointy tail.

"Our comet!" he cries. "Allie, I knew our kiss would be cosmic!"

You've been imagining our kiss? I think, laughing. "It's like something...alien."

"Alien, yes!" he chuckles. "It's Lovejoy!"

The first time you can see it in *how* many thousands of years?

We gaze after it until it has faded into the dark and then turn to each other, stunned.

"They said Lovejoy would not live," he tells me. "It's a sun grazer. This comet has come through the heat of the sun. And yet it's still here! I can't believe it."

"It's a survivor, just like you," I tell him.

He's kissing me again, drawing me closer and closer.

Until we remember we're in the middle of a seabed and he has his bosses to meet.

WE NEED ALL the power of Lovejoy behind us as we head back to the marsh. It's painstaking, slow progress as I illuminate a safe route to land. I won't allow our happiness to make me careless when sinking sand could ambush us again.

Each time I stop, before I swing my phone light around for him, I glance ahead at the streetlights, willing them nearer. *The last time he will be out here by night,* I repeat, a mantra to urge myself on.

At last, the marsh is in sight.

I'M BUOYED WITH relief as we step up onto the marsh. While we walk side by side up the grassy path towards the Kents Bank railway crossing, it really sinks in. We've beaten the Sands and their traps. Seen Lovejoy. Had our first kisses. Mission accomplished and so much more!

"No!" he says, low.

He stops; lays down his sack; turns to me.

"It's them."

At the fear in his voice, my heart falters, knowing all too well who he means.

A bitter stabbing pricks along my veins. In a snap, our thirty minutes of joy is obliterated.

"They mustn't be here. I should meet them in the lane, as always."

Do they somehow know I'm with Maren and have come to intercept us?

I enfold my arms tight around him. "If we can beat quicksand, we can face them off for sure. We aren't doing anything wrong, me going out on the Sands with you."

"They won't like you knowing about everything, including them."

His voice, his body language, they're taut with fear.

"That night, in the minibus," I tell him, "I named them Stringy and Stumpy cos one's so tall and one so short."

Now I'm trying to cut them to size for him as well as me.

"Jez and Bosko," he tells me in a flat tone.

WE UNRAVEL OURSELVES, and sombrely, he hoicks his sack back over his shoulder.

In silence, we trudge towards them, deep dread in my chest.

Their cigarette smoke wafts to us, along with deep-voiced guttural sounds, ever louder.

Words neither of us can understand.

Twenty-Nine

GOOD EVENING, LADIES and gentlemen," Jez says, his sarcasm as heavy as his accent, while Bosko smokes silently beside him.

Between them, they block the width of the ramp, looming above us in the patch of orange light cast by the lamppost at the level crossing.

Maren nods and rolls down his sack between him and them. The cockles rattle as if trembling themselves.

"Aren't you going to introduce your girlfriend?" says Jez.

Am I? If I am, I'm proud to be.

Maren sticks his hands in his jeans pockets and looks to the side like he's bored. A briny odour escapes from the sack as Jez opens it to shine his phone torch over its contents.

Bosko keeps drawing on his cig and eyeing me up. *Only because I'm standing opposite him*, I tell myself.

"They couldn't be larger," Maren says, his eyes back on the sack. "You pay me now."

Jez finally reaches into his jacket pocket. Making him wait, he holds out a few notes between finger and thumb before peeling a couple off.

"For your room," he says.

He hands them on to Bosko, who holds out his fat palm and thumb for them, a gold ring on his little finger winking in the lamp light.

"For your transport," Jez sniffs, looking only at Maren as he peels off one more and passes it across to his boss as well.

Maren will *never* pay off his debt at this rate, I realise, and any last trace of our earlier happiness is squashed out of me.

Now, at last, a faint sneer on his face, Jez hands what's left—one fiver—to Maren. Maren's hand shakes ever so lightly as he takes it.

"A little bet on the dogs later, eh?" Jez says to Bosko, who grunts as he pockets the notes.

My blood seethes. Maren could have lost his *life* an hour ago. How dare these two hold it so cheap, putting the proceeds of Maren's mortal risk to a disgrace of a dog fight?

This whole payment performance is clearly an exercise in humiliation. *Well, the only ones it humiliates are you, not Maren*, I tell them in my mind.

"It's not safe at night," Maren says, looking from one to the other, his voice fearless though I can sense him breathing faster beside me. "I was almost in quicksand tonight. You *need* me alive. I will go out in the light— no one will see me. I will go from further up the shore."

The two men look at each other askance and exchange grinding Polish words.

Bosko takes a step forward, draws on his cigarette and blows smoke in my face. I close my eyes against it. When

I open them, *he's* in my face, his stale, garlic breath bitter as his eyes travel inch by inch from my face to my feet.

My skin crawls.

"Hey!" Maren yells, stepping between me and him.

Now he's right in *Maren's* face.

"You go out when *we* say," Bosko growls.

Tossing down his cigarette butt, he stamps on it as if it were Maren and fires a tirade of words at Jez.

"We are sure we can count on you to stay alive," Jez translates. He takes a dramatic pause and gives a mock helpless shrug. "Unless you prefer to go to Rwanda? Or home to Albania? Taking your debt with you."

I finally understand how naïve I've been, and maybe Maren too—why they want someone working for them who's undocumented.

Diagonal from me, still higher up the ramp, Jez grabs the sack by its neck and drags it towards him.

Bosko is still looking Maren in the eyes, waiting for some sign of submission.

Maren doesn't even blink.

Bosko shifts his head to the side so he can see past Maren to me. A leer creeps across his bullish face, his tongue showing between his lips. He flicks his eyes back to Maren, jerks his head at Jez, and they're gone.

AT ONCE, MAREN pivots and steps towards the Bay as if he can't bear another second of them. Me, I watch the lumpy sack and the folds of Bosko's thick neck till they're out of sight. Even then, I listen for the Jeep's engine to roar, fade.

NOW COME TEARS, relief and frustration mingled: in a matter of minutes, they've snuffed out all our happiness. We're back to square one, only worse. We can't even hope he can go out in the day or see *any* other way out of this deadly trap.

And they know about me, every detail of what I look like. I feel as if Bosko licked the length of me, tasted me. A threat, obviously.

So much was said in such a short conflict, I have to replay it in my mind. Money for his room rent as well as his transport. Maren will never break free of them.

Sick to my stomach, I screw up my eyes, wishing I could erase what I've just witnessed—the syphoning off of most of his pay, the forced work.

Maren, this clever, independent, solitary young man, is *bonded*. Not to some 'bosses' but to exploitative gangmasters who deceived him about his debt, beguiled him with a legit job at the beginning only to betray him into darkest danger. And now he has to repay a 'loan' he should never have had to take—like the Chinese cocklers before him in even more ways than I imagined.

A violent tremor sets up in my shoulders and travels all down my body. Maren's trapped, and I'm the *only* one on his side.

Something shrivels to nothing inside me.

Hope.

But I can't let Maren know.

COMPOSING MYSELF, I go to stand alongside him.

Neither of us is saying the words, but they're in bright lights against the black of the Sands: Bosko, every bit as inhumane as the Chinese gangmasters, is *forcing* him to continue his nighttime fishing.

And once I'm gone, Maren will be totally alone.

What if he continues to mirror the Chinese cocklers right to their tragic end?

Maren suddenly roars words out in the dark of the Bay, sending my shoulders sky high.

Albanian's nothing like Polish. It's lighter, musical, even though his voice is raised.

"I *will* not do what they say," he tells me. "I will *not* risk my life for them."

Our hands find each other.

EVEN WITHOUT THE cockles, our steps are heavy as we stumble back across the train track. I can sense Maren's mind searching for *how* he can outmanoeuvre Bosko.

What an ugly knot binding him to them. I *have* to help him loosen it and escape. Before I go home tomorrow. My mind's bouncing, in overdrive, when I need it be calm and rational.

Too soon, we're at the crossroads where I should turn right.

Without either of us saying a word, we continue up his road.

Thirty

As we slip past Krys's motorbike in the front garden, the doors of sleeping Poles, and up into Maren's room, I'm determined those evil men won't taint the rest of tonight. Maren seems to be of the same mind, pushing his bedroom door firmly closed against the world. A world against us: the bosses, Krys, Courtney too. And, in case that's not enough, even the freakin' Bay did its damnedest this evening.

So much has changed in the three and a half hours since we left his bedroom—for the worst but also the best. How could either of us ever forget our supernova first kiss under a blazing comet?

By the glow of the streetlight, we push out of our shoes and shrug off our jackets.

Straight away, we're holding each other again, so tight, trying to cram a year into a week. I'm stroking whatever parts of him I can reach while he grips me closer and closer.

"Allie," he murmurs in my ear.

Through our kiss, this energy and euphoria grows. Nobody and nothing can stop us right now.

Except Maren's stomach, it turns out—growling loudly! We laugh and finally pull apart.

195

"BE … AT HOME," HE says, gesturing the little room, now our refuge, as he puts on the desk lamp and closes the curtain. "I'll find something to eat."

A happy warmth soaks into me as he smiles at me. This is *our* time. Our secret, middle-of-the-night party for two, and it could be an all-nighter!

I flop onto the mattress and edge back to prop myself up against the wall.

"Something to warm you?" he says, reaching beneath his desk.

He hands me a metal flask.

"Vodka?"

"Raki—what we drink in Albania."

I take a sip; splutter as it burns my throat. He laughs.

A packet of crackers in his hand, he shuffles onto his bed next to me.

I pass his flask to him for a much bigger swig. He offers me the packet in return.

"I'm so hungry," he says, cramming biscuits in.

"Did you eat before we went out?"

He chews and swallows. "Something, but the kitchen is too dirty to cook in. They expect me to wash and clean up after them. But I won't do it anymore."

"Good for you!"

Except it's stopping him eating properly. I wish I'd brought him something from the canteen.

"What's Albanian food like?"

"It depends who cooks!" he says, a spark in his voice. "My family eats a lot of fish, some lamb. My favourite is byrek, a pie with cheese and spinach. I could eat some right now!"

"And Albania itself—what's it like?"

"A big question, Allie." He munches another couple of crackers. "Heaven and hell, many of us call it. We have bad roads, bad driving, bad buildings from communist times. But around Bushat in the north, where my family lives, beautiful mountains rise up not far from the sea."

"Like the stunning bay you showed me where you fish with your grandad. But you can't cook the view."

"What do you mean, Allie?"

"Oh, it's a line from the play I'm reading this week. It means you can't live off beautiful scenery, I suppose."

"Ah! Yes, exactly. The mountains and sea are all I could ever want, except they give little work. And still we suffer from the past. My grandfather was seventeen years in Spac, a political prison, only for praising God."

Seventeen years away from his family? And not even for a crime. I can't wrap my head around all that time.

"Still we Catholics do not always...fit, you say? Politically. Even in our schools and universities, the Government controls what we can say."

I shake my head, struggling to imagine this different life he's left behind.

"And your home?" he asks.

I falter. I've got it so good—our lovely house, my bedroom with all my treasured plays and poetry books, Mum. But I don't want to think about being back there tomorrow. Not if Maren's not safe.

"It's a village near Leeds, with a stream, fields, a church and not much else," I tell him instead. "Except Finn." Home is people for me, I've discovered this week, not a place. "Finn's helped make it home. He's this unique combo of brother and best friend."

"Driton's something like that for me."

"Your brother?"

"Yeah. We hoped…" A quaver enters his voice. "Driton, like so many of us, dreamt of coming to the UK. But it's not…"

He trails off, unable to finish the sentence. Not *safe*? A twinge of pain spikes across my belly at how they must have pinned all their hopes on England being only a good move for Maren.

Fear has crept back into the room again. We've *got* to make this come good for him. I'm holding this in my mind whilst making the most of each minute of our night.

"Do you…did you play chess with Driton?" I ask, my eyes alighting on the board on his desk opposite us.

"Yeah, and I usually won."

"Well, you won't win against me," I tell him, scrambling up off the mattress. "Up for five-minute chess?" My hands are on either side of his chessboard.

"How does it work?"

"We each put five minutes on our phone clocks, start it when it's your turn, stop it when you've moved. You either win in the time or you lose if your clock gets to five mins first."

"You're on!" he says.

Carefully, I carry the board over to his mattress; we sit cross-legged with it between us.

"Okay. Ready on your clock?" I ask. "You go first cos I rarely lose."

He scoffs. "Is that right, Allie?"

He studies the board for a second, taps his phone and moves his first piece, a middle pawn.

Whenever he makes a good move, his eyes gleam; I raise my eyebrows at him when I'm happy with mine.

We fight it out, thinking fast and furious, shoving a player, tapping our phone screens, silent with focus.

"No!" he suddenly roars. "My time's up!"

I throw up my hands. "I did tell you!"

He sinks back. "Luck. And it was my first try."

Smiling, I give an unconvinced shrug and lean across the board to give him a consolation kiss.

"It's almost worth losing," he says.

"I'd have given you a winner's kiss anyway," I say, kissing him again.

When I finally sink back down, I'm still holding my queen. I rub its contours in my hand and think of Maren's family.

His eyes are on the chessboard between us. Is he thinking of the grandfather who made it? Or Driton? Or whether he'll ever see them again? I can't go home till I've done everything in my power to make sure he can. Looking at the chessboard, I wonder if I might just have found a winning move.

"My jeans are still wet at the bottom," he says quietly after a long moment. "I need to shower if you excuse me for five minutes, Allie."

Once he's gathered some clothes and his towel, he makes me lock the door behind him with a bolt I hadn't yet noticed.

PULSE OVERWOUND, I'M on Google the second he leaves. My thumbs are forming words I hate to associate with Maren, but I have to do this.

Anti-slavery charities

A whole list lines up on my screen—I know from my research, the Chinese cocklers' tragedy led to new laws and new protection. A word calls to me.

Unseen.

Just as Maren's plight is unseen by everyone but me.

From Unseen's landing page, black writing in an orange box jumps out at me:

**Call the UK modern slavery &
exploitation helpline on
0800 121 700**

No time to consider, my breathing all short, I press the number.

A gentle male voice answers, asks whether I'm safe; understand English; my age. I can choose whether or not to give my name.

Allie, I whisper. I've got five minutes at most.

Understood, he says. **Why are you calling Unseen tonight?**

I've been rehearsing this sentence in my head, but the only way I can say it is if I pretend I'm speaking about some theoretical person, not the lad in the next room I care so deeply for.

My friend's a modern slave, I tell him, my voice trembling. *And he's in terrible danger.*

Can you say what type of danger, Allie, please?

He's being forced to pick cockles in the dark. Tonight he nearly walked into quicksand. But his bosses are making him carry on because he's bonded to them.

I understand, Allie. Can you tell me a bit more about your friend?

He's male, Albanian, in his late teens.

I've got that. And where is he living and working?

Morecambe Bay.

And his bosses, what can you tell me about them?

The bathroom door opens right next to the bedroom. It closes; I tense.

Quick, tell me how to save him.

You need to report his situation to the local police, Allie. They'll take it from there.

A soft knock on the door. "Allie, it's me."

My free hand, shaking, goes to my mouth.

"Coming," I tell Maren.

First, I've one last question and it's crucial.

What will happen—will my friend be deported?

Not necessarily, because of the exploitation.

Okay, got that.

I've got the words, now I need to understand them.

Tell your friend we would do our best to support him—in a safe house or in the community.

Thanks, I squeeze in before I cut the call.

I puff out a quick breath as I push up from the mattress, willing my heartbeat to slow as I go to unbolt the door.

Now for my next challenge: what am I going to tell Maren?

Thirty-One

As I go to unlock the door, part of me thinks *yes, going to the police, this could be our move*; but his words—*not necessarily* and *we'd do our best*—gnaw at my mind. Nothing's clear-cut or guaranteed. Maren won't buy into that. And anyway, what's he going to think of what I've just done?

"Better?" I ask as he re-bolts the door behind him.

"I'm awake again." He's smiling, fresh and relaxed in a navy T-shirt and grey joggers.

I close my eyes for a second, hating to spoil his rare carefree mood by telling him about my call.

When he opens his arms for me, I shove everything else aside. We *need* these moments. He smells of soap and green, somehow; tastes fresh and minty as we kiss.

"I love this hair. It's what I first saw of you." He releases my hair from its scrunchy and combs his fingers through the whole length of it, to under my shoulder blades. "I love this mouth too."

My wide mouth I thought no one would ever want to kiss.

I burrow into him, slipping my hands under his shirt to the smooth skin of his back; I flood with…yes, *love* for him. And I'm wired because I must act on that love.

As he holds me close to his chest and I hear the strong thud of his heart, I know, no matter what his reaction, I've got to tell him what I've done.

"What is it?" he says, feeling the tension in me.

PROPPED AGAINST THE wall, he's not angry at me for contacting Unseen, but I can tell from the set of his mouth that he's resigned, not at all up for new suggestions.

"Thank you for trying, Allie. But I have to carry on as I am. I won't be deported. So no choice."

Those two words flip me. It's what the Chinese cocklers must have felt. But not Maren. Not if I can help it.

"You *do* have a choice," I tell him firmly.

The chessboard, still between us, sparks an idea.

I set out the black king and rook. "These are Jez and Bosko."

Their names should have no place in his room, but time's running out. I set out the white king and queen opposite them. "This is you and me."

"And *their* queen?" he asks.

"They haven't got one. Not trying big myself up or anything, Maren…" I grin at him, "but I *am* the only one with free movement here…"

He smiles at last. "True, Allie. But don't forget, they also have Krys and Leon who, I think the word is, *spy* for them."

Reluctantly, I add a bishop and a knight to the black side.

"Look, we are…outnumbered?" he says.

"It may look like they have the upper hand…" He half-smiles at the idiom in spite of it all. "But really, it's checkmate. And I tell you, Maren, we *can* win this game."

He shakes his head, serious again.

I move our queen across till I'm facing Bosko head on.

"I report them, what they're doing...to the police."

His hand shoots out and grabs our queen off the board.

"But then I'm busted too—you would have to involve me. We might stop them, but you heard Jez earlier. I end up worse than ever, back in Albania at best, owing thousands of pounds I cannot pay."

He slumps back against the wall.

My stomach all jittery, I wrap my hand around his fist, still clamped around our queen.

"It...it's different, Maren, if they're *forcing* you into dangerous work."

His eyelids are heavy. "Your government believes many of these claims are not true."

"But *yours* is," I tell him. "And we can prove it."

His face is totally sceptical, but he submits to hearing me out.

I move our king, him, into the middle of the board. "Tomorrow, you go out and cockle in the day, unseen, whenever's safe."

Now I replace our queen bang in Bosko's face.

"First thing in the morning," I tell him, "I ring the police in Kendal and tell them what's going on. They'll take it from there, but I think they should know about when you meet Bosko and Jez to hand over the cockles. They could come and *witness* Bosko taking almost all of your earnings, *making* you cockle at night. They'll be prosecuted, imprisoned. And we win!"

He throws up his hands. "Even if the police would do all this, how is it a win? I'll still be deported. We go in circles, Allie."

"It *is* a win, Maren. While it's being investigated at least, you get to stay, if you're…"

The phrase from Unseen's advisor sticks in my throat. Tears prickle.

"If I'm what, Allie?" he asks quietly.

We look at each other for a long moment, the phrase heavy between us. Nothing under the sun will make me think of Maren as a victim. I won't even say the word. But I think one of us has to name it if we're to move ahead with this plan. My eyes fill as I force out two of the choking words.

"A modern slave."

It *kills* me inside when tears glaze his eyes too.

Next second, somehow, we're clutching each other at a ridiculous, twisted angle, the chessboard and pieces in chaos between us.

I'm smoothing his shoulders, hair, trying to ease away the words. "I'm so sorry," I murmur. *Sorry this happened to you; sorry I've had to speak it.*

"But even if I was allowed to stay on, even then, it would all take so long, Allie," he says into my neck. "After Manston, I'd be waiting in some ferry or military base for a year or even eighteen months…" His voice breaks up. "And I just couldn't."

"No, no, Maren, that wouldn't happen." I clasp him even closer. "On the phone, he told me—he definitely said a safe house or in the community. And to tell you they'd support you. *I'll* support you. And, best of all, you'll be *safe.*"

Feeling my face wet on his, he pulls back to look at me; wipes away my tears with the side of his forefinger.

"You must wish you had never met me."

I give him my best *as if* face. "We *will* get you free of Bosko and the Bay."

He gives me a watery smile and the gentlest of kisses. "When you came onto the Sands on Saturday to warn me, you were the first person in the UK to care for me, Allie. And you haven't stopped since."

"I'll never stop, Maren." I kiss him again. "Sleep on it all?"

"I *need* to sleep."

"One day," I say, gathering up the chess pieces, "we'll have a proper, full-length chess game together."

A smile wavers on his face, as if he can't imagine a life where that would be possible. "If you're ready to lose!"

"I never lose," I say, returning the chessboard to his desk.

WHEN I TURN around again, he's collapsed into his bed.

"Come, Allie," he murmurs sleepily, holding up the side of the duvet for me.

I turn out the light and take off my jeans—no way can I sleep in them. Maren interweaves his knees with mine, warming my bare legs with his fleecy joggers.

"I think it's now safe to say we're involved!" I tell him.

He laughs. "I was involved from our first afternoon."

"Me too, but you know..."

"You had to listen to your head!"

He kisses me, shifts to rest his head on my chest. His hand grows heavy where it lies on my hip and he's asleep, my arms protecting him.

I have to struggle to turn my mind off—all tonight's unforgettable events, all I want to happen tomorrow and whether it's possible to win for Maren.

Day 7
Friday, 31st October

Watch your step, submarine. By rights they outa throw you back in the water.

Eddie to Rudolpho

Thirty-Two

A HAND'S STROKING MY back; gently shaking me now. *Nooooo, Luce. It's still night!* I hump away from her and go back to sleep.

The hand jogs me more strongly. "Allie, you must go soon or you will be busted."

This is Maren speaking. I'm in his bed.

I roll over and snuggle into his chest. His T-shirt smells of him and soap.

He smooths my hair and I focus only on this Maren moment.

"I never want to go," I murmur to him. He's so warm and solid.

"I never want you to."

On our sides now, he wraps his arms around my back, holding me so close our bodies are touching top to toes. Savouring the firmness of him against me, I imprint the feel, the scent of him on my mind.

"Allie," he stirs eventually, "I've decided."

My stomach muscles steel themselves. It's today, the last day.

"Whatever it means for me, we have to stop Bosko," he says quietly. "So he can't do this to anyone else. If you're still willing, I am too."

I nod, over and over. Today we set out towards a safe, legal life for Maren, still in the country where he wants to be.

Bit by bit, we work out our plan, one that protects Maren to the max.

Ten minutes later, I'm dressed.

"I'll message you as soon as I've made the call," I tell him, perching on the mattress next to him.

I hesitate. I've been pondering whether, with all that's going on, he'll want to meet tonight. We both have a big twenty-four hours ahead of us, trying between us, yet separately, to thwart two dangerous gangmasters. But I *need* to see him.

"I've got to escape this terrible Hallowe'en party Courtney's organising at the hostel tonight."

Torchlit PJ party in the lounge with truth-or-dare and ghost stories. #Courtney&FinnsLastNightofFun?

"You up for our own party?" I ask. "We could work out where later."

He leans up onto his elbow.

"I could bring fish and chips from the town," I add.

"Then yes! Plus a game of chess."

I shake my head sadly. "You know what will happen!"

We smile at each other, lighter now we have that to look forward to.

He pulls me to him. Our kiss is so sweet and gentle, lingering and just ours, it hums all the way through my arteries to my heart. We start to slide towards something, giddy like we can't stop, and...

We have to.

I TIPTOE DOWNSTAIRS, but one or two of them creak. Almost at the bottom, I fix my eyes on the panel of glass in the front door, through which a grey, wet day is dawning.

"Good morning, Allie," slithers a sarcastic voice.

My stomach does a painful somersault.

Krys lurks in his doorway in skin-tight, red-and-black-striped boxers, his pale belly hanging over the waistband—the opposite of Maren's hard, lean body. How can Courtney stomach him? He sees the distaste in my face, I know he does, but he doesn't speak. Like a Gorgon, he freezes me in place with a hateful glare.

I despise you more than you could ever hate me, I tell him in my head.

And look—you've brought Maren and me even closer together.

I won't let you expose him any further.

Still he fixes me.

Adrenalin courses through my veins. If he tries to yank me into his room, I'll scream for Maren. I'll scream the place down. But what if he covers my mouth?

Before he can make a move, I'm at the door. Can't open it, jangle the latch, glance over my shoulder. He stands watching, gross in his state of undress.

I twist the door handle and I'm out of there.

I STOP TO make my call just as it's becoming light, at the point on the prom where I first spotted Maren walking the Sands. If it had been foggy-cloudy then, like this grey early morning, I'd never have seen him and the whole week would have been different. Though I have no idea how. I could never regret having met him.

Talking to the police is even more nerve-shredding than talking to Unseen. The hugest of stakes—Maren's future—depends on me being absolutely convincing, not dismissed as some melodramatic teenager.

It helps that I can say Unseen advised me to go direct to them, and they ask me similar questions. Maren didn't want them to have his address or even phone number, so I've got to get the details right, especially where and when he's meeting the bosses tonight. They've *got* to arrest Bosko and Jez. Maren can't carry on risking his life.

Afterwards, still shaking, I slump onto a bench. They say if they find Maren genuinely is a potential victim of modern slavery, they'll get him straight to a safe house, and he'll be put in this process called the National Referral Mechanism. I decide it's better I tell Maren that tonight, *after* he's done his final cockling.

Wobbly with relief and hope, I message him.

> ALLIE: The police said to leave it with them—they'll keep you safe. I've explained when and where your meeting is. It's happening!

Vivid images appear in my mind from the night I first saw him handing cockles to his bosses on the dark, empty lane. Part of me is desperate to be there tonight. I don't know what the police are going to do with my information, but I have to trust them to help Maren from this point.

How to end my message? I decide against kisses. *Thinking of you all the time*, I write instead.

Only one tick appears, as I made him promise to turn off his phone and go back to sleep.

THANKFULLY, COURTNEY AND Lucy are asleep too. Leaving my kagoule on the chair and my phone on my bedside table, I sneak straight into the shower in the hope they won't even know how late/early I came back.

How am I going to survive the next twenty-four hours? I try to wash away my tension with steaming hot water. *Hour by hour—till I see Maren tonight,* I tell myself. *And with Finn.* I'm so relieved he has at least some idea of what's going on.

Courtney's on her side, comatose, and Lucy's at her wardrobe choosing today's outfit as I patter back into the bedroom wrapped in a towel.

She looks at me over the top of her glasses. "All right, Allie?"

I nod.

"How's Maren?"

So she *does* know I've just come back. Her simple question moves me, but my fuzzy mind fumbles around for what she knows. She'll mean from a romantic point of view, I realise. For a moment, I'm allowed to be a teenage girl with her first boyfriend.

"He's lovely." Even with everything going on, I smile at the thought of him. "We might have kissed too."

If only that were the most important event of last night.

"I can always tell!"

"But tonight could be the last time I see him."

"Grange isn't a million miles from Leeds, Allie."

How can I even begin to explain that Maren won't *be* in Grange? That we have no idea where he will be.

"Love finds a way," she says. "You know how it is with Shaf and me."

Wistful, I smile and nod. Both their families would go ape if they discovered the relationship they've managed to keep secret for two years now. They can see the end of it now, though, if they both manage to pull off a place at Nottingham Uni. Maren and me—our complications are on a whole new level!

I flop onto my bed in my towel and reach for my phone.

> MAREN: Couldn't sleep. Got your message. Thank you, Allie, for everything. I'm going out at 1 this afternoon so can sleep afterwards. Don't worry.

I scrunch my lips.

> ALLIE: I can't promise!

But this *is* his last time out there.

"I'm gonna give breakfast a miss," I tell Lucy, nesting under the quilt even if it is for only half an hour.

"Okay, I'll bring you some toast," she says.

Courtney stretches up with a loud yawn. I roll over, away from her.

Thirty-Three

AN HOUR LATER, my body's on the sofa for our morning drama session, but my heart and mind, both are with Maren. I've pulled up some lines I scripted yesterday on my screen but can't even begin to edit them.

Miss rolls up opposite me.

"Need some help with the cocklers' story, Allie?"

I nod. Part of me wants to come out and say it—*Because I'm right in the middle of a cockling story happening right now to this lad I care so deeply for*—to confide in her about this proud, resilient boy, whose fate I've become entwined with in a matter of days, and about the phone calls I've just made, the most terrifying and significant calls of my life.

Miss is looking at me, weighing up whether or not to probe further. Something stops her, maybe this sixth sense she seems to have. She says it's down to her having more opportunity to sit and notice these days, more time for people.

She holds out her hands for my laptop.

"*You go out there when we say,*" she reads aloud. "You think one of the cocklers objected to going out that night and this is what their gangmaster said?"

"I know it is," I tell her, though not to the cockler she has in mind.

215

"You've found the why, Allie—essential, as you know. You've nearly got this finished. Time to knit it all together, I think." She turns to the other four, scattered around the room. "Come and join us over here, the rest of you."

Finn comes to sit beside me, the other three on the sofa across from us. All the time, Courtney's giving me her beady eye: I'm pretty sure Krys has told her I stayed with Maren last night.

"So, our last day," Miss says, "and time for a title to unite our story strands. And remember, the right title will introduce *heart* from the outset. Any proposals?"

I look at my lap. A title's the last thing I've been focusing on.

"Yeah," Courtney says straight off. "*Happiness Seekers.*"

I'm intrigued in spite of myself.

"You mean, everyone who goes out into the Bay is seeking a sort of happiness?" Lucy asks.

Courtney only raises her eyebrows, arms folded.

You and Finn the afternoon we arrived, I think, gazing at her, trying to work out what she's playing at with this title.

"I think we *are* all seeking happiness," Finn says in a quiet voice, "irrespective of this Bay. But we're often looking in the wrong place."

"Happiness is something you find when you're *not* looking for it," I say, smiling because of how happy I am seeing him back to his real self now, even in front of Courtney, and of Lovejoy last night, and my dazzling moments with Maren, even in the tensest of situations.

"Tell me where the *right* place is," Courtney says to Finn, ignoring me.

He gives her a rueful smile. "Making others happy."

I've heard Finn quote his favourite humanist, Ingersoll, before. I wait for Courtney to scoff at it. She doesn't, but her mouth twists as if she's totally unconvinced.

A pause.

"Time to 'fess up, Courtney," Miss says, raising her eyebrows at her. "The others don't realise."

What the...? We all stare at Courtney.

She shrugs, clearly not up for explaining anything.

"*Happiness Seeker,*" Miss says, "is a phrase the press occasionally throws around—a derogatory term for economic migrants."

A pain shoots right across my chest. Courtney's attacking Maren because, technically...

Maren *is* 'only' a happiness seeker.

A hot, painful mix churns in my veins. Unable to bear Courtney's smug face a second longer, I make for the window. The Sands are still grey under a steady, slatey drizzle. Maren will be out there soon. And I have no idea how today is going to end for him.

"Like the cockle pickers," Courtney's saying behind me. "So fits our script perfectly."

"But they were fleeing poverty," Lucy points out.

"Yep, not war or persecution," Courtney says. I know her eyes are on my back. "So not refugees at all. Only economic migrants."

"Pioneers is what we used to call people who left their homes for a better life," Miss says. "And admired their courage. Until we invented borders, labels next, to limit and reduce people."

We all know what Miss thinks about the labels *she's* gathered that aim to render her *one* thing.

I re-join the room. "Yeah—refugees, immigrants, migrants and now *degrees* of migrants when we're all *people*. Some even leave the happiest of families…" I stare at Courtney to say, *Yep, I know this is all about Maren,* "because they're desperate for work and a future. Why shouldn't they have what we have?"

"Cos there's loads of 'em," Courtney says. "They're chancers, gaming the system."

I throw up my hands.

"There *is* no system for them! People like the cocklers don't know what they're getting into. They become indebted then exploited—and we know how that can end."

Her expression, totally uncaring, riles my blood still further. "If they want to be safe," she says, "they either stay at home or stick to the immigration rules."

My hands are in fists. Tearful, I look to Miss. What if I told them straight what's going on with Maren right in this Bay in front of us, twenty years on from the Chinese cocklers, simply because he was born in the wrong place?

"Otherwise," Courtney blunders on, "migrants'd swarm in from everywhere and anywhere poorer than the UK, sink our schools and hospitals, take all our jobs."

"Yeah, we're *queuing up* to risk our lives cockling in the dark," I say, looking anywhere but at her. I can't bear her smug, ignorant face.

Courtney fakes an exaggerated yawn.

"What?" she says, as *now* I glare at her. "Never heard of compassion fatigue?"

I'm gobsmacked. Until it dawns: I'm wasting my breath with Courtney. She's stuck forever in her inhumanity.

Finn catches my eye and pats the sofa next to him. Shattered, I collapse beside him.

"Another phrase I wish I'd never heard, Courtney," Miss says. "Our compassion can't fail if we strive *genuinely* to understand how it is to be in an individual's shoes."

At 'shoes', I find myself looking at Miss's trainers on the footrest of her wheelchair. When I first arrived at Leeds Academy, Miss didn't even know she had progressive MS. I glance at Courtney and grant you have to know a person, or at least their circumstances, to get anywhere close to empathising with them, as even she does with Miss. But Courtney hasn't even tried with Maren.

We've all gone quiet.

"What other titles have we got?" Miss asks eventually.

"I had one," Shaf says, "but it could be equally shocking."

"Try us," Miss says.

He looks slowly at each of us, playing his audience. Finally, he announces his title.

"*Last Words.*"

I duck my head to hide my face. Also too close to home—to Guo Bing Long, and to Maren and me last night.

Eddie—the one who dies in *A View from the Bridge*, not one of the foreigners after all but the tragic hero—simply gasps to his wife, 'My B!'

Maren—out on the Sands all alone—would have last words for no one. But his thoughts, they'd be for his mum. I know they would.

"'They have made worms' meat of me,'" Shaf's saying, quoting some of Mercutio's last words from when he played him in year eleven.

"I like *Last Words* as a title," Lucy says. "We could split our story strands into those who had the opportunity for last words and those who didn't."

"I'd rather not know about it when the time comes," Shaf says.

"Do you think hearing your last words'd comfort your parents?" Finn asks. "Or make it worse for them?"

Courtney licks a scornful glance down the two of them. "S'hardly something you're given a choice about."

"Anyone object to Shafeeq's suggestion?" Miss asks.

I rub under my eyes. I can't handle either title. Nor can I face another argument.

"Then let's take *Last Words* as our working title," Miss says.

Thank God it's finally break time and I can check my phone.

SHAF AND LUCY are off like bloodhounds to the canteen for drinks and chocolate biscuits. Me, I can't move, so Finn offers to bring me something back.

Courtney's still here, though, thumbing something on *her* phone. To Krys?

She looks up and our eyes lock.

You're completely off the rails now, aren't you, Al-e-the-a? hers say.

I wish you'd get the hell out of my sight, I shoot back, *and I never had to think about you again.*

Thirty-Four

"ALL RIGHT, ALLIE?" Finn says, handing me a mug of tea and a Twix.

"Better now she's gone," I say, of Courtney. I offer him half the Twix. "For frig's sake, Finn! *Compassion fatigue*?!"

He drops next to me. "To have compassion, you have to have received it."

I peer at him. "What does *she* need compassion for?"

"*Everyone* needs compassion, Allie, you know that. Her parents have never been together, and unlike ours, neither of them gives a toss about her." His face clouds. "Her mum used to leave her alone in the flat when she was far, far too young for it. This is why she hates ever being alone."

Ah, Finn, this is so you—to care about her when nobody else does. I'm sorry for what she went through as a child. But despite what Finn and Miss say, I have no compassion to spare for her right now. I don't believe her family situation gives her an excuse to hurt others or be so entirely unfeeling.

I sigh and rub my eyes again.

"How are things with Maren?" he asks lightly, edging his knees around onto the sofa so he can look at me.

I glance out of the window where the clouds are dispersing and the Sands are becoming visible. Soon he'll be out there again.

"Is he still cockling?" Finn prompts.

"For the last time today," I say.

Maren's got to get through today alone, but I've got a best friend I'd trust with my life. And Maren's. So I tell Finn all that's happened in the twelve hours since we were on this same sofa yesterday evening. The enormity of it sinks its teeth into me as I speak.

"My God, Allie," Finn says when I'm done, "I can hardly believe it. This is…extreme stuff. You've been so brave. And reckless. What if something had happened to you?"

"Or Maren," I point out. "But it didn't. And now we're going to," I throw up my hands, "save him."

"I…don't you think?…Is it time?…Time we told Miss Duffy about this?"

"Finn, no!" I all but shout. "It's all in place. If anyone interferes with it, the whole plan's ruined. Promise me you'll tell no one."

Chin in hand, he ponders. "Mum was asking after you last night."

I'm so raw today, I'm warmed and chilled at the same time. Poppy always has a heart for me, but if she finds out, she'll contact Miss—or even come here. And then our plan's up in smoke.

"You didn't, did you? Tell her?"

"No, but I considered it. You know what Mum would think, let alone your parents, if I knew what was going on and didn't look out for you. I just want to go home with you in one piece. So, you've got to promise me. You'll steer right away from the Sands and those bosses for these last—" he looks at his phone "—twenty hours."

"That I can do," I tell him, entirely truthful.

Now he smiles.

"Finn…" A question keeps nagging at me. "What does Courtney know about Maren?"

His eyes, so readable, darken. "She's too wrapped up in Krys at the moment to talk to me about anything outside drama."

God, what sort of friend have I been to him this week? Finn has *real* feelings for Courtney.

"It's only cos he's older and foreign," he carries on. "The forbidden. She'll forget him once we've gone home." A pause. "It's time we went home, isn't it, Allie?"

I look away from him, towards the Bay. I can't even think of home. And I definitely don't want to be there unless Maren's safe. Unless I know I can see him again.

"I get it," Finn says, reaching out to squeeze my hand. It's nothing like holding Maren's, but it's solid and reassuring.

"Coming for some fresh air?" he asks, standing up.

"I'm gonna stay here, thanks, Finn. Nap for a few minutes."

"ALLIE?"

I jolt awake, not knowing where I am or who's speaking to me this time.

Rue is kneeling in front of me.

I give her a weak smile.

"You look worse than me," she says.

223

"Gee, thanks! But listen, I was coming to find you later—wasn't sure whether you'd be back at school or not."

It's hard to believe it was only yesterday Maren brought Billy's body home to Rue.

"I need to ask you something, Allie."

I swallow, not at all sure I've got anything left to give.

"Would you…would you come to Billy's funeral? Please? I know this is last minute. I wasn't sure I could go through with it. But I'd like you and Finn and maybe some of the others to come to it. Which has to mean today."

I can't stop tears forming. "Oh, Rue."

"Dad's going to bury him in the garden whilst I play his requiem."

"It sounds…exactly right," I manage at last. "Nothing would stop me being there. I might have only known Billy for a short time, but I felt I got him."

"You did," she says quietly.

"And I loved his spirit and his beauty."

"I know," she says. "That's why I hoped you'd say a few words. I won't be able to speak."

Me neither, I want to say. Any other day, I'd have found this hard. Today, it's all but impossible. Yet I know I have to do it for Rue.

"I will," I tell her.

She gives me a faint smile. "Half-one—after lunch and before your afternoon session?" I nod. "And could you please tell the others, in case…"

"'Course I will. I know Finn at least will want to be there, and I'm sure some of the geographers too."

She manages a faint smile and straightens up off the floor.

"Rue." I stand too. "I can't say too much, but I have... we are, Maren and me, doing something to make sure Maren doesn't have to carry on endangering himself out there."

"I couldn't hear anything better on the day of Billy's funeral," she says quietly. "Do you want to ask Maren if he can come? I wasn't sure what to think..."

I don't either. My whole body leaps at the chance of seeing him once more, though, even at a funeral. Now I remember.

"He's got something on," I tell Rue.

His last cockling ever.

I FALL BACK onto the sofa. How Rue must feel, this final goodbye to her someone. Who could have ever foretold this week would end with her losing him? And my chest's leaden to think it's all wrapped up with us coming here. If we hadn't broken into the lido with Rue, Billy could still be alive. But then, I suppose he could have run off another time. What-ifs are the way madness lies.

DURING THE NEXT hour, Finn's right beside me, tweaking our scripts but running things past me so I'm still involved, whilst I try to find the right words to do justice to Billy's energy and love of life. I hold the main melody of Rue's requiem in my head and try out words about Billy being her someone. It's important—he was not 'only' a dog but a part of their family, her closest friend. It hurts me all the way down to my gut to think

JENNIFER BURKINSHAW

she's asking me, us lot, today because she seems to have no good friends at school. And now no Billy.

Tomorrow we're gone. How's she going to be?

And Maren?

It's cruelly abrupt to be on a train out of here in the morning, back across the viaduct that brought us to this place of extremes. When I fell in love with the golden scene in front of me last Saturday, how could I have foreseen the all-too-real drama this week would bring? Or we would bring to it.

Though Billy's life's tragically over, now I've recruited the help of Unseen and the police, I'm helping write a happy ending for Maren. Yet villains are lurking in the wings, poised to impose their own version on him.

Thirty-Five

A MESSAGE ARRIVES AS I'm following the others out to lunch, needing even the worst the canteen can offer to help me through the next hour or so.

> MAREN: Allie, can you come to meet me before I go out on the Sands, please? In the waiting room on the Bay side of the station at Kents Bank. x

The kiss jumps out at me—the first time either of us has put one in our messages, perhaps because we've kissed for real. He must need me, some moral support. This is the hugest of days for him, when all his plans for his new life in the UK are changing. For the better, we trust.

> ALLIE: Of course I'll come. It's lunchtime, so I'll grab a sandwich and I'm on my way. x

Only when I've sent it do I remember Billy's funeral. It's a good twenty minutes each way to Kents Bank. Even if I run, it's going to be tight for time. I could message Maren back to ask if he could meet me part way, but then it'd throw *his* timings out for the Sands. Nor can I *not* go—I'd never live with myself if I passed up on one more time with Maren.

It is possible to do both, I tell myself, stuffing down my sandwich as I jog along the pavement towards Grange.

The morning drizzle has given way to a feeble but strengthening sun. Shining one last time for Billy.

IT's COMING UP to twelve-thirty when I cross the railway at Kents Bank. I spot the waiting room I'd never even noticed before. It looks like the original Victorian one and a discreet place to meet, down at the far end of the platform.

No sign of Maren, but then he'll be trying to lie low.

"I'm here, Maren," I say as I get closer.

No answer.

As I approach the doorway, a face appears.

Not Maren.

Krys.

I pivot to run, but he grabs my wrist.

"Where's Maren?" I gasp, struggling in his grip.

"Maren couldn't come, could he, Allie? As you know!"

I shake my head, lost. "What? No, he *asked* me to come!"

In his free hand, Krys holds up Maren's phone.

"You make do with me instead."

Krys sent the message! Maren's already out on the Sands. He can't help me.

A black buzz of adrenalin shoots up my left arm to my heart.

"Help!" I shriek twisting around, looking for anyone on either platform. "HELP ME!"

But all I can hear is my breath, shallow and sharp.

He's going to rape me in there, I know he is—payback for the scorn and repulsion I've shown him.

And the tiny station, always quiet, is deserted today.

My free hand goes to my jeans pocket for my phone, as to a gun. He yanks my hand back out, digging his fat fingers in there to disarm me, lingering too long.

"I keep this safe," he says, shoving it in his jeans.

Now he has both my and Maren's phones.

"Someone help me!" I scream, twisting around in his grip again. Maybe someone in a house nearby will see or hear.

He clamps his huge, clammy hand over my mouth and manhandles me into the gloom of the windowless waiting room, pushing my face against the wooden wall and shoving his knee into my legs to keep me there. Is this how it starts? I want to vomit.

Cigarette smoke registers. Whilst he's been waiting for me, I suppose.

"If you are quiet, I will take away my hand," he says.

I nod.

He swivels my whole body around, keeping me in front of him.

"Now, say hello nicely."

I gasp. There in the half light, perched high on half-benches along the opposite wall, are Bosko and Jez.

"So, we meet again," Jez says, "girlfriend."

"She looks so sweet," Krys says, "yet she stayed the night with Maren."

He says his name as if it's dirty.

Jez tuts and shakes his head in mock shock.

"Maren," Bosko says, in his deep growl, his tone serious. "He has to learn I am boss."

Oh God! I suddenly realise. Krys has Maren's phone—has he also read my message to Maren? What exactly did I write? *I've told the police when and where you're meeting them.* It doesn't take a genius to work out who I meant.

My armpits and palms trickle sweat as my breathing quickens. Bosko must be boiling with rage not only at Maren but me too. *I'm* the one who involved the police. *I'm* the one who's here.

What are they going to do with me? A tremor travels up all the muscles of my legs. This is worse, worse by far than the quicksand last night. That I could escape if I was careful. No way can I predict what Bosko is going to do to me or break free of three hefty men.

"Yeah," Krys chips in. "Maren has to be put in his place."

He says this last bit proudly and slowly as if he's learned it and is saying it for the first time. He says something in Polish to the others—a translation, I think, as they nod their agreement.

"We are all sad and disappointed," Jez says. "Maren must 'play ball', as you English say. He owes us money."

"Owes you money?!" I spurt. "With the massive markup you make on his cockles and the amount you cream off for his poxy room, he owes you *nothing*."

Krys jerks my arms up my back.

"Ow!" I shriek. "You're hurting me!"

"Give some respect," he hisses in my ear. "Maren would not be in this country but for them."

At the same time, Bosko's off on one in Polish, his ring catching the light as he throws his hands around for emphasis.

"He says," Jez translates, "you know nothing. You think we lend Maren forty quid for an easyJet fare?

"Puh!" Krys scoffs in my ear. "They arrange for him secret transport so no one knows he is in the country. This costs big money—they have a lot of skin in the game."

My flesh crawls at the ugly phrase.

"And," Jez adds, "Krys and the boys, they welcome him as one of them, shelter him. You see, we are all nothing but kind to Maren."

"As long as he does what you say," I tell him, recovering my voice. "But he's risking his *life* out there for you at night and you—"

Bosko stops me with what sounds like a stream of swearing as he takes a step towards me and stares me right in the eye, his dark nostrils flaring.

"Enough! *We* make big risk for Maren."

I scoff my disbelief. Risk? On dry land?

"Anyway, he won't let himself be seen today," I tell Bosko. That much is true.

He snarls at me. I back into Krys.

"Fishery Patrol is out today," Jez says, translating Bosko's snarl.

I blink and shake my head, trying to make sense of this. Why? Why today of all days would they patrol the Sands? It's way too much of a coincidence. My hope shrivels—is it something to do with the police? Is this what happens when you involve another party?

I peer at Bosko through the half-light; at Jez too. So far, this has been only about Maren. *Do* they know about me involving the police or only about him being out on the Sands? I can't be sure either way. One thing I do know is somehow, I've got to kick, scratch, whatever it takes to escape this shelter. After which, I'll call the police again.

"No more talk now," Bosko orders.

My whole body chills and I clamp my eyes closed. What's he going to do? Stab me? Strangle me?

Someone lifts my chin, forcing me to open my eyes. Jez.

"You take a message to Maren at the cockle beds now."

The very last thing I expected. "Message? What message? Why?"

Bosko slams the flat of his hand against the wooden wall, making me jump.

"Too many questions," Jez says. "You listen and you obey."

The Kent, engorged with new rainwater from the hills, fills my mind's eye because, as Maren told me this morning, he's going right out to Priest Skear today so he won't be seen from the shore.

I shake my head vigorously. "I can't."

"You can and you will," Bosko says.

I stare at him without blinking.

"If I don't go back to the hostel, they will come looking for me. I'm due at a funeral."

"What?!" Krys says.

"It's true. My friends will all be asking me where I am."

The three of them confer in Polish, Bosko shaking his head. They clearly don't believe me.

"It will be Maren's funeral unless you do as we say," Jez says.

I swallow hard; breathe. At least they're not going to kill me. Not yet. I've got a chance to get help. Police. For Maren, for me.

"Okay." I bow my head, all meekness.

"Now, isn't this so much better?" Jez says. "So you tell Ma—"

Taking advantage of the drop in tension, I rip myself free of Krys and leap out onto the platform, hoping desperately for other passengers to be there or a train to arrive.

One, two strides away from the shelter...

Noooo! Krys has me again, by both arms this time.

"Get Maren away from them, Allie," he mutters urgently in my ear. " They've too much to lose here. If they are caught for hiring an illegal, jail for five years."

Five years? I wait, but he says nothing about the police or what else their bosses could be charged with. But I know now, the only sure way I have of keeping Maren safe is if I tell him what's going on. I've *got* to find the courage to cross the Kent.

I nod my understanding to Krys.

He swings me around and frogmarches me back into the waiting room to face the two bosses.

"What is all this?" Bosko demands, nearer the door now and thunder in his face.

He raises his thick arm. My only defence is to screw up my eyes again, but it's Krys he cracks around the head. I feel the jolt.

"All right, all right," I say quickly. "I'll take him your message."

"Our message to Maren…" Jez spits out his name. "Fishery Patrol is out, so he must not bring the cockles back to Kents Bank. He must take the cockles to Humphrey Head."

Yeah. And then what will they do to him? And me? It'd take but a moment to push us off the edge and both our bodies are lost. No one would ever know what had happened to us.

"Got it?" Jez says.

"Humphrey Head," I repeat.

"Good," Jez says. "We three will watch you safely across the river in case you were thinking—"

"Don't bother. I won't let Maren down."

THEY ACCOMPANY ME to the gate between the level crossing and the marsh. Now I'm finally free of them, on the stony path down to the reeds. Out of habit, my hand reaches for my phone. Without it, it's like I'm naked—and completely isolated. Until I reach Maren.

ONLY WHEN I get the edge of the grass do I look back at the evil trio. All three of them are still in a line, Krys in the middle, checking on me. I fully believe him when he says how urgent it is for Maren to escape Bosko. What confuses me is him tipping us off, though Bosko whacking him one proves at least some of the loyalty is forced on Krys.

This time, I can't stop to think. The step down onto the Sands, I just do it. The Sands' power over me has shrunk. Last night, they did their worst; failed. In the light, I can study them like a book as I angle myself towards where I'm guessing the cockle beds are, based on the crossing with Elijah. Now, though, it's the river giving my arms gooseflesh and my stomach knots.

I pause. I could run parallel to the shore back towards Grange. I'm pretty sure I could outrun any of them. But I'm going to cross the Kent. Not for them. For Maren.

Thirty-Six

T HE SAND UNDER my soles is soggier than I've known it all week. When I glance behind me, my imprints are two to three centimetres deep, so it's like running in sloppy snow. This is going to slow me down, sap my energy.

Checking each pace, I make as fast I can for where I hope Maren is, scanning the distance for his figure, all the time my mind whirring.

Would two gangmasters of a doubly illegal cockler really lurk around the shore if Fishery Patrol were out? Have they invented the story to ensure Maren *does* go to Humphrey Head?

He mustn't go. God knows what they'd do to him in such a remote spot.

It will be Maren's funeral today if you don't do as we say. What if Jez's words weren't only a figure of speech?

What our next is tactic is after this totally unpredictable counterattack from his bosses, I have no idea. No matter what, we mustn't let them get hold of him again. I know now Marco stabbed Eddie to death in *A View from the Bridge*, and I won't allow such violence to befall Maren. I won't have *his* life be a tragedy.

One step at a time, I think. *First of all, get to Maren.*

Without my phone, I can only guess the time. Billy's funeral must be underway right now, the heartfelt eulogy I wrote trapped in my phone, with Krys. Rue and Finn will notice I'm missing. Our teachers, though…I hadn't yet told them about the funeral, and even Finn doesn't know where I am.

But I've got a mission. Adrenalin urges me on, the all-too-real danger to Maren if I don't reach him.

I fix my eyes downwards for the telltale signs of sinking sand. Every couple of minutes, I stop and look up, craving a figure in the distance to confirm I'm following the right trajectory.

Still nothing.

One time I stop, my heart stops too: only a few metres in front of me is the Kent.

IT'S A DIFFERENT river from when we crossed it with Elijah. A bigger, fiercer river, swollen with rain and run-off from the Lakeland hills, tripping over itself and creating white horses in its eagerness to reach the sea.

If the middle of it's a foot higher than it was on Monday, it'll be up to my waist and I won't be able to anchor myself. I'll be swept away, and the only people who'll know are three pitiless criminals.

But if Maren's crossed it, he knows it'll still be safe for his return, my head reminds me.

NOW I'M AT the river's edge, I *can't*. Billy is being buried right now because he was swept down the Kent. If he couldn't survive it, nor can I. You need to be strong and confident, like Finn and Maren, to even think of taking on this river. I can't risk being tumbled like a garment in a washing machine till I'm reduced to a rag.

My pulse is racing as if I've been sprinting. Most people would shrink from this river, let alone someone with a phobia of water.

I'm the last person who should be doing this. Yet, as Bosko well knows, I'm the only person who would. Maren's life depends on me reaching him.

ONCE I'VE TAKEN off my trainers and socks, I step forward.

Energy surges through me and a conviction persuades my muscles this is better done fast: wade through the water, up and out.

I visualise myself at the other side and know I can do this.

For Maren, I say with each wading pace. *For Maren.*

I'D RECKONED ON the greater depth but not the greater cold. Just when I think I've felt its keenest bite, it intensifies, sinking its teeth through my jeans, which are weighing me down, slowing me down. To balance, I have to take short steps, my arms scarecrow-like with shoes on hands.

By the time I'm up to my knees, I'm having to brace my muscles against the force of the water to my left, but my legs are strong. Another step, another. Still ever deeper.

I'm looking ahead, always ahead.

Thigh-deep now.

Aghh! The river's got its icy jaws on my waist!

And I'm tiring.

I stop. Can't go any deeper. Going to have to turn back. Face the bosses.

One more step. I don't know much more I've got in me.

A big but sure step forward, I plant my right foot in the sand.

And it's shallower.

I've done it!

No!

Catching my toes in soft sand, I pitch

forward.

The cold snatches my breath.

Face in the water. I snort it in.

Arms scramble, legs whirr in

nothing

pulse drumming in my ears

underwater.

My kagoule, jeans anchor me

down.

Currents tug at me,
    on each side   on each side
Till I'm

flail...ail...ing.

Billy.

This was Billy too.

My chest bursts

for him

me.

All along I knew this about water.
No lifeguard here to fish me out.
No anyone.
Only me.
My lungs burn; legs kick but fail.
Will *my* body be found?

Got to live.
Got to find Maren.
I force my knees to straighten.
Feet down, some survival instinct commands—*you can touch the bottom!*
One tiptoe
on sand.
Then the other.
Push myself upright, gasping, spurting out water. Coughing and choking, I wipe it from my face with a sopping sleeve.
Only three, four more steps.
Arms up again, I shuffle one foot forward at a time, clinging to the safety of the sandy bed.
Thigh.
Calf.
Ankle.
Out.
I haul myself another metre further, clear of any thinner sand, before I collapse onto my knees... and forward onto my forearms.
And I cry, great, retching sobs of shock and relief. Wild, living water nearly got me, precisely as I've always

dreaded. My whole body, icy, sodden clothes clinging to it, starts to shiver.

Have to get my blood flowing.

I kneel up.

But what if you can't find Maren? Or you're hypothermic and run out of energy first?

I shake the doubts out of my head. I'm not giving up and dying here.

Stuffing my socks in my pocket, I put my trainers back on and force myself to my feet.

Thirty-Seven

*D*AD'D BE PROUD *of me,* I think as I jog deeper into the Bay, my blood flowing a little warmer. We never told Mum about me having to be rescued from the wave pool, a seventh birthday treat gone wrong. The secret formed a bond between us, but I don't plan on telling *either* of them about this!

Finn would go mad if he knew I'd come out here after all, and I can't see any way I can keep it from him now. Or Rue, or Miss—everyone come to think of it.

My brain's wandering. *Keep focused, Allie.* I force myself to alternate in a rhythm between looking down for quicksand, then ahead for Maren.

Down, ahead.

Down, ahead.

FURTHER OUT IN the Bay, the wind's fiercer, colder, blustering in from open sea. Instead of drying me out, it bores right through my clothes to my bones and bullies the charcoal clouds overhead, shoving them around.

The air's different. Saltier, wilder.

This is the sea's territory now.

ONE TIME I stop to catch my breath, I glimpse a black figure way ahead of me.

Maren!

I *know* I can do this.

MINDFUL OF LAST night, I keep my head down. If I get stuck, that really is the long, slow end for me.

Next time I look up, Maren's vanished.

I tremble again. Without him, I'm dead. I can't get back alone.

Nor have I any energy to spare.

I'M LOST IN the middle of a seabed.

Resentment mingles with my panic, my legs shaky. It's me who's going to end up dying out here. Like our comet, Maren's a survivor. He'll reach shore safely, not even knowing I was trying to find him. I'll be one of the hundreds whose bodies the Bay keeps. My parents will never know what happened to me.

Turns out this is *my* tragedy.

So, you're going to stand here till the tide takes you?

A doomed wanderer in a vast desert, I stumble on.

One time, I trip forward onto the sand. It's easy to lie here on my stomach. Peaceful.

But it won't be, Allie. Not when the sirens sound and the tide bellows.

And you'll never see Mum, Dad, Finn, Maren again.

I PRESS UP onto my knees; haul myself to standing; check the sand; take a few more bumbling, drunken strides.

Now I look up.

My fingers go to my mouth.

That scraggle of creepy rocks.

Priest Skear and the cockle beds.

I jog carefully towards it.

Beyond it is some slightly lower ground before it rises again to the skear where all the Chinese cocklers drowned.

In this dip, as Guo Bing Long twenty years before him, kneels Maren.

I HALT AND stare.

His dark figure, silhouetted against the low, grey skies above the infinite Sands brings a painful lump to my throat. To be forced to risk your life scratting around in wet, abrasive sand for a few shells for wealthy diners is something no one should have to do. And certainly not my Maren.

I don't wave or shout. Focused on the sand, he doesn't notice me until I'm only a few metres from him. He's too astonished to move.

I kneel next to him and we clasp each other till we're breathless.

"Allie! What the…?" He murmurs in my ear. "You are wet *all over*. The river?"

The tears come.

He shrugs out of his jacket and wraps it tight around me so I absorb his body heat.

"You came through the river. On your own?" he asks, shaking his head in disbelief.

He rubs my upper arms, trying to warm me, strokes my hair, my cheek so tenderly, kisses all over my face before wrapping me back in his arms.

"You give the best of hugs," I tell him.

"You didn't come all this way for a hug, did you?" he tries to joke.

When I've finally stopped shaking, we collapse in a unit onto the sand and I tell him why, from the beginning.

"Krys didn't touch you? Hurt you?" he interrupts, his tone tight.

I hesitate. He made me feel dirty and violated but not in the way Maren's imagining. I shake my head.

Now the lines in the middle of Maren's forehead deepen into grooves. "Krys, all of them, were at work in Kendal when I came out here."

I huff. I knew he'd have been scrupulously careful. "However Krys found out, Bosko's furious. The Fishery Patrol is out, they say, and you must meet them at Humphrey Head."

"Fishery Patrol," he says, taking it in. "And that's nothing to do with your call to the police about tonight?"

I squish my eyes closed trying to get this clear.

"I don't think so. I've not seen any sign of a patrol. I think Humphrey Head's a trap. Krys said…" I slow right down, emphasising each word. "Krys said I must keep you away from the bosses."

We gaze at each other. "He wouldn't say this unless it was serious," Maren says.

I tell him what Krys told me about the prison sentence they'd get if caught.

He sinks his head to his knees.

"They won't risk prison." He looks ahead, clamping his lips together. "I don't like this meeting place they mentioned."

"Bosko," I say, "he hit Krys round the head for letting me escape for a second."

How much greater would Bosko's punishment be for Maren's deception today, costing them their freedom for a long time?

Grim, he shakes his head. "I have become too much trouble."

My pulse speeds up. Bosko's going to eliminate the 'troublemaker' who could send them behind bars. And what of me, Maren's accomplice, a key witness?

"I don't go to Humphrey Head or anywhere on that coast."

"Where then? We're stranded in the middle of the chessboard!"

"That's it, Allie!" He's smiling. "We're not chess pieces. We keep going right to Arnside."

My stomach relaxes, a little. "Yes, they won't think of that. But then what?"

"Then I…disappear."

My belly hurts again as my mind thrashes around, trying to adjust. Our plan, our hopes for a safe future for Maren, are defeated before they began. Him vanishing somehow, somewhere—yes, it's obviously better than being beaten or killed by gangmasters, but it's so precarious, so much less than he deserves.

"Allie?"

He's waiting for my opinion, I realise.

"It's…it's…it gets you away from them." I shrug a sigh. "But…"

You'll always be undocumented. And how will you earn a living? And how will we ever see each other again.

"I know." His chin's shaking a little. "The way things have worked out today, I no longer have any choice."

Maren without choices. Exactly what I wanted to avoid.

I hug my knees into my chest.

"And your belongings?"

To think of him with only the clothes on his back, not even his phone or his precious chess set, it kills something inside me.

He throws up a hand, helpless. I rub my eyes, also at a loss. This is so not what I wanted for him. What *he* wants.

"I'll collect them," I tell him. "Meet you … somewhere, sometime."

He smiles faintly, but it's one of his evasions, I know.

"Okay," I squeak in a strange, small voice.

Nothing more to be said, we hold each other briefly. This is the best we can do, and at least we'll reach land together.

We stand up, and he takes a last look at his cockling equipment and the sack part full of cockles he's picked, a phase of his life now over, thank God.

He reaches for my hand and we set off for the far side of the Bay. *Not a retreat,* I tell myself, *but an advance of sorts because even though it doesn't solve his undocumented status, it does mean he's safe from his gangmasters.*

The sun suddenly appears over Arnside, cheering me. I swing our hands between us. He's going to be safe. And one day, we'll see each other again. I can give him my phone number once we reach the shore.

Maren stops abruptly.

I catch a breath. "Not more quicksand?"

"No, a voice. I heard someone behind us."

"Not them? They wouldn't come out here after us. Would they?"

Maren turns. I keep looking forward. Maybe if I don't see them, it won't be happening.

"Allie!" a voice yells, faint but distinct.

Thirty-Eight

W HAT THE *HELL* ...?"
Finn straightens up, wiping his hand across his face.

"When you weren't at Billy's funeral," he pants, "I was worried..."

I shake my head. "You shouldn't have come. I'm safe with Maren."

"That's not all," he says, having caught his breath now. "I asked Courtney to take me to Maren's place, but she said he was out here. And confessed."

My throat dries at the ominous combination of Courtney and confessing.

"Confessed what?"

"She'd read Maren's message on your phone. Rang Fishery Patrol."

His words knock the air out of me.

"*She* did it?" I could kill her, genuinely. "Why?"

Finn shrugs, at a loss. "I wanted you to know they might be around today." He glances at Maren. "So your... plan for tonight wasn't spoilt."

"We know, Finn," I tell him, "and the plan's already ruined. His bosses know he's out here too." I look at Maren now. "And they know because Courtney told Krys."

He looks almost resigned, like the how doesn't matter as much as what's next. But his jaw twitches with tension.

"Oh God, Allie, I'm so sorry." Finn's face is strained and white now.

"Finn," Maren says, taking charge, "you come with us, to Arnside. After, you can take the train back to Grange with Allie."

"No," Finn says.

I step towards him. "What? Why? You've got to, Finn. We have to stay together."

He shakes his head. "It's Courtney. She's stuck back there."

"For God's sake!" I turn to Maren in horror. "This can't be happening."

He's already scouring the Sands in the direction of Grange.

"Why did she even come?" I ask Finn, incredulous.

He gives me a sad smile. "She was trying to make sure *I* was all right." He pauses. "That and to 'clean up her mess,' she said."

I bray out a *puh*. "Yeah, and look how that's turned out!"

"Okay. She's on a sandbank," Maren says. "I have equipment in the backpack I left."

After what she's done to you today?

He checks his watch. "We have two and half hours before the tide starts to flow."

My stomach turns over. Elijah said people need to be off the Sands at least three hours before the tide.

"Let's get to Arnside," I say, "send the coastguard for Courtney."

It's all her fault she's stuck out here.

Finn gives me one of his looks.

Maren takes my hand. "We still have time enough for Arnside, once we have Courtney."

THE THREE OF us set off at a brisk pace back towards the cockle beds and Courtney, Finn's trainers making a squelching noise that'd be comical in any other situation.

From plan A to B to friggin' C, each one a bigger compromise, all because of her. And with each new plan, the worse Maren's future will be and the less chance we have of ever seeing each other again.

Focus, Allie, let's get out of the Bay first.

Hang on! A hope strikes me. "Won't Rue have raised the alarm?" I ask Finn. "When I didn't turn up for Billy's funeral?"

We need help *now*. Not to-ing and fro-ing on this sodding seabed!

"Sorry, Allie, but no. I told her something had come up with Maren."

My mind casts around. "What about Miss? We're supposed to be with her this afternoon."

"Lucy was going to tell her we were doing some last-minute research at the library and we'd be back for tea."

My whole body slumps. We're on our own.

NOT BOTHERING TO remove our shoes, we splash through a channel of water, ankle-deep, and slow right down as we approach Courtney. As I now know only too well, sinking sand can go in patches, a lethal, contagious rash.

There! A couple of metres of puckered sand loiters between us and her. I thrust my arm out to halt Maren and Finn. We all stop dead as if she's in a deadly magic ring.

Courtney's a statue. Still and as pale as marble. Up to her chest in sand.

Up to your waist... the odds are against you. Elijah's voice echoes in my head.

"She's further in than when I left her," Finn murmurs to Maren and me.

"We can try," Maren says.

"YEAH, THANKS FOR coming," she croaks.

I screw up my mouth, and my blood seethes. She sounds so friggin' entitled, I want to grab both lads, turn our backs on her and march right away to Arnside. What she really means is thank God Maren's here. *Now* she wants him around, now he can be useful to her!

She wipes away the snot running down to her lips with the sleeve of her denim jacket. *This is what it is to be cut down to size, literally,* I think with a kick of satisfaction. *Hubris.*

"Keep still!" Maren commands.

She freezes.

He kneels on the Sands and pulls his cockling gear out of his rucksack.

"Allie," Maren says. "First, I need you to pass me this rake. If it doesn't work, this water to free the sand." He hands a small pump to me and a coil of rope to Finn.

On his belly, he wriggles across the sand towards Courtney.

I have to grit my teeth, witnessing him lowering himself for her and her stupidity.

Once he's within arm's length of her, he twists his head around.

"The rake, Allie," he calls.

I scutter it across to him; he digs away at the sand directly in front of her.

"How long are you stuck?" he asks her after a while, though I've lost track of the time.

She shakes her head.

"Twenty minutes," Finn calls.

"This sand is set." He turns to me. "The water."

Crouching, I roll the pump gently sideways towards him. It only reaches his knees, but he gropes behind him and grabs it.

"Now the rope," he says.

Finn tosses the thinnish coil to Maren, who leans forward to loop it under Courtney's arms. Once he's tied the two ends together, he slings them back towards me and Finn.

"Finn, over your head, around your waist," he says. "While I put the water into the sand and dig, when I say three, Finn, you walk away from us with all your strength. Courtney, when the sand is more...loose, you must push forward.

"One, two, THREE!"

Finn heaves away from them till the rope tautens, then heaves some more.

Courtney shifts slightly forward. Yes!

"Stop!" Maren shouts.

Why?

But now I see. Finn can only pull her forward, not upward. Now she's simply stuck in a different position, still petrified, a listing masthead.

Maren half turns so we all can hear him. "She needs Bay Rescue."

Thirty-Nine

COURTNEY WHIMPERS.

I look to Maren.

"Kents Bank is nearer. But..."

"The river," I finish.

"I'll go," Finn says.

"He's a strong swimmer," I tell Maren.

"Okay," he says. "When Bay Rescue comes, they can take all of us to shore."

Plan D—a plan tossing Maren's entire future up in the air.

"Finn, I need your phone," he says briskly. Finn passes it to him.

Maren thumbs it fast then shows Finn the screen. "Our..." He holds up his hand for the word.

"Coordinates," Finn finishes. "So I'll screenshot it, yeah?"

Maren nods. He's got his compass out now. He balances it on the back of his hand and swivels it slowly, totally focused.

"Put these in your phone, and memory too," he tells Finn.

In case anything happens to his phone, I suppose.

He reads Finn the compass bearings for the viaduct, the island near Grange and the lido, which I can just make out with narrowed eyes, along with his best guess for each of the distances. My chest tightens in horror—we're sooo far from any land, but Maren's calm and precise. He's making sure we can be found.

Finn repeats the places and numbers as he thumbs them in and tells Maren them again, three times. I memorise them too.

"Go now," Maren tells him. "Check your phone before the river and after. We may have luck with a signal."

I stand astonished as Finn belly crawls to Courtney. After all she's done! He puts a hand behind her head, whispering something to her.

No time for goodbyes, I urge him. Every second is nearer to the tide flowing up the river.

Courtney nods. Finn reverses back to us.

"I'll make sure they get you all out of here," Finn promises.

I believe him, but my throat clamps against words, so I give him the briefest of hugs and watch his back fade into the distance. It fades fast too: the day's much hazier than it was when I left Kents Bank; than it was even when Finn appeared.

"He'll be okay, won't he?" I say to Maren.

He nods, but his mouth is tight. Part of me wants to say, *You go too, Maren. Two is better than one.*

But I don't. I can't be here without him. With Maren, I feel safe.

Almost.

"Courtney," he calls to her, "can you reach your phone without moving too much?"

She slowly unzips one of her chest pockets and holds up her phone just a little way.

"I'm going to come for it," he tells her. To me, "I want to check the battery, the torch."

He snakes his way fast to Courtney and then straight back to me.

"She is shaking badly," he tells me. "Shock. I need to think. Can you go and…?"

Keep her morale up, distract her, I suppose he means, and while he thinks about what?

When I wished this morning I never had to see Courtney again, I meant it. Now more fiercely than ever.

But for Maren, for Finn, I squirm towards her.

THIS WEEK, I'VE done many things I *never* expected or wanted to do, but this could be the weirdest. Prone, I'm propped up on my arms to speak to Courtney, who's in so deep we're on a level.

"I know what you're thinking," she says.

I give a hollow laugh. "I sincerely doubt it."

A large part of me wants to put my hands around her neck and squeeze. Me, who's never felt a violent urge before in my whole life!

"I'm proper sorry," she says. "For all of it."

I scoff. Sorry's a word I've never heard pass Courtney's lips before, and now it does, it's meaningless. She wouldn't be saying it but for the position she's in.

"You've ruined Maren's future. Do you realise? And for what? Why the frig would you phone Fishery Patrol?"

She looks down at the sand, then forces her eyes back up to me.

"I…I thought Maren should be stopped if he was on the make."

"On the make?" I splutter. "He's being forced to cockle at night for next to nothing."

"I didn't know that! Not till this afternoon when Finn told me."

"But why would you even think it?"

Her eyes slide to the side. "Cos he's Albanian, I s'pose."

My hands clench. "So how do you account for his evil friggin' gangmasters being Polish?"

She swipes at her eyes. "I know, I know. I get it now."

"Whatever. You had no sympathy for the Chinese cocklers either, even after what happened to them."

"But Maren's not going to die."

"He could have done last night if I hadn't been out here."

Her eyes widen. "On the Sands? Weren't you in his room?"

Yeah, between her and Krys, they've tried to have us taped.

I shake my head. "I don't understand why you were spying on us, passing on info to Krys. To get at me?"

"Yes…no…I don't know." She twists her head from side to side. "To Krys as well as me, you and Maren are both so smug and superior. And sensible. This golden couple…"

"Yeah, a slave. Right. Who now has to disappear with nothing but the clothes he has on. And me—I'll always be in fear of my life from his bosses who seized me today, threatened me, forced me out here to Maren."

I won't hear another word from her. My veins buzzing with hot rage, I reverse around and, on all fours, track far away from her.

I ease up from the sand. In front of me it's a grey murk. Where *is* Maren?

Forty

"Here, Allie," he calls.

His hand warm and strong, he tugs me up alongside him.

"Oh."

Grange is no longer visible ahead of me, and even Courtney is a smudge.

"The change of tide is bringing a little fog," Maren says.

Disorientation in fog, one of the big killers—the headline of the *Guardian* article I read whilst researching this week. The tragic drowning of a father and son here when fog meant Bay Rescue couldn't find them in time.

"Oh God, Maren!" I wail. "Now what? Finn! He won't know which direction..."

He puts his hands on my shoulders. "He'll be through the river now. The Kent will show him the way forward. He will not cross it again, will he!"

I nod and try to believe him.

"Allie," he says.

I've never, even in all the perilous situations we've faced this week, heard such a serious note in his voice. It strikes dread into my core.

"What is it?"

He wraps his arms around me, murmurs in my ear as if to soften his words.

"We have to go. You and I. To Arnside. The fog, the time… Now it needs the rescue machine from the coastguard there to reach Courtney."

"But won't Finn's message be passed on to them?"

"We have to be certain."

I can't argue with that. It'll mean two rescue operations, one from each side of the Bay. Belt and braces for Courtney. And safety for us!

He pulls away from me and starts to put on his head torch.

"I'm going to tell Courtney," he says. "I hate to leave her, but better that than…"

Now I know we're going, my thigh muscles flex, raring to get off these Sands.

"Be quick, really quick," I urge him, all tight in my skin.

He drops to his knees.

"I'll take her phone back to her for the torch and my whistle. And…" he hesitates. "My coat too? Without moving, she'll become cold."

My chest twinges with both guilt and jealousy as I unbutton it and drape it around his shoulders. I'm giving up the warmth and comfort of his jacket for him. Not her.

My legs continue twitching to get the hell out of here as Maren worms towards her.

Come on, come on! I mutter under my breath.

Alone, my mind darts to Finn. Poppy would be proud of him. But thank God his parents, and mine, don't know we're AWOL. Yet.

After what seems five minutes but is probably only two, Maren's straightening up next to me.

He holds out his hand for mine. "Time to go, Allie."

I glance one last time back at Courtney. This mortal danger we're in, her in particular, isn't *all* her fault. This last bit, yes. But somehow, weirdly, I don't want to lay all the blame on her anymore. Not when bigger villains are involved. She's done something unbelievably stupid today with serious consequences, but she's not evil like Bosko and Jez.

If I put myself in her submerged, captive shoes, I know the terror I would feel to be left alone. And I also know, from what Finn has told me, she's been abandoned by those who should care most for her. She'll be scarred for life if we both leave her cemented and stranded.

And Finn. If he wasn't already trying to rescue us, I know what he'd do.

Those words from Donne repeat in my mind. *I am involved in mankind.*

"I can't," I tell Maren. "I can't say goodbye to her."

"Then don't. She doesn't expect it."

"No, I mean I can't leave her."

"Allie! I know you're scared, but I promise you, we can do this."

"I believe you. And I want off these Sands like nothing I've ever wanted before. But I can't…desert her."

His shoulders sag. "Oh, Allie. I would stay with her, but you can't go to Arnside alone. Not in the time we have."

"You go," I tell him. "You'll be faster anyway on your own."

"I can't let you stay."

"Is she going to be rescued or not?"

He hesitates for a split second. "Yes. But…I only know you are safe if you're with me."

My eyes well up. "Thank you," I whisper. "But if I come, she'll think we're not sure she can be saved. Which is… unbearable. For anyone, even her."

I try to make light of it at the end, but even though my every cell wants to go with him, it doesn't make it right.

"Now *you* are stubborn," he tells me with a half-smile. "And *all* heart."

He holds me to him. Against his sweater, I take in his warmth and unique Maren scent for one last time. He pulls back to speak to me.

"When you see or hear any sign of rescue, whistle, shout, flash the phone torch all around you both. If you are still here by four-thirty, do it continuously."

My head shakes in a shudder. That can't happen. "Wh… when…" I gulp. "When will the sea reach here?"

"The channels around you, around five-thirty." He looks me full in the eye. "Allie, come with me."

I try for a smile. "Go now, Maren. Go fast and bring help for us."

He takes both my hands. Shakes them up and down between us, a vow. I can't let go of his. I notice he's still got my scrunchie on his wrist when I've nothing of his.

He leans in, kisses me, tender and firm at the same time and so achingly sweet that tears prickle.

"Not a goodbye kiss, Allie, my *besa*—only exists in Albanian. An absolutely unbreakable promise. We will finish this kiss."

"*Besa*," I repeat. Now I'm properly smiling. *Why are some of our best moments in the middle of these goddamn Sands?!*

His fingers slide away from mine.

He makes off into the fog.

Forty-One

I STAND AND GAZE after him. My fingers go to my lips, to where his have been. I know Maren means what he says, but what if our kiss *was* the last time I ever see him? What if something gets in the way of his *besa* and what we had was as brilliant and brief as that comet?

"Maren!" I yell.

I take a stride in the direction I think he went, but the grey's closed behind him. I shift my angle.

Nothing.

I've burnt my boats.

My tummy rolls and rolls. I'm a prisoner of the fog.

Slowly, I turn right around. I *can* still see Courtney. The girl who gave me stomach aches every day for a term when I started at our school, who called Maren *just* a happiness seeker. Someone with whom I have less in common than anyone else on the planet.

But I stayed to be with her.

"WHAT THE HELL? Get out of here, after Maren."

Her teeth are chattering.

"I can't," I say, reaching forward to button Maren's jacket at Courtney's neck.

"For God's sake, Allie," she mutters, then jaggedly, realising, "Thank you."

On both counts, I suppose.

Now I'm with her, I don't know what to say. I just want this wait to be over with.

"Maren's a proper hero, yeah?" she says after a while, a little stronger now. "And totally into you."

I glow hopelessly inside.

"You're dead lucky," she adds.

I gasp. "How d'you work that out? If we even survive today, I'm unlikely to ever see him again."

That shuts her up.

"And anyway," I say, "what about Finn? He's so into *you*. You *know* he is."

"Finn," she murmurs. "I think I've finally blown it with him today."

"I doubt it. But he isn't some backup, you know."

"I know now. I do. How..." Her breathing's ragged again. "How the hell did I miss what a lowlife sleazebag Krys is?"

Exactly! But I'm not going to rub it in now.

"Because he can buy you alcohol, take you on his motorbike?" I say instead. "Plus he can dance and play table tennis a damn sight better than Finn!"

She tries to laugh, but it turns into a cough. "Krys had already pied me off." She chews the side of her mouth as if just understanding something. "Passing intel on Maren this morning, I was trying to get Krys interested again before we went home."

My head sags onto my arms. Of all the possible reasons for the four of us being in danger of our lives today, this is the most pathetic. I know what Poppy would say because she says it of Finn's younger brothers when they're acting up. It's the only way Courtney knows to win attention.

"But then," she picks up again, "he was only livid that I'd phoned Fishery Patrol."

"I'm not surprised. You've meddled in stuff you didn't understand with catastrophic fallout, especially for Maren."

"I know. I've been a complete idiot. I'm surprised any of youse are helping me at all."

In spite of myself, the teeniest twinge of pity for her twitches in my chest. She's never known unconditional caring before. And anyway, it turns out to be impossible to continue being angry at someone when you're alone with them, especially when they're stuck and you're both marooned in fog!

"Even Krys isn't all bad," I tell her. "He tipped me off about getting Maren away from the bosses. I think Bosko has some hold over him too. He hit him, right there in front of me."

She shakes her head and is quiet for moment. "Maybe Finn will give me a second chance—if I come through this. I'll never take him for granted again."

"Finn will always be your someone if you want him to be," I tell her.

And I fill her in on Rue's concept of a someone-just-for me. Because I understand now. Her mates at home, the boys she's hooked up with—they've not been *real* friends.

"Awesome," she says. "I've definitely never had a someone. Prrh! And certainly not my mum."

I wait for her to say more. She doesn't.

"Finn, I'm proper worried for him," she says hoarsely.

"Maren said he'll already be across the river by now. He'll be phoning the coastguard any minute. We've gotta focus on getting through the next…hour. Tops. Then we'll be out of here."

And I genuinely believe that, I try to convince myself. Finn must have already got to Grange. And I know how fast Maren walks. Both boys have our bearings, plus rescue services have a thermal-imaging thing, don't they?

"If only I could start today again," she says.

"The week more like. It began when we both got involved with Maren and Krys, I suppose."

"I screwed up, Allie. This thing with Krys. I was thirsty to…be seen, I suppose. Maybe him too. Cos we never…"

She trails off.

"Never what?"

She shrugs. "Never were at home. I never met me dad. And all my mum did was tell me how I'd ruined her life. Yet somehow she managed to keep me alive." She grimaces. "Look how I've done without her!"

I bite my lip. *I just don't get life—how we're having conversations like this now, when it's all but too late!*

That's what Finn's been trying to get me to understand. A splice of gratitude flickers warmth through me for the love I have: from my now-distant dad; from Mum, whose pushing me towards a 'sensible' degree is caring too; of course it is. My parents are split but always *bothered* about me.

"Finn's so tight with *his* mum, isn't he?" Courtney says. "Belling her every day."

"Yeah." I nod. "Both he and Maren have got like this... cushion of love, which gives them caring to share."

I think again of the irony of Maren maybe never seeing his family again.

Courtney's gazing down at the sand directly in front of her. She looks so forlorn, I reach for her hand. It's frozen. I try to warm it with my fingers.

At my touch, she looks up again. "Best believe it, Allie, once we get out of here, after all this real-life research, a contemporary cockler, gangmasters, our near-death experience today, we'll really be able to smash our script!"

Despite the mortal mess we're in, I have to smile at this trademark Courtney cockiness. At the same time, I'm seeing the best of her—humour, ambition, optimism— and I have to admit, as Finn's been trying to tell me, I should never have written her off. Any more than she did all Albanians.

"Will we even be allowed to continue the play?" I ask her.

"We'd better! We'll rewrite it bigger, with *all* the feeling. And we'll make it count—for Maren and all those others who have no choice."

I smile. A script to change lives *would* count for something.

But I can't stop my mind trying to project what's going to happen to Courtney, Finn and me—the interrogations and recriminations—and to Maren now his bosses won't be caught.

"I don't think your party's going to happen," I tell her. Or my own last night with Maren.

Courtney gives a hollow laugh. "The Hallowe'en party's happening here instead!"

She retrieves her hand from mine and picks up her phone from between us.

"Three-fifty," she says. "Only eighteen minutes since Maren left."

I collapse my head onto my arms again. I want time to both slow down and speed up.

THE MURK'S THICKENING. I shudder. Can't stay face down on the cold sand. Sitting up's a risk, so I roll onto my back, but now the fog's like the lid of a tomb, close, far too close. Its chill, clammy hands creep at my face and neck, slither down my arms and legs, clawing through my flesh.

Shaking, I turn back onto my front. My feet are cold bricks. I hutch off my sodden trainers and manage to tug my socks out of my pocket. At least they're dry. As I contort myself to peel them back onto my claggy feet, my soles get at least a hint of warmth.

"Take Maren's jacket," she says. "It's more yours than mine."

"NO!" I shriek. "Keep still or you'll sink further."

But I long for it! To smell its metallic grittiness, *him*, instead of the fog's dry, chemical-chlorine muffling our voices, locking us in its soundproof prison.

"What will happen to Maren?" she asks.

"No idea." I'm still shivering. "Our plan was to prove to the police tonight that he's a modern slave. But now…"

"Maybe we can prove it another way, when we're out of here."

I can't see it. Can't see another winning move for Maren. And if he's deported, not only is there no future for him, but not for us either.

I compose the ending we should have had. While we wait for his asylum, we're constantly in touch, and I visit him every couple of weeks in a bright, modern safe house, somewhere quiet and rural, where he can have big, long walks in open fields. When he's granted leave to remain, he finds a job in Leeds and we're always together. We play chess. Enjoy millions more kisses.

"TIME?"

Courtney drags me back onto the Sands.

"Four-sixteen."

"I can't stand it, I can't!" she wails.

My heart bumps. If she panics, flails, she could go right under. I can't be alone here.

"They must be looking for us right now. You whistle while I flash the phone torch around."

Even though no one's going to hear or see us through this rat-grey fur of fog.

Forty-Two

F OR OVER THIRTY long, *draining* minutes, we whistle and shout. I shine the phone torch in every direction; we swap the whistle around when our voices are hoarse. It's sapping, but it's not as if we have anything else to save our energy for. Emotionally, it's exhausting when each minute you hope, but minute after minute, no one comes.

It's 4:49 when we…peter out. I lie spent on the sand, facing Courtney, who's waxen.

We're done for.

ALL AT ONCE, a lightening. From my left, open sea.

"Courtney, look!"

My whole body thrills with hope. Parting the grey, at sky level, the sun's slanted rays, translucent bands of gold and ruby, as if through a prism, light a shimmering pathway across the Sands.

The fog's beginning to clear!

I shuffle towards the light. There's enough sun to warm my face, if only a little, and to wash Courtney's in a pinkish blush.

I will the sun on in its battle against the fog. *Come on! You're almost there!*

If you can do it, so can I. When you break though, I'll run for it, run along the silvery path. I can't be the fog's hostage for another second.

I'll leave Courtney.

Rather drown running for it than lie here like…some sacrifice to the Bay.

No! The hues are steadily fading as if someone's turning down a dimmer switch. I push to standing, stretch out my hand to cling on to the jewelled colours.

"Stop!" I cry out loud. "Please don't go!"

But the grey curtain swishes closed on the sun, as on my grandad's coffin at his cremation.

Fog, thicker than before, shrouds us.

Now it's me who hasn't grasped how real this all is. Now I may as well be cemented in sand too. No going anywhere now. No rescue from either side of the Bay.

We'll die in the fog.

I SWIVEL ALL the way around me, trying to make out something through the gloom. It's not darkness, not uniform. There are different shades, from off-white to slate. Phantom shades.

When I've turned 360, I still can't see her.

"Courtney!" I scream.

"Here! I'm here."

"Keep talking. I'll find you."

"Be careful, Allie. Stay where you are if you can't see what's in front of you."

"No, I'm coming."

I drop to my knees. We can't die alone!

Caterpillaring forward on my elbows, I test the sand with my fingertips while Courtney spurts out words to guide me.

Another sound sidles through the fog. My shoulders leap. The siren from last Saturday, muffled but unmissable. Eerie as the gates of hell; a sly, insinuating sound, saying…

Here's a warning, but much good will it do you!

Twenty minutes before the sea comes for us.

Our death knell.

"Allie!" Courtney screams over the top of it. She's close by now!

I stretch out my fingers towards her, find one of her hands. I push mine forward until we're clasping left hands. Hers is corpse-cold even against mine that's icy from the fogged damp of the sand.

Our hands climb up each other's arms till we're clamped together as close as can be, head-to-head as if we're in danger of losing each other; as if we're saving each other's lives.

Perhaps we are.

The alarm stops.

The silence is worse. A breath before the sea unleashes itself on us.

"I don't want to die," I wail.

"Where's our rescue?" She sobs. "Maren and Finn both have our bearings."

"They can't have got to shore," I whisper.

And if they haven't, it's because *they're* not safe either.

"No one else must die out here today!" she cries into the stillness, a plea. "It's all my fault!"

Her panic, somehow, calms me. I ease back from her a tiny way. In these last minutes of my life, I've got to make sense of my death.

"No," I tell her. "We all made our own choices today."

But I don't believe that either, not completely. Some of them were thrust upon us.

There's a horrific inevitability to it all—as if once the week began, this was always going to be how it ended, only it was never meant to be *me* dying! Especially when I had a get-out card with Maren. What was the point of me staying only to die with her, just so she wasn't alone for her final hour?

My whole lifetime for one hour of hers.

Could I have lived with myself if I'd left her?

With my every cell, I'd take that risk now!

If only I'd not got involved—with Maren, her. I let go, lost control, and I'm paying with my life.

TIME'S RUNNING FASTER; running out. Only minutes left. Like plays we've performed at school, once the opening line's spoken, the action can't be stopped. It has a momentum of its own until, suddenly, you're at the final words, then the bow.

What kind of a curtain call is this?

I *recognise* my death now it's in sight. It was always going to finish this way.

My despair is ash-like. At seventeen, I'm tossing my life away in a place I knew to fear as soon as I learned of all its tragedies, and there's nothing we can do to stop it. Our names are destined for the registry of drownings in the priory. Mine, Courtney's. I've achieved nothing, left nothing.

THE TRAGIC HERO this week, isn't Maren at all. He'll survive. I know he will. It's Courtney and me.

Only there's nothing heroic about our deaths. Not even tragic. More like idiotic.

"ALLIE," SHE WHISPERS. "I *am* going to die out here."

"If you are, I am." My voice is thin and grey.

"No, *you* can swim for it, Allie. You're free."

"I can't swim."

Her eyes widen in shock. It's true, after the wave pool ten years ago, I refused to ever be submerged in water again.

"Water petrifies me," I jibber. "I'll go under and…"

Juddery sobs jolt their way up me. I haven't read of *anyone* swimming to safety in this Bay.

She strokes my cheek, her hand glacial.

"You've got to live, Allie. No one's ever put me first as you have today."

When I decided to stay, I trusted Maren we'd be saved, I think, still weeping.

"Fight for your life," she urges me.

I whimper on and on. "I'll try," I tell her thickly through gritty snot, even though I know I have zero chance.

"Good." She sounds almost cheerful! "Because I need you to pass on my last words."

"Courtney!"

"Seriously, I want you to film my last words, now."

"Whatever happens," I say, swiping away my tears, "the phone won't survive."

"Please, Allie. And show it to my mum," she says. "I need to tell her something. And Finn. Put it in our play. Stick it on TikTok! Let the world see what it's like to die out here. Maybe it can save someone else."

Forty-Three

I DO FILM HER—IF only to distract us in the final minutes of our lives.

By the time she's finished, it's clear she knows exactly what she's done.

And at last, I see the Courtney Finn knew she would be, given even a little of the love he's had. But how can you be a work in progress if you're dead? I read somewhere that hearing someone's last words creates a bond between you, but what's the point of a bond that only lasts minutes?

I'm not going to record my own last words. Not because I'm going to be saved when Courtney isn't. Saying my goodbyes, it's an acceptance I'm not brave enough for.

In the irony to end all ironies, my last words are for Courtney—from sworn enemies to the closest of friends.

"Life is random," I tell her. "Last night, Maren was lucky. He escaped quicksand because I was there. Today, you were unlucky. Plus, you were the brave one, at the front, else it could have been Finn. If you hadn't come, it could be him stuck here now, alone, and no one would ever have known.

"And it wasn't all down to you I was out here today. It's cos I met Maren in the first place. It was *my* idea he went cockling this afternoon. Krys chose to pass on your info to their bosses, but they could have found out some other way Maren was out here. And they had this power over him for massive reasons way bigger than us.

"A horrific, twisted tragedy created by those who hold others' lives cheap. Not you."

Her usually beady eyes are big with tears. She can't speak but there's the ghost of a smile.

I lean forward. Kiss her on the forehead.

WHEN I NEXT look at her phone, it shows 5:19.

I won't look at it again. I won't let my mind revolve through all the disasters that could have befallen Finn and Maren.

As I make to push the phone right down into my jeans pocket, a crackle of something in paper is in the way. Mint cake from when we walked the Sands with Eli— two squares! I hand one to Courtney. The other I suck, relishing its sweetness on my tongue instead of bitter fog, making it last as long as possible.

The sugar soon fades from my mouth.

"Can't believe that was our last meal," Courtney says in a tiny voice. "Or that I'll never have another burger."

"Never see another play again," I murmur. "Or the sun."

"Never down another shot…"

"Never kiss again." My chest hurts for Maren and what will happen to him. How he'll feel about…what happens to me today.

"Never go clubbing legally."

"Never finish our A' Levels, go to uni, grow up."

"That was never gonna happen anyway," she says, which makes us both laugh. Gallows humour.

"Never play Monopoly again with Finn."

Never see Finn again. I hope he mourns me. But not too much.

"Never go to New York."

I don't tell her I've been.

"And we'll never be famous now," I say.

Except in death. I write the headline.

Two girls from visiting Leeds school drown on Sands.

"Never see Mum again," she says.

My throat dries out, and I could vomit. No bravado left in either of us now.

"I want my mum," I whimper, "and my daddy."

Save us, God, I whisper in my head. *Let us live and I'll never take it for granted again. Maren believes in you, and I don't know where else the power to create planets and comets would come from.*

I turn my face to my right as if for the answer to my prayer.

Only black.

And a briny freshness, the scent of the sea, now all but upon us.

Mum, my mummy, I mutter over and over, an incantation.

My solid, steadfast mum. What will she feel? Do? All on her own now. She'll never understand what happened this week. Finn will tell her, try to make her see I did everything for the best of reasons. Didn't I?

I'll never have a chance to tell Dad how much I've always missed him, how he made everything all right. If he was at Morecambe Bay now, he'd find me. My daddy.

But if anyone *could* find me, it'd be Maren. Which is another reason why I know with such certainty how this ends.

My funeral. My poor mum and dad, their foolish only child, throwing her life away.

Oh God. My body! I *have* to have a funeral. These Sands can't be my graveyard too. I could never rest here.

As DARKNESS FALLS, the fog sucks up that too till we're in a pitch-black tomb.

We're silent. I crunch my limbs up into a resigned, terrified hunch.

We don't join hands again. When the moment comes, we will. You die alone, they say, but the faint warmth of another person has got to make it a little less terrifying, surely.

The second siren sounds.

Five minutes left, it warbles, on repeat.

My body's boneless, my blood no longer flowing. As if I'm already dead.

"Courtney!" I sob as the siren moans to its sinister end.

I wrap my arms around her neck.

She weeps in my ear. We've no more words.

Another silence.

Now this growl

a monster making for us

a gurgle—

a watery rumble—

a bellow

like a colossal waterfall, only there's nothing lovely in this.

The tide's coming for us.

I clamp my eyes closed, hide my face in Maren's jacket. The sea is filling the channels all around us, trapping us on an island.

Slowly, certainly, it will reach us.

No quick end for us. Icy waves will rise up my legs, engulf my waist, my arms.

Even if I sit tall, stand, crane my neck to its furthest reach, in the end, the water *will* enter my nose, my mouth, fill my lungs. A burning will follow, I've read. A long, gurgling torture of a death.

Still clinging to Courtney, I try for some happy image to…end with.

My grandad in a rainbow aura, leading me gently into the bright light of the afterlife, where everything's only happy and I don't even miss everyone I've left behind.

But no! No grandad. Only the anguish of drowning. Black. Not being.

"Allie!" Courtney says, hoarse, urgent.

My heart halts. The sea's on her back already.

"Look!"

"No!" I bury my face into her collarbone.

"Now! To my left."

Forty-Four

HIGH IN THE fog, a blue light.

A man-made colour! Rescue! My whole being bounds with hope.

"Whistle!" I tell Courtney, disentangling my arms from her.

My legs want to leap up, but I must keep my cool, not end up stuck too as the sea circles us like a shoal of sharks. Fast as I safely can, I belly-crawl backwards.

We mustn't be missed, like castaways on a remote island watching the only search ship sailing off into the distance.

Muscles numb and stiff, I clamber to my feet.

"Here!" I yell, still unsteady. "Over here! We're here."

I scan the phone beam all around, bawling at the top of my voice.

We scream and whistle for our lives.

Two golden suns now.

Headlights.

My face turns to them like a sunflower to the sun. *Am I going to live?*

Now the low throb of an engine.

The first hint of a huge, high vehicle, a tank or nothing I've ever seen, big enough to find me in its beam.

It's come for us.

"STAY PUT!" A voice yells to me. "We see you."

Don't lose your head now, Allie.

"We'll be with you soon," another voice calls. "Just keep still and calm."

I stand stock still, not trying to return to Courtney behind me.

A kind of track appears to the side of me, black with yellow edges and like an elongated Li-lo. The ghost of a person emerges through the fog, on hands and knees, coming along the plastic pathway.

The figure, in red and orange, reflective strips glowing, is crawling straight to me. The top of his yellow helmet is near. He slowly straightens up in front of me.

I'm shaking, massive, violent shudders, my legs still as if the bones have dissolved.

The man puts a hand on my shoulder. "It's okay. I'm Tony." He's putting a lifejacket on me while he speaks, tying it around my waist at the front. "You're safe now, Allie."

He knows my name! From Finn and Maren. Thank you, God.

But I don't feel safe. The tide's got us surrounded, thundering with menace. It could sweep over us at any moment. I grab tight hold of Tony's arm. I don't care. I can't be on my own in the sea.

"C...C...Courtney. She's over there. Stuck."

"We know. My colleagues are on their way to her."

Without moving my legs, I twist around. Like an actor in a broad spotlight, Courtney's illuminated by the headlights of the rescue vehicle. All around her are those inflatable platforms, two rescue crew, laden with equipment, nearly with her. So it's not too late?

I'm out of my body now.

Everything's not real. Or too real.

Sloooowed right down.

Too bright flashing multicoloured

too LOUD

noises I don't recognise all around me.

Wind, now I'm standing, blasting my face.

I don't know what's going on and I

definitely can't move.

"Let's get you into our vehicle now," Tony says, "Sherp."

Voices blare from a radio on his jacket.

The sea suddenly booms so loud I clutch at him again.

"It's all right," he says. "It's our search helicopter overhead. Helped us find you."

Tipping my head back, I glimpse what looks like a giant insect with six legs and flashing feelers.

"To Sherp," Tony says.

THE ORANGE TANK has massive black wheels to transport you through anything. Except deep sea. The back door is open, like a huge boot lid.

"Foot on the step," Tony tells me.

A woman in an orange safety vest reaches out a hand and hauls me high into warmth and onto a black cushioned seat.

"We've got you now, Allie. You're safe," she says, putting her arm around me. "I'm Sue, the driver."

I break into jerky sobs I can't stop, quaking uncontrollably.

Tony closes the door against the bellow of the sea, the cruel wind.

Sue wraps a metallic blanket around my shoulders.

"What…about…Courtney?" I manage.

"They're still working on her," Tony says on the other side of me. "Injecting gallons and gallons of water into the sand to try to loosen her."

"They'll get her out, won't they?"

A pause. I know how set the sand is around her, how low she is and how deep the sea will be by now.

"Two of them are working on her, doing everything they can," Tony says.

He sounds like a doctor who soon after tells you the patient's died, despite their best efforts.

I LOOK UP at that rhythmic rumble again. "Why's the helicopter still around now it's found us? Will *it* be rescuing Courtney then?"

An image of her being winched up into the sky plays through my mind. Sue and Tony exchange glances over my head.

"No, no," Tony says.

"We've thrown everything at finding you," Sue says.

She's pouring steaming liquid out of a flask into its metal cup. When she passes it to me, my hands drink in its heat but are shaking so much the hot chocolate splashes out onto my jeans. I push it back towards Sue.

Snatches of blurred voices keep beaming into the cab from the dashboard behind us. My chest tenses. "What's happening?"

Sue smiles and shakes her head. "Just crew keeping in contact."

"How did you get our bearings?" I ask. "From Finn and Maren?"

Have they even sent a message for me?

"We don't know such details, love," Tony says. "The coastguard coordinates it all. We get the info, scramble to Arnside, mobilise Sherp and start the rescue as fast as ever we can."

"And our Sherp'll get us safely back to Arnside," Sue says brightly. "A big boat on wheels so it floats. A right Chitty-Bang-Bang!"

"Apart from the flying," the man says. "It'll be a hovercraft, though, before we arrive back at shore!"

A hovercraft! I hide my face in my hands. I know their banter's meant to reassure and distract me, but a hovercraft means the Sands are sea. Waves will smash against the windows. The tide must already be at Courtney's level now. The image of her gulping in water is so grotesque I'd throw up if my stomach wasn't empty.

My mind torments me with every wasted minute earlier that could have saved Courtney—the discussions between the four of us, Finn saying goodbye to her, Maren to me.

Tears seeping from my eyes, I lean back into the seat.

And I know the day's not over.

Not by a long way.

2:08 a.m.

A RARE COMET streaks across the sky. Alien-green, it trails a pointed tail. Lovejoy, they call it, but no one sees it. Not this night. Not with all the commotion right in the middle of the Bay.

Close to the inky water, a helicopter circles, adding its beam to the yellow splodges three lifeboats splash onto the waves.

On dry land, a small group is fixated on these distant lights. A girl quakes so violently, the arm around her shoulder tightens over the foil blanket, yet still she trembles.

What chance do they really have of finding her friend in these hundred square miles of pitch-black sea?

As time rolls on, one boat returns to shore. Later, the others must retreat before the grey tide ebbs. The girl too is made to leave, lie down before she collapses.

Jaded now, the moon is a ghost as orange fingers reach over the horizon.

Two more helicopters have joined the first to scour the newly bared Sands. Finally, they too whirr away home.

At last, the Bay is at peace.

The Sands are left to themselves with all their secrets.

In their bottomless depths, so many bones.

And in the bones
    the why.

Day 8
Saturday, 1st November

Eddie Carbone had never expected a destiny.

Alfieri

Forty-Five

WHY?
      everyone's been asking us.

Police.

Parents.

Teachers.

Why were you out there?

As if it were a question with a one-line answer. Or a question with the same answer from each of us. Or an answer that makes any sense.

As if it even matters when not all four of us are accounted for.

Because until there's any evidence, like Rue with Billy, I won't believe it's true.

MY DADDY, THOUGH, he's not asked why. At least, not yet.

Maybe he already knows enough through Mum, who got here first last night, because without one question, he's agreed. As he drives me along the Esplanade back towards Kents Bank, I avert my eyes from the Bay, the Bay that's won yet again in a cunning connivance of circumstances, and from the orange glow of the sun that has no respect for the lost.

I'm in a numb state of almost-disbelief.

Last night, after I was released by the senior medic at scene in Arnside, into Mum's care, after she'd taken me to a tiny bed and breakfast, after I'd showered and eaten and acted as if I was coping, I made her take me to the shore to watch the search. How could I not?

I only went to bed when Dad arrived. And the search had to pause.

TODAY, I CAN only focus on one thing: this.

This final act I must do before I go home from this place I loathe and fear; will never return to.

My empty, poisoned stomach rolls as I tell Dad where to stop.

Outside what was Maren's home for a few short months.

"You don't have to do this," Dad tells me, gripping my shoulder as I peer up at the window, curtains still open, where I stood with Maren only thirty-six hours ago.

And I know he's not there. Not ever coming back.

MAREN WOULD HAVE said something similar to Dad. *Leave the stuff—it's only things.*

But they're *his* things.

And I won't let Krys throw them away as if he didn't exist or leave them for the police to take, label and store in plastic bags somewhere.

"I do," I say. "It's just…" Only a little squeak comes out.

We're silent for a long moment.

I pull out from under Dad's hand. He nods at me and comes around to open my door, somehow knowing I need his prompt.

He takes my hand through the crook of his arm as if I'm elderly or an invalid as we walk through the open gate and slowly up the path. Krys's motorbike is next to the door; his curtains closed.

I reach out to the doorknob, twist it carefully.

It's off the latch! My heart trips right over. I nod to Dad. He's to stay at the open door, as we've agreed.

UPSTAIRS, I BURY my head in Maren's pillow, taking in his spicy scent. My body yearns to lie here under a quilt that also smells of him, remember our one night, forget everything else and never come out again.

But I have these responsibilities. Massive ones of anguish that must be faced.

I stuff as much as I can into my backpack: his towel, toothbrush, razor, geology book; I'll carry his joggers, shirts and kagoule in my arms.

I check the drawer of his desk in case there's something precious in it. His passport—he'll need that. Only an open notebook with something *he's* written in what must be Albanian. A pen and some loose change.

All I leave are the thin quilt and pillow. I remove the pillowcase and hold it to my face for a long moment. I tip the chess pieces into it. The board fits into the top of my rucksack.

I'm out of there. With Dad. Back on the front path.

I breathe out a shaky sigh as Dad closes the door behind me.

One last look.

No! The curtains shift, and Krys's fleshy face fills the side pane nearest me.

I can't move even when he shoves up the sash window.

His arm reaches out.

In his stubby hand are two phones. Mine and Maren's, of course.

He bows his head as I reach for them.

Epilogue

GUO BING LONG speaks his last words to the silent, sombre audience sitting in darkness, while the translation in English is projected onto the massive screen at the front of Grange's Victoria Hall.

It's the first time we've been back since.

Since that day.

I swore I never would. I could never have anything to do with drama again. But this, today, it's more than a performance. It's a memorial, and memorials have to be made by those who love the one lost.

Hey Ho replaces the words on screen with a big close-up of Courtney.

A gasp in unison from the audience—from those who've not heard her last words before, who've not seen her deathly white face and black hair plastered, wool-like, to her head.

"Weird though it may sound, last words are a privilege," she tells us. "So I'm counting on Allie surviving to bring you mine."

293

She tried to smile at me as I filmed her. I remember shaking my head at the bravado she was trying to infuse into me even as she was set in quicksand. But that was her last shred of spirit.

"I'm not gonna lie," she whispers. "This is really bad. I'm scared. I've been so dumb, I hate myself. Life is the best, I want more of it. But I'm about to die."

I'll never forget the iron-cold certainty that I was too. But for the fog, we'd have seen the tide on the horizon at that point.

"Even worse is knowing as I drown that three others could die too—because of me."

She collects herself one last time and looks direct at the camera.

"So don't *you* do anything to endanger someone else's precious life."

She pauses, and a moment of realisation and panic arrives, unmissable in her eyes, as if her executioner has just arrived. She speaks faster now, running out of time.

"Please, tell everyone goodbye.

"Sir, Miss, forgive me for deceiving you—*none* of this was your fault.

"Finn, of *course* I love you too. I'm *so* sorry I cocked up this week.

"Mum, please forgive me for being a bad girl and so difficult to love. I want you to know how much I love you."

She looked at me, her voice giving out. "It's a wrap."

She could say no more, and I stopped the camera.

While her image lingers, frozen on screen, yet again I find myself replaying all the things we could have done differently that week. I scratch at them like a fingernail returning to the sorest wound.

How, without any one of them, the outcome would have been different:

If only we'd never come to the Bay.

If only Maren had never come.

If only I'd not met Maren.

Or even Rue. Befriending her played its part in the domino-like tragedy none of us will ever get beyond.

If only the world wasn't sliced by borders that rendered Maren here illegally.

If only his gangmasters hadn't exploited him.

If only Krys could have played a different role that day.

Courtney's is *not* the only responsibility. She made a late, bad move in what in reality was a Game of Life. But it was me who drew Maren, Courtney and Finn into the game.

We—what's left of our drama group—allow the silence to continue, for the audience to absorb it. When it feels the right moment, we step from the wings onto the stage for our finale.

My heart's yammering. The gristly mass that started life in the pit of my belly that darkest of October nights swelled even more this morning. Now it rises up my gullet.

But I *have* to say my words.

On the second row, my dad gives me a little nod; next to him, my mum raises her gripped fist in her lap for me.

Courtney's mum raises her chin. On the end, Miss gives me her calm smile. And I know, the show must go on.

I WALK TO the front of the stage and look towards Sir in the lighting box at the back of the hall. I force my lump back down.

"And now," I say, "we're going to hear from…"

I started strong. The clump in my throat blocks the end of my sentence.

Courtney steps forward. We clasp hands as we did much of the time we were stranded on the Sands. Once I was in Sherp, it took fifteen endless minutes for two heroic rescue crew to free her, in the very nick of time, the sea up to her neck. But we went to Arnside, to land, *together,* separated only when she had to spend the night in hospital in Kendal for hypothermia.

"Now we're going to hear from Finn," Courtney finishes. "Finn didn't have the luxury of last words…"

That he died alone, no one to share his last thoughts, is part of the tumour of guilt in my stomach.

The guilt that our dear Finn had to meet the tide alone when it barged up the river and swiped his feet from under him, spinning him head over heels so he couldn't tell up from down; carried him down river where his body was washed up three days later, not far from where Maren found Billy.

"So," I join in, "we're going to hear from him through the last words he spoke to…those he loved."

A tall figure rises on the back row. I look down at the wooden boards, unable to see Finn's dad so stooped with sorrow.

"To me," he starts. His voice is clear but thin, so thin. People from all over the hall twist around towards him. "To me, Finn said, 'You're in charge this week, Dad.'" He coughs. "'I'm going off duty!'"

Davy, Finn's youngest brother, stands small next to his dad, looking lost without his role model. Audience members from the front crane their necks, resulting in scattered 'oh's.

"Finn said to me, 'I'll bring you a pressie back from the seaside, Titch,'" he says in one squeaky rush. "'See you on Saturday.'" He clatters onto his chair, hides his head in his hands.

On the other side of Davy, Poppy gets to her feet. My heart shrinks into a hard, twinging nut.

By now, the whole audience is facing backwards.

"'Happy birthday, Mum,' Finn said to me." She gulps. "'Hope you've baked yourself a cake! I've left your present with Dad.'" She holds up a book. "It was this, *Humanly Possible*."

Shafeeq steps alongside me. He clears his throat to get the audience facing front again. "'You're a total numpty, Shaf.'"

A mild titter from the audience at this one speck of lightness this afternoon.

"'New dress, Lucy?'" Lucy says. "It wasn't!" she tells the audience.

Another weak chuckle.

My turn. If Finn's family can do this, I must.

"'I just want to go home with you in one piece, Allie.'"

Each time I recall those words, it inflates my ball of guilt—the irony that it was Finn who wouldn't come home.

Courtney has the last of Finn's last words. Her fingers clamp around mine. "Finn said," she pauses, "'Love you, Court.'"

The three words he crawled over the Sands to tell her before he left to get help.

And had he not phoned in our bearings when he did, Courtney and I wouldn't be here today, it took so long to find us in the fog.

HEY HO RAISING the lights again is Rue's cue. Head down, she trudges to just in front of the stage. She tunes her violin, the sliding slur of notes already saying all harmony's gone from the world.

Soft, she plays the notes of the requiem she composed especially for today, a new requiem, for Finn. Rue, her name means 'regret'. She only knew Finn for a few days, but I suspect she held a torch for him. Yet another loss for my poor friend. Both of us, we share this instinct not to become involved with people. Why in God's name didn't we remain islands? Then we wouldn't be part of a memorial today—Rue's third.

Rue's tremulous notes, drawn out so slowly across the strings you can't see her elbow move, echo how my feelings follow their engrained habit of reaching for Finn, like a plant's tendrils for the light.

Only he's not there.

His body is under an oak tree in a beautiful woodland burial site to the north of Leeds. The plaque includes the meaning of his name.

Courageous fair one

But where is *Finn?*

Rue's music shifts now from expressing our sorrow to the *essence* of Finn; high notes weave together his energetic, wild streak with deeper notes that reflect his steady caring for people.

Finally, her bow hums wistful, single notes. This is the cue for Lucy to start the final segment of *Last Words*: our roll call of many, but only some of the drowned of Morecambe Bay. As Rue fades out her notes, we too draw to our end.

> LUCY: Guo Bing Long, 5th February 2004, aged 28
>
> SHAF: Henry Turner, 22nd August 1768, aged 19
>
> LUCY: Robert Harrison, 3rd March 1782, aged 24
>
> ALLIE: Billy Rainer, 27th October 2022, aged 9
>
> COURTNEY: Finn Yates, 31st October 2022, aged 17

As Hey Ho slowly dims the lights for the last time, Rue bows her head and returns to her seat. The four of us remain frozen in darkness on the stage as the song Finn's parents chose to end with fades in—'He Ain't Heavy, He's My Brother'.

Behind us now is projected a quotation Finn's parents also chose, by Robert Ingersoll:

> Happiness is the only good. The time to be
> happy is now. The place to be happy is here.
> The way to be happy is to make others so.

Some of the audience start to sing along, but my voice will never sing again. I grope again for Courtney's hand, the hand I've held so many times since that day, my new someone; my new best friend.

Because, of course, I lost both mine at once that day.

Each and every time I take a hand, however much I resist it, I'm jolted right back to the sensation of Maren's callused palm on mine, how he would take the weight of my hand. And I miss his touch like a smothering homesickness.

Courtney's hand is a vice around mine. We battle together against our frequent flashbacks, our vodka oblivion more effective than the counselling that doesn't even begin to touch our guilt.

As the song draws to an end, footsteps. Someone's coming down the right-hand aisle of the hall.

A spotlight picks out the figure.

Poppy, a haggard ghost of her plump, energetic, upbeat self.

I squeeze my eyes closed. Finn would hate how his beloved mum has aged a decade in the ten months since he died.

Now, though, she's walking with strength and purpose. She comes right to the front, up the steps onto the stage, and slots herself between Courtney and me. She takes both our hands; hers are shaking.

"I'm not part of the performance," she tells the audience. "This wasn't planned. But there are things I have to say." She glances at me, then Courtney, tightening her hand on mine.

"Finn was our firstborn." She looks to her family at the back. "He was special, a one-off. And that's not just a mum speaking."

A ripple of agreement runs though the audience. Poppy raises my and Courtney's hands a little higher.

"A huge-hearted young man with huge plans."

His plans. He missed his Turing programme; his degree course will begin in the autumn without him. He will never work for the UN on peace through collaboration.

He'd hate missing all that! I look down at the wooden boards of the stage, trembling all over. If Poppy wasn't clasping tight hold of me, I'd have fled already.

"Finn had plans to make the world a better place," Poppy says. "And didn't he do that already?"

"Absolutely, he did." I hear Miss's voice above many, answering her question.

Poppy turns to her right.

"Courtney, my love, may I build on what you said about not endangering another's life?"

Blinking, Courtney nods *of course*. Poppy looks out front.

"We need to go further, I believe, than not only jeopardising others. As the song says, 'his welfare is my concern'. The welfare of his friends was Finn's concern that day. He went for help. As he got closer to Grange, he managed...in case...to phone in the bearings of the three out on the Sands. Finn got involved for his friends' lives. Just as Allie got involved for *her* friend's life. And as you know..."

She falters now, her hand moving to her heart as if to stop the pain.

"Greater love has no person than this, that they lay down their life for their friend."

My shaking's so violent that Poppy notices and puts an arm around me, then Courtney, drawing us close to her.

"Of *course* we wish every waking hour that Finn's involvement hadn't cost him...everything. But..."

She pauses to gather everyone's attention, though I've never felt such a focus from hundreds of people at once.

"But the outcome changes nothing." She's speaking each word so slowly; each word is so important. "Finn made his own decision, the right decision."

I gasp out loud. Finn's *mum* says he did the right thing. She nods, emphatically.

"Finn was almost eighteen. A man who knew what was right and did it. I believe he would have stood by his actions right to the end. And we, his parents, his family, we too stand by his decision. We could not be prouder of him."

A swollen stillness sinks across the hall.

A FEW SCATTERED, tentative claps break through. Members of the audience glance at each other—*is this all right or not?* The clapping slowly gathers momentum until it's one united applause that grows so big, it lifts people to their feet.

On the front row, my parents and Courtney's mum stand. Miss rises up out of her wheelchair, tears streaming, as they are down almost every face. Not mine. I've been beyond tears these many months.

Lucy takes my hand. Poppy joins hers with mine and Courtney's again, till we're linked with Shaf across the stage. Poppy raises our chain high; raises it for Finn.

Hey Ho lowers the lights for the final time.

POPPY GATHERS COURTNEY and me into a tight circle.

"Allie, Courtney, I need to know you believe what I just said."

My head's so blocked with tears, it's shaking of its own accord. "In trying to save Maren, I never thought I'd lose Finn." I was so intent on Maren not being a tragic hero, it never crossed my mind it could be someone else, and never *ever* Finn.

"And how could you have, Allie, love? You also did the right thing."

I PERSUADE MY parents I'm all right, strong enough to go down onto the prom. Rue offers to go with me, but I need to do this alone.

Poppy's words echo in my brain as I walk through under the railway underpass:

You also did the right thing, Allie.

So you can do the right thing with the wrong outcome?

The glib, amber sun gleams off ribbons of water on the bared Sands the way it did the time I fell in love with the glorious view from the train.

As I trudge along the prom towards the lido, I can see the green of Maren's top out on the Sands on the day I met him. And I remember the moment he spotted Finn and Courtney; *he* called them back to safety.

For the first time, I want to make a start on shrugging off the grey, weighted blanket I've worn ever since, woven of grief and guilt. Both are selfish emotions. They don't benefit Finn's family and they don't benefit Finn.

But how *do* I peel off this clothing that's become a second skin?

PASSING THE LIDO, I remember Finn's plunge from the diving board. And what could have happened to him then.

The café's closed, but I remember Maren's face that Sunday. Now I know Jez had just told him he had to cockle by night.

Beyond it is the bandstand where we had our first 'date'; where he later told me he was Albanian.

Finally, I reach the point where I first met Maren. I lean on the rails and gaze at the Sands, washed with a burnt orange as the sun sinks.

Do I really mean I wish I'd never met Maren?

Not meeting Maren = Finn alive

It's faulty logic, I know somewhere deep in my core. It's trying to work out an equation that isn't solvable. Once, when I was tussling with some maths homework around at theirs, Finn's dad told me some equations just can't be solved—they're called transcendental. He was being kind. The equation *was* solvable; I needed to try a different method to tackle it.

Transcendental sounds right, though! Algebra will never work with people, I'm beginning to realise.

At heart, it's me trying to convince myself there was a way, if I'd got everything right that week, Finn would still be here. Because some things are too awful to grasp, and Finn gone is the most awful of all. I grapple daily with the concept of him not being.

I look towards the horizon, where the tide will return from, and now I know. Just as I wasn't responsible for quicksand and fog colluding against us, nor could I have factored in what everyone else would do that last day, especially the gangmasters.

I glance to my right, and there's Maren's smile that first afternoon. The tears I've blocked since the first horror of Finn's death, now they trickle down my cheeks.

EVERYONE WANTED TO talk to Maren. After. My parents. Finn's. The coastguard. The police.

Me, I *needed* him.

HOW, WHETHER, HE managed to contact his parents, I just don't know when he had no phone, no money, no anything beyond his clothes and my useless scrunchie! I keep all his belongings safe by my bed. All except his jacket, which the tide took as Courtney was hauled from the Sands.

What I do know is, like our comet, Maren's a survivor. One day, he'll contact me, I know he will.

Through Rue, maybe.

Or he knows the name of our school. Every afternoon when I come out, I check across the road, on the edge of the park, in case he's there, waiting for me, under a tree.

One day I'll look up, and he'll be there.

He gave me his *besa*.

Ends

Warning: If like me, you read the notes and acknowledgements at the end of the book first, then don't! Don't turn the page, as everything that follows contains complete spoilers.

You have been warned!

who can he tell?

If you need help or think someone could be a victim of modern slavery, call the free and confidential Modern Slavery & Exploitation Helpline

WE'RE OPEN 24/7
365 DAYS A YEAR

 modern slavery &
exploitation helpline
08000 121 700

If you think someone may be a victim of modern slavery call the 24/7 modern slavery & exploitation helpline.

08000 121 700

 **modern slavery & exploitation helpline**

Working towards
a world without slavery

Modern slavery covers a wide range of abuse and exploitation: sexual exploitation, domestic servitude, labour exploitation, criminal exploitation, slavery, forced labour, and organ trafficking. **Victims** of modern slavery can be any age, gender, nationality or ethnicity.

some general indicators

Behaviour – withdrawn, scared, not willing to talk, doesn't speak English
Appearance – unkempt, malnourished, few possessions, health concerns
Work – inappropriate clothing for job, long hours, little or no pay
Fear of authorities – doesn't want to speak to police or authorities
Debt bondage – in debt to, or dependent on, someone else
Accommodation – overcrowded, poorly maintained, blacked-out windows
Lack of control – no ID, no access to bank account, work transport provided
Lack of freedom – unable to move freely, unwilling or scared to leave

More information at www.modernslaveryhelpline.org

Author's Note

'Why' is a thread running through *Happiness Seeker*.

Why an Albanian economic migrant? Why modern slavery?

Economic migrants, it seems to me, are part of a grey area. While it's relatively easy to empathise with refugees, many people, like Courtney, struggle to find the same sympathy for 'happiness seekers'.

I've had the pleasure of visiting Albania once—so far. As Maren says, it is a beautiful country with a traumatic past—the most repressive Stalinist regime—still affecting the present, stacking the odds against its people. It leads to many of its young people getting involved in dangerous situations they haven't 'signed up for' when they (part) pay for undocumented entry to the UK and other countries.

If Maren's story had to be tied to a particular year, it would be the autumn of 2022.

The National Referral Mechanism (NRM) is the framework Maren would have been referred to if his and Allie's plan had worked out on their last day. July to September 2022 saw a 38% increase in referrals compared with the preceding year. This was the highest number of referrals since the NRM began in 2009. UK, Albanian and Eritrean nationals were the most commonly reported potential victims.

The number of Albanian nationals was the highest since the NRM began, with the most common exploitation type recorded for potential victims being labour exploitation, which Maren suffered. A *Guardian* article from 2022 describes young Albanian men as being 'viciously exploited' after arriving in the UK from 'a poverty-stricken former communist state'.

There is a reason for the majority of Albanian nationals who are referred to the NRM being recognised as genuine victims of trafficking and modern slavery, for Unseen's helpline statistics revealing Albania as being one of the seven most common sources of potential victims of modern slavery. Romania is the most common, then—along with Albania—India, Vietnam, Sri Lanka, China and the UK.

As I was revising *Happiness Seeker* in the first half of 2023, I read articles on almost a daily basis that scapegoated and vilified Albanians. Once viewed as taking our jobs and benefits, Albanians in the UK were now viewed as criminals, cheating the system.

If Maren's story was set in the second half of 2023, following the Illegal Migration Bill becoming law in July, he would have had even less confidence about trying to get help and even more justified fear of being returned to Albania, sent to a safe third country or detained in unsuitable accommodation for years.

Slavery may be closer to you than you think. Modern slaves may be hidden in plain sight, rife in rural areas and cities alike. They could be the car washers, nannies and pickers you see around you.

It is up to businesses to ensure modern slavery is eradicated from their supply chains.

And it's up to each of us: many modern slaves do not realise they have been trafficked and enslaved. Don't leave it to someone else. Your information could save a life.

Acknowledgements

Happiness Seeker has been with me in some form for longer than I care to pin down. It certainly wouldn't be in your hands today without the help of *a lot* of people, chronologically more or less, as follows:

I will always be grateful to the late Ian Craddock for his idea of bringing an illegal, contemporary cockle picker into the plot, and for his ongoing interest in and support of my writing. I loved reading his writing, notably his musical *Pals*.

Thank you so much to the Golden Egg Academy, particularly Imogen Cooper, for all her editorial help and encouragement with earlier versions.

My sincere thanks to Meryl Lovatt for giving me such personal insights into living with MS. I hope I got Miss Duffy's experiences of MS somewhere near authentic.

Thank you to Emily Ould for her editorial help and suggestions with the first quarter of the book.

This year, I have met for the first time, both in person and online, an inspiring array of people who have humbled me by being so willing to lend their expertise to my story:

Two people without whom you definitely wouldn't have been reading this story are my two beta readers, Sarah Dodd (*Keeper of Secrets*) and Paul Rand (*Joe with an E* – coming soon). I have been blessed with these two wonderfully talented writers, who have taken me by the hand and dragged me and the story up out of sinking sand. You both know there are times I thought of giving up on it, and I thank you both from the bottom of my heart for all the time and thought you have given me in helping this be a far, far better book. Sarah, you kept me focused on story and pace, character motivation and arcs – thank you for your much-needed honesty and for helping me cut at least some of the deadwood! Paul, you *always* had wise solutions to offer and would always be up for yet another read. You ended up knowing my characters and what they would and wouldn't do at least as well as I. I defy anyone ever to have had better beta readers!

Thank you to my writing friends at SCBWI NW for all their insightful critiquing and encouragement, including but not only Helen, Anna, Eve, Sue, Will and Ruth. Ruth, thank you for being a constant support; always on the end of an email, you've been the best writing buddy.

I'm hugely grateful to Catherine Makinson, English teacher and librarian extraordinaire at Brighouse High School, and to her wonderful Year Nines, now in Year Ten. Thank so much to all of you all for all your help during two visits with the blurb, epigraphs and opening chapters. You were incisive and decisive, and by giving your honest opinions, you made a huge difference to the beginning of the book. I'll bring the finished book to show you as soon as ever I can!

I'm immensely privileged to have had further expert help with *Happiness Seeker* from Unseen, the anti-slavery charity that runs the Modern Slavery Helpline and works with survivors. My sincere thanks go to Will Robinson in particular for always being willing to answer yet further questions, for so tactfully suggesting changes needed, for reading the relevant parts of the story and for his enthusiasm for and encouragement of the story. It made ALL the difference, Will.

Many thanks also to frontline workers at Hope for Justice, another vital organisation aiming to end human trafficking and modern slavery, for their input in terms of some extremely insightful comments and suggestions about my plot outline. My thanks to Adam Hewitt for coordinating these responses for me.

I am honoured to be supporting both of these crucial charities.

Just this summer (2023), I have had the great pleasure of being put in contact with John Stokes (thank you, Julia Rampen, for connecting us). John, who has fostered two Albanian 'lads', did me the great honour of reading *Happiness Seeker* in a matter of days. I am so very grateful for John's encouragement and for his great sensitivity in helping to deepen my understanding of how Maren might be feeling at various stages of the story. John, I'm looking forward to reading your memoir, already well underway.

A massive thank-you to Gary Parsons, the founder of Bay Search and Rescue, and all of this heroic volunteer team. I spent such an inspirational hour at the station in Flookburgh on a sunny evening in late June, the whole place buzzing as the team did some training. Thank you so very much to Gary, who not only patiently answered my questions about so many things from the moon and tide to Sherp but even offered to read the inciting incident and rescue chapters. Gary, you know where I am when you find the time to write your memoir.

My thanks to Janet Carter and Sally Houghton at Save Grange Lido for their interest and support of *Happiness Seeker*. Didn't we have an unforgettable Bay crossing in August? No one got stuck this time, though I did walk over three patches of dizzying quicksand. I was relieved the guide had us set off half an hour late to allow the Kent to empty further after the heavy rain.

Also in August, I had the privilege of spending a few days in Grange-over Sands with my cousins, including Jonathan Green, a brilliant young photographer. Jonjo, I will never be able to thank you enough for all your skill, creativity and hard work on the striking cover for *Happiness Seeker* and the interior photos – your own inspired idea. Thank you, too, to cousins Rachael and Lauren for their contributions and for being prepared to be in some of the photos. We are grateful to the staff at the Victoria Hall, Grange-over-Sands, for enabling us to take photos of the hall, where the epilogue of *Happiness Seeker* takes place, and for their interest and encouragement.

My sincere thanks to Chris, Izzy and all at Daisy Roots in Grange for their support of the book and allowing me to launch it in their wonderful bookshop with its breathtaking Bay views.

Writers are *the* most supportive community when, arguably, they have the least time for reviews. So I'm all the more appreciative to all the hugely talented writers *and* book bloggers who've made the time to review *Happiness Seeker*.

Thank you so much to Liz, my wonderful sister-in-law, for being willing to give some of your time and skill to creating trailers for the book, especially after all you put into trailers for *Igloo* only a year ago! You're the best.

I'm so very grateful to Douglas McCleery for saving the day at the last moment by agreeing to lend his skill and time for the stunning map and plan at the start of the book. A thousand thanks, Doug.

My final thanks are to Debbie McGowan at Beaten Track. Debbie was already my all-time hero for publishing my debut, *Igloo*, in Nov 22. *Happiness Seeker* is a story close to my heart, and I thank Debbie from the bottom of mine for enabling me to bring it to readers.

Because of all of you, *Happiness Seeker* has become a much better book and in the hands of more readers than I could ever have managed alone. Thank you.

Readers, including teachers who might be interested in a school visit, please do get in touch if you have any comments or would like my readers' questions on the story, exploring character, empathy, modern slavery, tragedy, 'No Man is an Island' and *A View from the Bridge*:

jennifer.burkinshaw@gmail.com

and/or see my website:
https://www.jennifer-burkinshaw.com

Content Warning

Please note that the following content warning contains spoilers.

- Death, including the death of a dog and a secondary character.
- Exploitation of migrant workers and racism related to this.
- Disability related to a progressive condition.
- Bereavement.

About the Author

Jennifer Burkinshaw grew up in Lancashire and taught English, Drama and Classics for twenty years in several schools, including four years in Paris. She later completed an MA in Creative Writing for Children at Manchester Metropolitan University and is also an alumna of the Golden Egg Academy.

Now retired, at least from teaching, Jennifer lives with her husband in West Yorkshire but enjoys being by the sea, in the mountains and, most of all, with her growing family.

Website: https://www.jennifer-burkinshaw.com

Beaten Track Publishing

For more titles from Beaten Track Publishing, please visit our website:

https://www.beatentrackpublishing.com

Thanks for reading!

Printed in Great Britain
by Amazon

29594136R00192